D0546192

THE LOST CHILD

9 40163744

Suzanne McCourt grew up on the wild southern coast of South Australia and now lives in Melbourne. *The Lost Child* is her first novel.

The
Lost Child

Suzanne McCourt

TEXT PUBLISHING MELBOURNE AUSTRALIA

textpublishing.com.au

The Text Publishing Company
Swann House
22 William Street
Melbourne Victoria 3000
Australia

Copyright © Suzanne McCourt 2014

The moral rights of the author have been asserted.

All rights reserved. Without limiting the rights under copyright above, no part of this publication shall be reproduced, stored in or introduced into a retrieval system, or transmitted in any form or by any means (electronic, mechanical, photocopying, recording or otherwise), without the prior permission of both the copyright owner and the publisher of this book.

First published by The Text Publishing Company, 2014

Cover design by Imogen Stubbs
Cover artwork © copyright Jeremy Miranda
Page design by WH Chong
Typeset by J&M Typesetting

Printed and bound in Australia by Griffin Press, an Accredited ISO AS/NZS 14001:2004 Environmental Management System printer

National Library of Australia Cataloguing-in-Publication entry:
Author: McCourt, Suzanne, author.
Title: The lost child / by Suzanne McCourt.
ISBN: 9781922147783 (paperback)
ISBN: 9781922148773 (ebook)
Subjects: Families—South Australia—Identity (psychology)—Fiction.
Dewey Number: A823.4

This book is printed on paper certified against the Forest Stewardship Council® Standards. Griffin Press holds FSC chain-of-custody certification SGS-COC-005088. FSC promotes environmentally responsible, socially beneficial and economically viable management of the world's forests.

For my mother and sons

PART ONE

On the mantelpiece, Mum is a bride with a mermaid tail and a frothy veil, her hands hidden behind big flowers. There are two bridesmaids with more flowers: the one with the grumpy face is Mum's sister. Dad is standing next to Mum but it doesn't look like him.

'Who's this?' I ask when I climb up to get a closer look.

'Your father. Who do you think?'

'It's not his face.'

'They got the airbrushing wrong.'

'What's airbrushing?'

'Improving the photo.'

Dad's improved face is dolly-smooth with lipstick lips like Mum and her maids. The dimple in his chin looks like a spider hole. You could pick a whole nest of spiders out of that hole. He doesn't look happy with his improved lips and his spider hole. He looks like a stranger to himself in a black suit and bow tie, gloves like cocky feathers in his hand.

In the other photo, Dad is a boy with his own lips and chin. He is standing next to a chair, stiff and straight as a fence post, wearing a jacket, short leg pants and socks pulled up to his knees. He looks as if he thinks it's silly being dressed up in a suit with slicked-down hair, holding on to a chair instead of sitting on it.

He looks as if he wants to be outside, being a boy instead of a little man.

Next to him is a photo of Big Red winning the Muswell Cup. This is before Big Red fell at Reedy Creek and broke his leg and Dad had to shoot him to put him out of his misery. In the photo Big Red nuzzles Dad's ear as if he wants to eat it, as if he loves Dad as much as Dad loves him, and Dad holds up a silver cup, grinning fit to burst. In his other hand, he holds a folded whip.

It's his whip from the kitchen dresser, his whipping-whip!

'What sort of hat did she have?' says Mum.

Dunc throws his bag on the chair and unbuttons his shirt. His face is shiny hot and he smells of summer grass. 'I dunno. Yellow.'

'What about her dress?'

'We had to sit on the oval for ages and when the plane flew over we had to wave. The Queen was in a car and you couldn't see anything, except everyone waving. It was dumb.'

'What about the Duke?'

Dunc makes us wait while he drinks a full glass of water. 'Why didn't you go yourself? The whole school went on the train and half the mothers too. You could've taken Sylvie. Mrs Winkie took Lizzie.'

'I'm not Mrs Winkie.'

I know this and Dunc does too. Mrs Winkie has grey hair, three chins and a strawberry birthmark on her neck shaped like a beetle. Mum has reddy-brown hair, one chin and a mole called a beauty spot near her mouth. Marilyn Monroe has two beauty spots.

Dunc unbuckles his bag and gives us presents from Coles in the Mount. 'I hope you didn't waste your money,' says Mum, sucking on her ciggie.

Mum's present is a cup with the Queen's head, and a saucer with a gold crown underneath. She says Dunc shouldn't have. Dunc has a new pocketknife with a gold crown on a red case, and blades and hooks and things that he snaps out and back under my nose. My present is a locket with a Queen's crown on top, when I really wanted a skull ring like his. I wish I had money to waste from trapping rabbits like Dunc, instead of sixpence inside a pig that I can't get out.

Dunc presses my locket until the top pops up. Inside is a hole covered with a cellophane heart. 'This is where you put the photo.'

'What photo?'

'Your boyfriend's, of course.'

'I don't have a boyfriend.'

'Or a lock of hair,' says Mum.

My hair has dead ends from the Toni Home Perm that Mum gave me when she permed hers. Mine didn't take properly, which is why it is straight with frizzed ends. Dad says I'd be better off bald.

In the bedroom off the kitchen, where Mum sleeps in the big bed under the window and I sleep in the bed against the wall, Dunc clips the chain around my neck.

'Don't lose it,' he says, making slitty eyes at me in the mirror as if he can't decide whether he is pleased with my locket or not. I move my head in the mirror light and make the gold glint. I wonder if there is time before tea to take my heart up the street to show Lizzie. She has a gold bangle, and her own bedroom. Her mother is Mrs Winkie with the beetle birthmark. Mrs Winkie also has a gold tooth.

When I turn from the mirror, Dunc is on my bed, bouncing my dolls all over the place. 'Don't,' I say as I rescue Ted, but now Marilyn is bouncing on her head and Blue Rag Doll's arms and legs are twisted and I am full of scorching air and angry words. I squash everything inside my mouth and rescue Marilyn and ask myself why Dunc is always being nice then turning mean and tricking me. Then his new *Phantom* comic slides out from under my pillow. This is not meant to happen.

Dunc bounces to a stop. 'What's this? Didn't I tell you to leave my comics alone? Didn't I?' He rolls the *Phantom* into a tube and flicks my head—*flick*—arms—*flick*—ears—*flick*. 'Anyway'—*flick*—'you're not even five'—*flick*—*flick*—'you don't go to school'—*flick*—*flick*—'and you can't even read'—*flick*—*flick*—*flick*.

'I can read pictures.' I climb onto my bed and back into the corner against the wall. 'Mum!' I yell, holding Ted over my head to shelter me from his hits. 'Mum! Dunc's messing up my bed.'

Still she doesn't come. Dunc stops hitting and I peep through Ted's legs. 'Anyway,' he says, 'this was my bed before it was yours.' He pokes out his tongue so close to my nose that I can see his dangly tonsils thing. 'I slept here for five years before you were born, and Dad slept here too, not in the spare room. You didn't know that, did you?'

His breath smells of licorice and mint leaves. He must have bought them at Coles and eaten the lot.

'Dad used to sing me to sleep every night.' He whispers with a licorice hiss as if it is a dirty secret. 'He never sings to you. Does he?'

He picks up Marilyn and holds her in front of my face. 'You don't even know she married Joe DiMaggio. You don't even know who he is!'

When I don't answer, he whispers: 'You don't even know how babies are made.' I know about the stork but he doesn't wait for me to speak. 'A boy puts his red hot poker in your black hole of Calcutta.'

Suddenly he is gone, sliding across the floor on his socks, and my breath dropping out of me.

In the kitchen, I hear Mum say: 'What did you get your father?'

'A beer mug with a crown in a coronation box.'

'He'll like that,' she says.

He does. I am fed and in bed when he comes home from Hannigan's. I am keeping quiet and being good like Mum says I should. From my bed, I can see the stove and mantelpiece, half the table, two chairs, the bubble-glass dresser, the door to the laundry porch. When Dad comes in, I can see him but he never sees me.

'What'd I do to deserve this?' he says, messing Dunc's hair and play-punching him. 'It's a beaut. Better baptise it right away.'

'Haven't you had enough?' says Mum.

Dad pours beer into his new mug. When he sits at the table, Fluff hops onto his lap. I send Fluff magic messages. *You are my kitten. Jump down and come to me.* But Fluff rolls on his back and puts his legs in the air and Dad tickles his tummy like Faye Daley's dad tickles her.

I put my head under the blanket. I am a wombat in a hole full of hurt and hot air. A bird is squeaking and beating inside my chest. When I burst out, the hurt is a slimy toad and Dad has finished his tickling.

'Come on, Dunc,' he says, tossing Fluff onto the floor, 'better see what's happening with the weather.'

I take a running leap onto Mum's bed so the bogeyman underneath won't reach out and grab me. When I lift the curtain, the night is still summer-hot with no breeze; there is a smell of dry mud from the lagoon and waves boom on the beach behind the dunes.

On the back step, I can hear Dad telling Dunc that a ring around the moon means rain in two days. The moon is low over Shorty Manne's shaggy pines, with no ring anywhere. Dad says a star close by means wind will blow up next day. There are star spots everywhere, pale and white, with a bright one not far from the moon. But how close is close by?

'Should be an okay day. Worse luck.'

'You don't like fishing, do you, Dad?'

'It's a mug's game.'

Mum's voice: 'Duncan, you've got school tomorrow.'

A beer bottle clinks. 'With horses you can tame 'em. But the sea's ya master. You're nothing out there.'

'Can we get another horse, Dad?'

'No point, mate. Racing's a mug's game.'

Then Dad begins singing, softly, hardly more than a hum, his honey-brown voice sliding in through my window like a warm breeze. 'In the cool, cool, cool of the evening...tell 'em I'll be there—'

Mum again: 'Come on, Duncan, bedtime.'

'Stay where you are,' says Dad and then he tells Dunc a story about a monster he saw out past Ten Mile Rocks. A flash beneath the wave's curl. Something lurking. 'Could've been an old, sleepy hair seal swimming on the edge of the deep. But when the seagulls fly up, flapping and squawking, you can bet there's something big about. And probably pretty darn mean.'

'Duncan! Bed.'

'Was it a monster, Dad?'

'Could've been. Augie reckons he saw a tentacle curl outta the water big enough to wrap around the whole boat. Could've been a squid that grows up to fifty foot and weighs a couple of ton. I says to Augie, we're getting out of here. And we did. Faster than a cut snake.'

'I wish you wouldn't tell him things like that,' says Mum at the back door. 'You'll give him nightmares.'

'You're the only nightmare around here.'

There is a drop of silence. Then Dad laughs. And after another drop, Dunc laughs too. Their laughs cackle high into the sky and now there is a laughing ring around the moon, which means rain in two days. But that laughter booms in my head like the surf behind the dunes and I curl in my bed against the wall and wonder if I smashed open my pig, could I buy Dad a present for sixpence?

Water is up to my shins and hidden things—periwinkles, crabs and maybe stinger fish—wriggle beneath my feet. 'Dunc!' I yell. 'I want to go home.'

Dunc jumps off the reef with a silly scream. Pardie and Ken scream on their tractor tube. Gulls scream for sandwich crusts.

'Du-u-u-u-u-nc!' I scream.

Suddenly there is a hole in the reef and water over my head. I choke and grab at weeds and kick and scream and swallow sea and try to swim and sink with water in my mouth and ears and suddenly no sound of anything.

Then Dunc is there, yanking me out with strong arms, thumping me on the back.

'Shit,' he says as I cough and choke. 'Didn't I tell you to stay on the beach? Didn't I?' Thump, cough, thump. 'Shit,' as he leads me ashore and sits me in the shelter of the old boat that lies on its side in the sand. 'Shit,' as he wraps his towel over my shoulders with kind, clumsy hands. But when Pardie and Kenny come to gawk: 'Now stay here, like I told ya. And don't tell Mum.'

When they leave I watch the jetty dancing on criss-crossed legs all the way to the end. The cold has climbed up my nose, even my hair shivers. I try to find Dad's boat in the middle of the others, but although the *Henrietta* is the biggest in the fleet, there are too many boats. The sun warms the top of my head but my teeth still rattle in fright and my fingers are witchetty grubs, wrinkled and white. Then, as I dig in the warm sand, right there under my hand is buried treasure, paper money with the new Queen's head on it.

I run to the change sheds. Two big girls are smoking in the dunnies but I dress with my back to them and don't let them see my money. I leave my bathers and towel in the old boat with Dunc's towel, then I run along the sea wall, past Denver Boland's big white house, past the rotunda and the harbourmaster's house, over the road to Mrs Cronk's shop.

Mrs Cronk looks like a fox with bushy, red hair. Her eyes behind her glasses are bigger than her mouth. Her shop is opposite the playground, near the roundabout with the big pine. Once she told us to stay off the slippery slide if we couldn't use it properly, that we'd break our necks going down backwards. Faye Daley gave her the rude sign and Mrs Cronk called out that she'd wallop the living daylights out of us if she had more time. Her shop smells of mothballs. The holiday people who stay in the rooms above smell the same. So do the cottons and wool and knitting needles, the hats and beach towels.

My friend Lizzie is at the counter with her big sister, Mary, who is home from boarding school in the Mount for the weekend. 'A pound!' says Mary when I show her my money. 'Finders keepers. What are you going to buy?'

'A present. A present for my Dad.'

Mrs Cronk looks at me with her magnified eyes as if she recognises me from the park. Then she says she has just the thing; it is a piece of round glass with the Queen's head inside. She says it is a paperweight to put on your papers. I can't think why Dad would want the Queen sitting on his paper because when he's finished with it, Mum tears out the crossword and screws up the pages to start the fire. Mrs Cronk says one day it will be a collector's piece. Mary and Lizzie don't say anything and when I look up, they are at the shop window.

'The circus,' says Mary, grabbing Lizzie's hand, turning to me. 'Want to come?' Then she sees my pound on the counter and Mrs Cronk's fox fingers scratching towards it. Mary gets it first. 'Don't lose it,' she hisses as we push through the door. 'You give it away when you buy something.' She pulls Lizzie and me past the petrol bowser.

All the way from Stickynet Bridge to the harbourmaster's house, people are running off the beach to watch the circus crawl into town. Dunc is propped on his bike across the road when he should be looking after me and not letting me out of his sight for one minute. I want to show him my pound but he is blocked from my view by a car with fins bigger than the white pointer Dad caught off West End. Then vans with curtained windows and trucks with high sides covered in painted lions and clowns with fat lips and sad eyes. Then an elephant on a tray truck with chains on his feet and one angry eye that looks right into mine. And a camel with a long waving neck and yellow teeth, but no real lions or tigers or monkeys or bears.

Mary says they are inside the cages with boards on the side and we have to get to the oval to see them unloaded. She says there are jobs and free tickets but we have to hurry.

'Come on!' she says as the last truck turns at the roundabout pine. Pardie, Dunc and Kenny are already tailing the trucks and vans on their bikes. She says we'll take a short cut and yanks Lizzie and me across the street, through the park and under the pines near the fish factory. At the goods shed, with its wide-open doors and black hole under the floor that sometimes hides tramps and once a dead dog, she pulls us onto the railway track. 'Hurry!' she says, showing us how to jump from sleeper to sleeper.

I don't like this two-handed closeness. I try to get free but I am tied to Mary like an extra-long arm. I am afraid the train will come and we'll be squashed flat but when I look back there are only two rail tracks running into the scrub and a huge blue sky above.

When we get to the spot behind the oval where the circus sets up, Dunc and the others are already there. 'Damn, shit, damn,' says Mary, going straight to the man in the cowboy hat. He says she is too late, that he has all the help he needs. Mary says she worked for him last year, doesn't he remember? He says for God's sake he travels all over Australia, does she think he remembers every kid he meets?

'I'm not every kid. You said I was the best girl worker you'd ever had. You put your hand up my jumper and told me I had the juiciest apples you'd ever seen. Remember?'

Lizzie and I look at Mary's apples. So does the man. 'Creep,' she says, pulling us away from him.

Lizzie and I pretend we can't see angry tears on Mary's freckles. We follow her past the monkeys cage without stopping; Mary says she hates their red bottoms. Behind the vans, the circus people are stringing up clotheslines and unpacking pots. A lady with yellow hair says: 'Clear off out of here.'

'Make me,' says Mary, and we run, cheeking and giggling, towards the clearing where the big tent is spread on the ground with circus men banging in pegs and Dunc lumping a hay bale towards the animal cages. Then a loud shriek and a fur ball leaps onto a van before running along the top and swinging onto a cable connected to a trailer.

A man yells: 'Free tickets to anyone who catches 'im!'

Mary is off like John Landy. Pardie, Dunc, all the big boys, Chicken McCready too, everyone yelling at everyone else to cut it off here, there, somewhere, but as the monkey bounces off a truck onto the grass, Mary is way out in front, racing across the clearing, Lizzie bobbing behind.

Before I can follow, everyone disappears into the muddy shadows beneath the tea-tree on the edge of the lake. The sun sparkles on the surface; on the far side, yellow dunes slide into the water. It is warm behind the cages with no wind and no one except me. The circus people hammer. The lion roars in his cage.

Then I hear a kitten cry.

I look behind the vans; it is tied to a wheel with a black leather lead and a red collar. It is the most beautiful kitten I've ever seen, more beautiful than our Fluff, a soft brown like Lizzie's old cat, and with big yellow eyes. I pat the circus kitten and it stops crying. I tickle it under its collar, under its chin, behind its ears, until it purrs and tries to nibble my fingers. I think about how much Fluff likes Dad and he likes Fluff. I untie the circus kitten. I tuck my pound under the kitten's bowl and leave a bit poking out for the circus people to see.

I have the best present for my dad.

On the pockmarked land behind the oval, the kitten sniffs down rabbit holes. At the rail tracks, it pulls on its lead and gives a loud *miaow* that makes my neck shiver. Before crossing the street, I scoop it into my arms. It is bigger than Fluff and has a horsy smell. It needs a good wash.

You're mine now, I tell it. *You'll like living with Fluff and my dad better than a circus.*

Hannigan's veranda has red and blue tiles that are good for hopscotch. I don't like the bee-swarming noise in the bar or the beer smell that creeps under the door, but I have a rest on the bench under the coloured glass window. The kitten stretches at my feet and licks its paws. I think about a kitten being a better present than a beer mug. I have to get it home before Dunc gets back from the circus. And I need a box with air holes in the side like Lizzie's silkworms have for a house. I need a ribbon to tie up the box like a proper present.

Just then Augie Moon pushes out the door. He is Pardie's father. He sways as he looks at me, as if I am swaying too. 'Waitin' for your dad?' he says, and, before I can reply, he tosses his butt in the gutter and lurches off the step. 'You'll be waitin',' he calls as he heads down the path to the dunnies.

A dusty black car drives by, full of farm kids with laughing heads and arms and legs and beach towels hanging out of windows. They hoot and wave and make so much noise that the kitten takes fright and almost tugs the lead out of my hand. It hides under the bench and when I reach down it hisses at me with white teeth bared; it has a lot of them. I pull gently on the lead and whisper words like Mrs Daley's sister whispers to her new baby. *There, there, you funny little thing, it's all right, you've got me to look after you, there, there.* The kitten puts its teeth back in its mouth but still won't come out. I remember Grannie Meehan's kittens that were put in a bag with a brick and dropped in the dam at Bindilla, but I don't want to think about drowned things so I get bossy and give the kitten a good hard yank.

It walks over the hill past Mr Hammet's house, then hears something in the boobialla and drags its belly on the ground in a prowling stalk. I tell it we need to hurry and when it doesn't, I bundle it into my arms and carry it like a parcel, down the slope, along the lagoon path, past Shorty Manne's house. It doesn't wriggle too much but when I try to open our gate, it twists and scratches, then leaps onto the grass. There is blood on my wrist but I don't stop to lick. I pull the kitten up the drive, saying, *Hurry, hurry,* the whole time.

Mum is at the well behind the hedge. She doesn't see me creep through the nasturtiums and into the old shed that backs onto Shorty's fence. She doesn't see me creep out again and return with a bowl of milk. She is dribbling a bucket of water over her veggie seedlings when I slide out of the shed and ask if she has a box with air holes.

'What for? No I haven't.' Then from the well: 'I need you in the tub. I want you fed and in bed before your father gets home.'

In the bath, I decide that when Dad comes in I'll say I have to go to the dunny, then I'll untie the kitten from the post. Already I can see Dad's surprise. *What'd I do to deserve this?* He might even pick me up and swing me around like Blue Daley does with Faye. *What a beaut. We'd better give him a name. Whaddya say?*

'How did you get that?' says Mum, soaping my scratched wrist.

I almost tell her. It is hard keeping something so good locked inside. But then Dunc bangs into the laundry porch. 'I've got a free ticket for the circus. I caught a monkey that escaped. I have to be ready at seven. I'm going with Pardie and Kenny.'

'Get the milk,' says Mum, 'or you won't be going anywhere.'

When Dunc returns from the kitchen with the billy, his eyes are as big as tombowlers. 'Someone stole a lion cub. What if it escapes into the bush and becomes a sheep-killer like the Tantanoola tiger?'

'What if you're not home in time to go to the circus?'

'What's a cub?' I ask when Dunc leaves. But already I know.

'A baby lion,' says Mum, towelling me.

'What colour?'

'Brown, I suppose.'

'Where's my black hole of Calcutta?'

'It's not yours. It's in India.'

'Where's India?'

But Mum has finished answering and when I am dressed I let her feed me peaches and cream without once biting the spoon and telling her I am old enough to feed myself. I try to find her eyes, to ask what I should do about the cub, but she is lost in her bubble where she smokes her ciggie and feeds me in a dreamy way as if her bubble has floated away and I've gone too.

In bed, I pull up the sheet and squeeze my eyes tight. I try not to think about the lion in our shed but still I can hear it begging to go back to the circus; it is the sound of cats drowning in dams and tearing open bags and ripping my skin into soup-bone meat and no hands to save me.

Then Dad's jeep stops at the gate and I poke out my nose. Mum has a tea-towel bunched in her hands. She sets Dad's plate on the table. I hear him kick off his boots and splash water in the laundry trough. Then: 'Bloody hell! What was that?'

Mum sucks her top lip right into her mouth; she does this when she has no words.

Then again: 'Bloody hell! It's a rat, big as a cat.'

Mum shakes her head and covers Dad's plate with a saucepan lid. I follow into the laundry porch. Dad is bent over the trough, poking behind with a broom.

'Watch out!' he yells, jumping back. 'It's a rat, a big bugger.' He has bleary eyes and a skinful of beer. 'Get a trap,' he tells Mum.

Mum says she won't set a trap in case they catch the cat. She flicks on the light near the kitchen door. She says Dad's tea is on the table getting cold. She says it might be an old house but they've never had rats before, it's probably only a mouse. 'You're so worse for wear,' she says, 'you wouldn't know what it was if it bit you on the nose.'

Dad is spread on the floor like a starfish, poking under the trough and the shoe cupboard in the corner. 'I know what I bloody saw.' He climbs to his feet and steadies himself with the broom. 'It's a bloody rat. And if it climbs into your bed, don't blame me.'

Mum marches me back to bed and looks all around with a worried frown. When she is gone, I search with prowling eyes, under the dressing table, in the corner, in the dark place next to the wardrobe. Then I pull up the spread and look under my bed. Lion eyes stare back at me.

What now? Can I toss him out the window? What if I do and he grows up and steals sheep like the Tantanoola tiger did until he was caught and stuffed and put in a glass box in the Tantanoola Pub? What if Constable Morgan finds out and I am taken away like Lanky Evans was when he stole sheep? Since he's been back, he has to live in a van in the caravan park because Mrs Evans won't have him in the house, he's a disgrace.

Dad plops onto a kitchen chair, pulls off his smelly socks and drops them on the floor. Once he rolled them in a ball and tossed them through the open door to the bedroom for me to catch like a football. Once he threw them out the kitchen window. Once they landed on the chimney clock and fell onto the stove. Tonight, he throws his pants at the sink. He takes off his shirt, rolls it in a ball and tries to hit the wall. Mum picks up his socks, his shadow legs and shirt and walks them to the laundry trough.

When Dad is in a throwing mood, I keep very quiet. When he is in a throwing mood, Mum talks to herself. 'It's stew from the lamb flaps. I thought we'd get some rain this morning, the garden needs it, but it blew over. I ran into the Old Girl at the post office, her ankle's on the mend. She should stay off ladders at her age. Not that anyone can tell her.'

Then Dunc is back with the milk. 'Look,' he calls from the porch. 'Look what I can do.' He is blocked from my view by the frame of the door, except for his arm holding the billy.

He is doing his milk trick!

Mum turns from the stove. Dad's fork stops at his mouth.

Dunc's arm is the spoke of a wheel, silver and shining, spinning up and around and over his head and still the milk stays in! He says it has to do with centrifugal force. He says I can't try because I am a girl. He says the dangerous bit is when you slow down.

Just then Fluff shoots under Dunc's feet and into the kitchen. From under my bed the lion cub gives a loud *Mi-ao-ow-ow*, more like a howl. Fluff's fur bristles into a brush. He stands on stiff legs and hisses into the bedroom, hisses at me in bed, at the lion under the bed.

Dunc's arm stops turning too soon, stops with a jolt. Milk splatters the table, the walls, runs down the dresser, slides over the lino and settles in a white-paint puddle at Dad's feet. Fluff steps through the milk, flicks his paws and hisses some more.

Dad's hand snakes out and scoops Fluff off the floor as if he is a ball of Mum's soft black knitting wool. Pushing back his chair, he lifts Fluff above his head and throws him hard against the chimney wall.

Fluff is not as soft as knitting wool or socks. He cracks like a chopped mallee root before he falls to the floor. Before Mum closes the door.

Dunc opens his sloppy gob full of porridge and milk and mouths words at me that Mum can't hear. 'You're a drongo fart,' he says when she leaves the room. 'How do you think it was for me? Having to take that cub back to the circus with everyone knowing I've got a thief for a sister?'

I wonder if hateful words can split open a head if there are enough of them. I wish his ears would fall into his porridge. I make myself look into his eyes so that he can read my mind but he is red-faced angry, as if he has been saving it up for a long time.

'Don't speak to me ever again,' he says. 'From now on you're DEAD. Understand?'

That night I am dead and in bed before Dad comes home. Dunc has been sent to bed too but it is still light outside and I know he is reading comics or sorting his egg collection on the sunroom floor. I am colouring Noddy's hat a nice bright blue. I am not wearing Dunc's heart crown and from now on I never will. I am not sure how to get the colour right for Golly's skin.

Dad's jeep stops in the street and Mum fumbles his plate off the simmering saucepan and sets it on the table. Golly's skin is really a kind of brownish grey. I can get the colour right by mixing black and blue. It is important not to colour too close to the lines.

Dad clumps in without taking off his boots in the laundry porch. His boots scratch the lino like chook claws. He shoves his plate and knife and fork into the centre of the table. Mum turns from the sink, her face a squashed grape. Dad arranges things that look like sticks, all around the table edge. When he's finished, he stares at Mum without saying a word. I slide down in my bed and hide in the silence that squeaks up a storm on the roof, that is a ticking clock in Shorty Manne's voice, that calls out to Mrs Shorty in spoggie talk.

'That's the last time you're going to whip my kids.' Mum folds the tea-towel into a cushion and turns away to wipe words off the bench, over and over. Then I know! She's chopped up Dad's whip! His Muswell Cup whip! His whipping-whip!

'She's a mongrel thief.'

'She found a pound. I asked Mary Campbell. She thought she was buying you a present.'

'She's a mongrel liar, and a mongrel thief. Whatever people say about me, they'd never say that.' He picks up a bit of his whip, a handle piece, plaited and thick. He is facing the doorway, facing me. 'This…is the only thing'—his voice croaky as a frog—'You knew…' His eyes bulge too. I am afraid he might cry. I press fingers into my ears but still his croak breaks through. 'Big Red… you bloody knew…the Cup…you knew…'

Mum stops her wiping and stands at the sink fidgeting with the tea-towel. Her fear creeps into my bed as if it has nowhere to go except into me. She says: 'I'm not having my kids whipped.'

Dad gives a spluttery laugh. 'I never touched her!'

'You would've. If I hadn't got her out of here. You did it to Dunc.'

'It never hurt me.'

Now Mum splutters too. 'You said you had welts for weeks.'

'Toughened me up.'

Mum shakes her head, unties her apron and hangs it on a chair. From nowhere a piece of whip hits her hard in the back. I slide further down in my bed: now there will be yelling and no stopping. Then Dad is in the bedroom, flicking on the light. And straightaway Mum hisses, 'Sylvie's asleep,' and flicks it off again.

Dad is at the wardrobe, grabbing Mum's fairy dresses with the net petticoats that she wears to the dance. Hangers fall to the floor, and still he grabs more. 'You and your fancy dresses. Workin' my guts out floggin' crays around the Mount. Floggin' apples around here to make an extra quid.' Mum grabs at her dresses but still he bundles more. 'Everything saved for best. For one day. For never. Well,' he calls as he stomps through the kitchen, dresses piled high in his arms, 'never's just come.'

As Mum runs after him, I leap onto her bed. My stomach wobbles in fright, but it is the best leap. Outside, a big bowl of stars hangs over our house; dresses are piled in the drive. Dad strikes a match. Mum's dresses flare up in a fizz of flames, in a cloud of crackling and sparkling. Dad reels back and his shadow prances around the tank-stand, the shed, walks along Shorty's fence. He is a giant with thrashing arms and legs and no head. Shorty's dog barks at the giant, the stink of him, the blazing sky.

Slowly the flames die. The giant shouts: 'Whaddya doin'? Get back to bed.'

Under my blanket, I choke on dead fairies. There is a cry in my mouth but no sound in my head. It is Dad's cry, shouting at Dunc to go back to bed.

Then his jeep starts up. 'Don't come back!' Mum yells from the back door. 'Go and live with her. See if I care.'

Who is her?

Mum stands at the sink and looks out the window but it is black mirror glass and there is nothing to see except her face staring back. Sid McCready rides past on his squeaky bike. Dunc's bed squeaks as he climbs in. Mum snaps the blind down fast and covers up her face. Through her fingers she sees me at the door and pulls a chair close to the stove.

'All right,' she says, 'come here.' She sits me on her lap and holds me tight. The fire is warm on my back but Mum is all cold bones and stiff arms. She squashes me close to the soft part of her neck where she smells of Pears soap and black nights.

'It's not much to ask,' she says, squeezing me so hard that my bird cries out inside. 'Not much.'

Mum tells Mrs Winkie about the whip and about the horse Dad gave her when they got married and lived at Bindilla, how he broke that horse in himself. 'Knew it had a novice on its back. Tetchy the whole way. Then it just reared up and threw me. Split my head open on a rock.' Mum searches through her hair with her fingers. 'I've still got the scar.'

'Some present,' says Mrs Winkie.

Mrs Winkie is really Mrs Winkie Campbell. Her chins wobble when she walks. She has tiny feet with pudding toes. She married her cousin, which you shouldn't do because it makes your children slow. She has nine children—Mary, Lizzie and Colin— and plenty of others who've grown and left home. Sometimes Lizzie can be a bit slow. We are playing with our dolls on the floor and Lizzie wants to play mothers and fathers. She says I can be the father.

'This is a game without fathers,' I tell her.

Mrs Winkie says: 'I remember when he turned up at my place with that whip in his hand. One of the times I was glad to be a good axe-handle wide. I stood in the door with Dunc crouched behind and I looked him in the face and told him a whopper without thinking twice. *He's not here*, I said. *Haven't seen him since early afternoon when he rode past on his bike.* I waited until I heard Mick drive off and I sent that boy home with three Hail Marys following him. And no doubt you had him in bed before Mick got back with his itchy whip.'

Mum snuffles a cry. 'You did the right thing,' says Mrs Winkie, reaching for Mum's hand. 'Don't think you didn't.'

Marilyn has wet her pants. I give her a good smack and Lizzie smacks her doll too. Our dolls cry out with wide staring eyes. They cry louder than Mum, drowning out her bird squeaks. I am deaf and dumb like the fat girl in the Hammets' house.

'He wasn't always like it,' says Mum.

'The war,' says Mrs Winkie.

'It was only Darwin. Only for a year.'

'He was there for the bombing.'

Mum wipes her nose and drinks from her Queen cup.

'Get on with it, Cele,' says Dad. 'You're eating into my drinking time.'

Aunt Cele moves her camera stand and looks into the box on the top. 'Be eating into a lot more if you'd had to book in at the Institute like everyone else.'

'Wouldn't have got me within cooee.'

'We know that, don't we, Nell?'

Mum makes a clucking sound in her mouth and fluffs out my dress. She says it's a good opportunity, and good of Cele to take our photos in her own time. Cele says she'll get better shots here because the Mechanics' Institute is a dark hole even with backdrops and lights set up on the stage. Though it's not as bad as some of the places they have to use, travelling around some of the towns.

We are arranged against the sunroom wall, down the garden end, away from Dunc's bed. Dad's leg is close to mine. His hand rests on his knee. I try not to look at that hand. *He didn't mean it, he was drunk,* says Mum inside my head. My stomach is a heavy lump. Dad has had a bath and put on his grey suit. 'Hasn't seen the light of day since Spog Ward's funeral,' he tells Aunt Cele.

Aunt Cele straightens his tie and smiles into his eyes. 'Well, that's a crime, Mick. You look a million dollars. Doesn't he, Nell?'

Mum pulls up my socks and folds down the tops. I wonder if

a million dollars is the same as a million pounds but I don't ask.

'Pardie's got a new *Phantom*,' says Dunc. 'He's waiting to swap.'

'Well, let him wait,' says Mum.

'Pardie Moon's a weirdo,' says Dad.

'Mick!' says Mum.

Aunt Cele puts her head on one side. She has slip-sliding blue eyes and red lips. 'Sylvie, smile. You look gorgeous. You too, Nell. Two pretty pink peas in a pod, same eyes.' She looks into the camera. 'Heads up. Ready now? Watch the birdie. Chee-ee-se.' She snaps, flashes, snaps. 'Lovely,' she says, 'and cheese again.' And we cheese and flash and blink, all of us, and Dunc by himself, and me by myself, and Dunc with me and both of us holding hands and cheesing even though I am dead, and then one of Mum and Dunc and me.

'Now one with Sylvie, Mick, and that'll just about do it.'

Dad looks at his watch. 'I'm already done.' He stands, squashing my skirt against his chair as if it is a frill-necked lizard neck that he can stomp on if he wants, as if it is nothing. I fluff out my skirt until it is a perfect frill and I am a mouth in the middle that will bite off his leg if he steps on me.

'You're hopeless, Mick. Can't sit still for a second. Same as when you were a kid.' But Aunt Cele smiles at Dad and he smiles back with boy-shy eyes, the way he never smiles at Mum or me.

Mum tells Dunc to change before he goes out to play. In the bedroom, she widens her eyes and smiles at herself in the mirror. She is beautiful, like the Queen, everyone says. I am freckle-nosed with a small mouth, squinty eyes and my dead ends. Lizzie has straight black hair. Faye Daley and Colleen Mulligan have sausage curls. I am the only one with a perm.

'Come on,' Mum says with a sigh, 'better get you changed too.'

In the kitchen, Aunt Cele says she'll have a beer like my father. He is still wearing his suit. 'So who's this galah you're travelling around with, Cele?'

Mum says I can have a biscuit outside. I dawdle near the door and she says she can see through walls and doesn't want crumbs on the floor. I sit on the back step and listen through walls but I can only hear Dad and Aunt Cele laughing with loud bursts and no words in between.

Over our fence, on the other side of Shorty's house, I can see Mrs Major bending around her backyard. She is Wanda the Witch. The dead rose bushes in the front garden are witch's wands, everyone knows. The well with the tin cover near the back door is where she drowns children—probably Mr Major too because no one's ever seen him and that's why the well smells. And the creeper all over the lean-to has a crow's nest hidden deep in the tangles and everyone knows black crows never nest in towns unless there's a witch with a cat who needs them for spells.

Two rosellas swoop into our peach tree and fly off again. Fluff is buried under that tree. Mum says if Lizzie asks about Fluff, I'm to say he ran away. Mrs Winkie knows about the whip and Mum's dresses but not about Fluff. Mum says the world doesn't have to know everything. Fluff gets stuck in my throat and makes me cough. *Not another cold. What's wrong with you?* There are ants running around my sandals and crawling through cracks in the cement. I put my head between my legs and think about ants living together in one big nest and how I'd like to live in the Skull Cave in the Deep Woods with the Phantom and his family and have Phantom powers.

Right then Dunc and Pardie bang out the back door. Pardie has a stack of comics with Dunc's new *Batman* on top. Dunc forgets he's not speaking to me. 'Stay out of my room. You're still double-banned. And don't go near my comics.'

Pardie gives me a secret smile, and a *Dick Tracy*.

'Give her *Wonder Woman*,' says Dunc.

'No, it's new.'

'It's girly stuff.'

Pardie's face pinks up.

They are going nesting and when I ask if I can go too, Dunc talks to Pardie as if I'm not there. 'Can she ride five miles on a two-wheeler? Can she climb a tree?' He jumps on his bike and rolls down the drive, legs stuck out either side like a fathead dingbat. 'Sylvie Alice Cackie Poo-ooo…Sylvie Alice Cackie Poo-ooo…'

I blink at my *Dick Tracy*. It's the one about Tonsils in the underworld. The baddies are trying to make him jump into a pool with a man-eating barracuda.

'He doesn't mean it,' says Pardie.

When I look up, he finds a *Phantom* and gives me that too. At the gate, he looks back and waves. I love his red hair, the way it blows in the wind like a Jesus halo. Sometimes I wish I could have him for a brother instead of Dunc.

I watch them cross the road. The lagoon is full to the brim with oily brown water and fat ducks everywhere. My eyes are full to the brim but no one can see. I wish Dunc would take me nesting in the tea-tree where he finds the spotted plover nests, and in the dunes behind the surf beach where there are blue wrens, spoggies and red-beaked parakeets. I wish he would dink me out past Five Mile Drain to the bottom paddocks of Bindilla where hawks and crows and wedge-tailed eagles live in the eucalypts. And I would hide amongst the heaths and bracken without making a sound and watch for emus on the farming flats. *They're so stupid,* I would tell Dad when we got back, *that half the time they lead you straight to their nest.* And I wish Dunc would let me help him carry the eggs home. I would take off my sock and carry them in the toe, the small ones in my mouth. I would arrive with bulging cheeks and spit the eggs onto his bed—if he would let me, which he doesn't. But I have watched from the spare room, which is Dad's bedroom, with the window to the sunroom. I have watched Dunc take a sewing needle and prick the eggs at either end. Then he leans over a bowl and blows gently, trying not to blow too hard in case the yolk and egg-white slime come out too quickly and make a ragged end. And when the yolk is blown, he checks for the spot of blood, the bird that might have been. Sometimes it is too late and all the blowing in the world can't get the yolk to move. Then he breaks the shell and flushes out a white-boned thing with bulbous eyes and frail blue claws, a heart and transparent things beneath a pale pink skin.

Dunc has the best collection of birds' eggs in all of Burley Point. He keeps them in shoeboxes on the shelves next to his bed where I am double-banned.

He has gone. I could sneak in. I could look for his skull ring. I could lie on his bed and read his *Phantom* comics and smooth the spread when I had finished.

I am ready to go in, when Mrs Winkie comes down the side path with Lizzie. 'You two play here,' she says, opening the wire door and walking right in. 'You there, Nella?'

Lizzie and I follow into the kitchen. Aunt Cele is trying to lift her camera legs but Dad says for once in his life it won't hurt him to be a gentleman and he lifts them for her. He says hullo to Mrs Winkie but his eyes slide over Lizzie and me. He is still wearing his good shoes. I know his toes inside those shoes are as white as crayfish meat. I wish his toes would grow into crayfish legs and get caught in a crayfish pot and cooked and cracked open at the fish factory and his white toe meat plucked out by the women picking fish: that is my wish.

When he has gone, Lizzie and I are allowed to have biscuits at the table.

'So what's her story?' says Mrs Winkie.

'Photographer's assistant. All over the state.'

'Separate rooms at Hannigan's?'

'What's that got to do with it?'

'Just wondering what else she gets paid for.'

Mum's eyes smile over her cup. 'She wants to take more photos of Sylvie. Wants to work by herself one day. That's what she says.'

'Big ideas,' says Mrs Winkie.

Aunt Cele drives fast around corners and laughs a splintery laugh. She wears pants like a man and a brown scarf at her neck. Along Main Street, the tops of the Christmas-tree pines poke into a pearly sky. At the beach, she slams the car door hard and says, 'I love Burley Point, don't you?'

I am a dumbcluck without a tongue. On the moorings, the dinghies are waiting for the boats to come in. The sea is soapy green and speckled with sun spots. Surf is spraying up a mist on Eastern Beach and all around the bay to West End. I follow Aunt

Cele over the foreshore lawn to the sea wall, which runs all the way from the jetty to Stickynet Bridge. Gulls wheel and scream above the fish factory then settle on the rotunda roof and fly off again.

'Scat,' says Aunt Cele, waving her arms and running from their flapping wings. She lifts me off the sea wall and pulls me along the beach but she has long horse legs that gallop over the sand. There are pillows of black kelp everywhere. I trip and fall.

'Upsadaisy.' She brushes sand from my knees and finds a sponge washed in on the tide. 'Look at this.' She throws it to me to catch like a ball. 'Let's build a castle.' And while I do, she clicks at me. 'Look,' she says, 'Sylvie, look,' and when I do she click-look-clicks.

'Now the back beach.' She pulls me along the sand, past rocky reefs and pools full of green lettuce weed. On the path over Poppy's Lookout, wind tears at our hair and flattens our faces into monkey masks. From the headland, we look across to the lighthouse on Seal Island where Mr Hammett has to take the gas bottle to keep the light flashing at night. Aunt Cele says there is no land between us and the bottom of the world where everything is white ice and there are penguins as big as men, but I know this already because Dunc has told me.

Turning around, we look down on Burley Point. 'Almost an island,' says Aunt Cele and, although I've never thought of this before, I can see what she means. There is water on three sides of our town—the big scoop of bay with the long jetty and beach where we play, the back beach behind, the houses squashed in by Lake Grey with pale scrubby dunes where the town ends, the farms a blur far away.

'Water everywhere,' says Aunt Cele and she tells me that Lake

Grey is one of a bracelet of lakes linked to the Coorong in the north. I have a gold bracelet with a key heart and chain that I keep for best, and I've seen the Coorong from the train on our way to the city. She says there are underground rivers and caves, with swamps and lagoons that dry and disappear and reappear. This is true about the lagoon. It is a brown egg in the middle of Burley Point. But she is wrong about the salty lake near the dunes where we learned to swim; it never dries up.

'Who's that?' says Aunt Cele, dropping my hand.

It is Pardie's mum, high on Postman's Rock, standing close to the edge; I can tell by her red hair. But Aunt Cele doesn't stay to find out. 'Wait here,' she says before charging onto the back beach.

I follow, running to catch up. On the Rock, she creeps up behind Pardie's mum and grabs her. 'I'll let you go,' she says as Pardie's mum struggles to get free, 'if you won't...' She nods at the cliff.

Pardie's mum laughs like a parrot, a screech, then silence. 'There's a stingray down there, a huge one, trapped by the tide.'

Aunt Cele is a popped balloon. 'Careful,' she tells me as we walk to the edge. And in a rock pool below, drifting and swaying in the shadowy weed, is a huge black stinger.

'I'm sorry,' says Aunt Cele. 'I thought you...'

'I don't think I'd do it that way,' says Pardie's mum.

'No,' says Aunt Cele, 'it's too...'

'...far down.'

'...cold.'

'...dangerous.'

Now they both laugh, silly and soft as the pigeons in the goods shed. As we step back from the edge, Aunt Cele says she's my aunt and Mick's cousin and why haven't they met before? Pardie's mum says she's married to Augie, who fishes with Mick. She opens her hand and gives me five creamy cowries she's found on the beach.

Aunt Cele says: 'I'd love to photograph you.'

Pardie's mum giggles and says the boats will be in soon and she has to get to work.

We watch as she walks along the beach, her footsteps following on the wet sand.

'What's her name?' says Aunt Cele.

'Pardie's mum,' I say.

When I turn five, I go to school with Lizzie Campbell, Faye Daley and Colleen Mulligan. We are the mid-year intake for Grade One, in the same room as the other Grade Ones and Twos with Miss Taylor, our teacher, and the blackboard divided down the middle for the two grades. I know the answers to the Grade Two sums but I don't say anything. Dunc is in Grade Six in a different room and his teacher is the headmaster, Mr Tucker. I walk to school with Dunc but he doesn't play with me because I am a girl.

In my double-lined exercise book, I write rows of beautiful 'f's, trying to keep their backs straight, curving their hats, tying them in the middle with bows. If my 'f's are the best—better than Lizzie's and Colleen's, better than Roy Kearney's and Chicken McCready's—I will get an elephant stamp. I will take my book home to show Mum. Dunc and Dad might see.

Miss Taylor says: 'Beautiful work, Sylvie.'

Miss Taylor is as beautiful as the 'f's she writes on the

blackboard. She has creamy white skin and glossy brown hair like the pageboy in the story about the king's court. Her voice is soft but firm and even the big boys in Grade Two know not to be naughty.

When I show my 'f's to Mum, she says, 'I could have been a teacher. Margaret Taylor's not that bright.'

'So why didn't you?' says Dunc. He grabs my book and looks at my 'f's but he's humming and doing hip swivels, not looking properly.

'Because,' says Mum, lighting a ciggie, 'I didn't have a grand-mother offering to send me to boarding school. I had a mother with bad nerves. I had to leave school as soon as I could and I was lucky to get a job as a telephonist, that's why.'

'I'm going to Muswell High,' says Dunc, dropping my book on the table, 'same as Pardie.'

'We'll see about that.'

'Good 'f's,' says Dunc, sliding towards the door on his socks.

He spoke! I'm not dead!

Later, when Grannie Meehan comes to visit, she brings us meat from Bindilla. I show her my 'f's and she says: 'I had the best copperplate of anyone in my class.'

Aunt Cele's photos are on the table in a brown envelope, with no airbrushing. Grannie holds them close to her nose because she's left her glasses at home.

'How's Dunc? Still top of his class?'

Mum says he is. She unpacks Grannie's meat; it is a dead sheep. Grannie doesn't visit very often because she can't drive a car or truck and has to wait for Uncle Ticker to bring her into Burley Point. Uncle Ticker doesn't come inside with Grannie because a long time ago he had an argument with Dad and they don't speak. Before their argument, Dad and Mum lived at Bindilla and Dad used to ride his horse into the pub. The horse could find its own way home to Bindilla with Dad drunk on its back, the whole twelve miles, crossing Stickynet Bridge and following the path around the lake to the bottom paddocks, never once getting lost or tossing Dad off.

Grannie squints at Dad's photo. 'He could've done law, he had the brains. All he wanted to do was ride horses. How'd he end up fishing, that's what I want to know? And blessed with that voice. I wanted him trained, I told you that, didn't I?' Mum nods and slides bits of dead sheep onto a plate. 'Wouldn't listen. Might as well've saved my breath.' She takes the next photo from me. 'Boys need a father to whip them into shape, simple as that.'

Mum sucks in her top lip and turns to the sink. Grannie studies the photo of Dunc and me. 'Maybe Dunc'll be the one. I'll pay to put him through law, you know that.' Then she looks back at Dad's photo. 'Well, let's hope he makes a go of fishing. Horseracing's for kings. And fools. And he's long past singing for his supper.'

Mum takes ages washing her hands. Grannie puts three spoons of sugar in her tea and stirs up a flurry.

'I suppose you've heard about Cele? She's left Jack and she's squatting in the sand hills out near Stickynet in that old shack of Spog Ward's? Have you seen her?'

Mum shakes her head.

Grannie says: 'After all I did for her. You can't keep running, that's what I told her when she called into Bindilla the last time she was here with that dodgy photographer. And you know what she said?'

Mum doesn't know.

'She said: *Sometimes the gas oven looks pretty good.* I told her not to talk rot. Her father ruined her, traipsing her around the world at fourteen when she should have been in school. More like a wife than a daughter. Only thinking of himself, that's what I said. And you know what she said?'

Mum shakes her head again.

'*A ruined woman, that's me.* I said you will be if you don't do the right thing by Jack, he's a good man and a good husband, and you won't do better than a banker. He could've gone to Tokyo, did you know that? She could've gone too. Now she ups and leaves. Well, there'll be no welcome mat for her at Bindilla. Marriage is for life and that's that. And what's she come back here for? That's what I want to know.'

Mum still doesn't know. But I do. 'Aunt Cele loves Burley Point.'

They stare at me with owl eyes. 'She's not your aunt,' says Grannie, 'she's your third cousin, twice removed, which makes her nothing to you.' She puts down her cup with a clatter and pushes back her chair. 'And she's nothing to me either.'

4

Other times I've looked under his mattress, in the jar with his marbles, but never in the boxes on the shelves next to his bed. They are labelled in Dunc's curly writing. *Red Wattle Bird. White Browed Scrub Wren. Rufus Bristlebird*, which Dunc calls *Hopping Dolly Bird* because sometimes they fly so close to the ground that they look like little dolls hopping along. Would he hide his ring under an egg? I lift a lid. Inside are five eggs on a nest of cotton wool, marbled blue and pink, spotted black and white. *Grey Shrike Thrush. Butcher Bird. Red Brow Firetail Finch.* No skull ring. I lift more lids. *Singing Honeyeater. Silvereye. Tawny Frogmouth. Rufus Bristlebird.* Still no ring.

A shadow at the window of Dad's room! I jump back with guilty speed and press against the wall, harder, flatter. Mum making up his bed? Or has Dunc come home from Pardie's?

Dad! He should be pulling pots? I flatten smaller, my head a spin. Then the door opens and he walks right in. 'Whaddya up to?'

'Looking.'

Taking the box from my hands, he sits on Dunc's bed. *Common Coot. Hooded Plover. Superb Blue Wren.* He lifts out a willy-wagtail egg.

'One of the few that build two nests a year. Ever seen one?' I shake my head. 'Here.' He pats the bed next to him. I don't move.

He looks up and beckons with his head. I sit beside him carefully, warily. He smells of Brylcreem and whiskers and the soapy scent of his shaving brush beside the basin.

'They're this big.' He shapes his thumb and forefinger into a small circle. He smells of something secret like a bird's nest might smell of if you sniffed inside when the bird had left. 'Made out of grass and cobwebs and hair. When they're building their nests you see them cleaning the cobwebs off rafters and gutters and flying back with full beaks. Good-looking nests they build too, smooth and strong, you'd think they were made of cement.' He returns the egg to the nest and examines another. 'When I was a kid, I saw them build a nest inside a dog kennel. You know why they did that?'

'They liked dogs?'

He laughs, more like a snuffle. 'Maybe. Could be. Mostly it's because they're not stupid, they know they're safe near a dog. Safe from rats and cats and foxes. And dogs don't seem to mind birds chirping above their heads. Whaddya think about that?'

I think he holds that egg gently as if it might break. I think he has fingernails bitten like Lizzie's. I think he might like Willy Wagtails better than me and my head is a muddle and the cat's got my tongue.

'Once I saw them build a nest in a shed at Bindilla where a pair of Sparrowhawks were camped. Hawks are mouse-eaters and the Willies knew they were safe there too. Another time, they built a nest on the tractor and every time I drove the tractor, they came for a ride.' Is he telling a lie? When I look up his black eyes are smiling into mine. 'It's true,' he says before I look away. 'When the eggs hatched, the young came too, squawking their heads off.'

He replaces the egg in the box and carefully fits the lid. 'I reckon those Willies learned to fly a whole lot sooner than they should've.'

He returns the box to the space between *Brush Bronzewing* and *Western Whipbird*. Then he reaches to the top shelf and takes down a box marked *Emu*. 'This'—he opens the box and holds it out so that I have to stand and move closer—'is one of the best emu eggs you'll ever see. I found it for Dunc at Bindilla.' Again he sits on the bed and places the box on his knees, carefully lifting out the egg. 'You want to hold it?'

It is warm and light, greenish black, a precious thing. 'You probably don't know this,' he says, 'but every season emus lay several batches of eggs. And you know who sits on the eggs?'

'The mother?'

'The bloody father. Doesn't even get off the eggs to eat, and loses half his body weight over eight weeks. And then he's the one who raises the young. The female goes strutting off to find another mate and lay more eggs.'

He takes the egg from my hands and places it back in the box. 'Sometimes nature gets things a bit wrong, but that's how it is. Anyway,' he says, returning the box to the shelf, 'you'd better be careful. You'll be in the poo with Dunc if you break something.'

When he's gone, I sit on the bed, empty of air. I hear him whistling in the kitchen, his footsteps on the drive, then his singing. '*...shake hands with your Uncle Mike, me boy...da da, da da, da da...you're welcome as the flowers...da da...*' The car drives off. I think of him taking baby Willies for a ride on the tractor, their squeaky beaks and scrubby feathers. *Da da, da da, da da.*

'Haven't I told you to stay out of here and leave his comics alone?' says Mum. 'Put them back where you found them. You're staying with the Daley kids while I go to Muswell.'

Mrs Daley is the tiniest mother I know; she comes up to Mum's shoulder. I like Mrs Daley but not Faye, who bosses me around worse than she bosses her sisters, Dawn and Dot. Faye and her sisters are the dead spit of each other, only one year apart, with the same curly brown hair. At the Institute Fancy Dress, they went as Snap, Crackle and Pop, wearing big cereal boxes decorated by Mrs Daley. I wore my bathers and Mum wrote 'Miss Burley Point' in red lipstick letters on a white satin sash. I threw up in the dunnies and smudged the words and had to go home with Mum pulling me by the arm and not speaking.

In the sunroom, I take my time and read Dunc's new *Phantom*. The Ghost Who Walks is feared by bad men everywhere. When Mum calls out again, I stack the comics next to Dunc's bed. The Phantom moves as silently as fog. At the door to the Deep Woods, I wait with the cunning of a fox and a thousand eyes and ears.

In the kitchen, Mum is dying. 'I'm dying on my feet,' she tells Mrs Daley. She puts her head in her hands and talks to the table but the Phantom can hear a whisper through the jungle. 'I have to see a solicitor. Get some advice. He's playing around with that trollop again, I know he is.'

'What's a trollop? What's a solicitor?'

Mum lifts her head and stares at me.

The Phantom can knock a flea off a warthog at a hundred paces without hurting the beast. There are no warthogs in Burley Point but Bullfrog Fraser and his deckhand are first in with their catch, pushing their trolley along the jetty then crossing the road to the fish factory. Bullfrog's muscles bulge and the legs of his frog tattoo threaten to leap right off his arm.

He says: 'Hullo, Blue Daley's kids.'

Faye, Dawn and Dot stop licking their toffee apples long enough to singsong: 'Hullo, Bullfrog.'

'Mister Bullfrog, to you,' he says with a croaky laugh.

Bullfrog has a bigger beer belly than Denver Boland, who is the Council Chairman and lives with Mrs Denver in the biggest house in Burley Point, opposite the beach. Bullfrog lives with Mrs Bullfrog Fraser near the Point. He doesn't speak to me because Dad says he's a creep. My hand is hurting from the toffee burn. On the trolley, the bags are piled three high, wet and dripping. Feelers, legs and beady eyes poke through the hessian and the crays thrash about inside. They smell of dead rabbit bait and deep, rocky reefs. Bullfrog lumps his cray bags onto the weighing machine which stands guard outside the fish factory door. I hear the crunch of broken arms and legs and wonder if the hurt from my burn could be as bad as broken crayfish legs.

Mrs Daley is picking fish, filling in for Merle McCready, Chicken and Sid's grandma, who is sick. We wait just inside the door while Ron Quigly lifts the big basket with the pulley chain from the boiler in the corner. Mrs Daley is first in with the others, scrambling to get the biggest spiders as soon as they're dropped hot and hissing into the trough, grabbing them before the steam has time to clear. Gert Nobel and Hazel Bird push past Pardie's mum, who doesn't seem to care. In their white rubber pinnies and boots and gloves, they look like factory ghosts, their hair tucked inside plastic hoods. Mrs Daley lugs her crate back to the picking table and beckons us over. Already she is separating tails and spiders, smashing her hammer onto claws and poking out meat with a long skewer spike. In no time she fills a box with cray meat, slaps it onto the roller belt and begins again, cracking, poking, picking. Faye yells in her mother's ear and because we weren't meant to be making toffee by ourselves, I keep my hand hidden behind my back. The fish stink is up my nose and when Mr Quigly starts hosing the floor I push out the door.

On the jetty, I lean over the rail and watch sunlight rippling the shallows below. Three gulls are riding the swell, chests puffed out in full sail. When I look up, Aunt Cele is standing outside the fish factory door, talking and laughing with Pardie's mum. Then Dad's jeep swings round the roundabout. His hair is swept up like a cocky crest and I wonder why he didn't go out with the other fishermen to pull his pots, and why Dunc is with him, and where they've been, and where they're going. And I see how they look like each other and I wonder if I look like Dad? Or Mum? Or anyone? And why Dad looks at the jetty but doesn't see me, and why he doesn't want me for a sunbeam like Blue Daley wants Faye?

When he's gone, I blink dust from my eyes and see that his boat and Bullfrog's are the only ones riding their moorings. *What are we going to live on,* says Mum inside my head, *if you don't pull your pots for three days? What about us?*

'Come on,' calls Faye. 'I've got the lines. We're allowed to go to Stickynet.'

The inlet is full of secret underwater things swirling near the surface. Halfway along, we find the shady place where roots reach into the water. It is quiet except for dragonflies *whip-whipping* as they dip and dart, and sometimes the rumble of a car crossing the bridge. On the lake, there are pelicans and black swans with fish-hook necks and, further out, a fisherman pulling his net, his dinghy heavy in the water.

There is no bait. Faye says we should get a stick and dig for worms. She doesn't say how to carry them back when we find them or who is going to put them on hooks while they're still wriggling. I walk along the edge of the inlet, poking about, not finding anything. On the corner where the track disappears into the tea-tree, two cars are parked in the shadows. One is Dad's jeep.

When the jungle sleeps, the Phantom wakes. The jeep smells of dead soldiers and garage grease. On the back seat, there's a girl with big boobies smiling a faded smile from the cover of the *Post*. There's a green army blanket and a glass lobster pot with broken rope webbing, and on the floor in the front, a squashed packet of Camel ciggies. The other car is new and blue.

Where are Dad and Dunc? On cat's paws, the Phantom moves through the Deep Woods, taking care not to rustle the reeds. She creeps under hangings of Old Man's Beard. Suddenly, a low grunt behind a whiskered curtain and she folds into the trunk of a tree. Only a fool crosses the Phantom: she takes a silent step and parts the curtain a slit. A man's bottom in the air! Two hands with painted nails, pink as salmon fish, are pressed into his skin. They're doing the same as the dogs at Bindilla. The lady lifts her head and I see it's Mrs Bullfrog Fraser without her Sunday-school

44

clothes! But who is the man? A bull ant climbs up his leg. 'Shit!' he says, bucking up, slapping his knee.

It's Mr Sweet the butcher, Kenny's dad! But who's minding the shop? Mr Sweet has the stick thing between his legs and two hairy eggs either side that bounce on the ground as he scratches. Mrs Bullfrog props on her elbows and her boobies drop down to her belly. Then a car starts up.

Dad's jeep! I can tell by the way it revs and roars. Mrs Bullfrog and Mr Sweet look at each other like rabbits with heads cocked to the side. And I'm off like a rabbit too, hopping over dead branches, leaping through reeds, twisting around trees. I creep along the bank. I am The Ghost Who Walks.

Of course Faye sees me coming. 'Where were you? We've caught two flatties. You're s'posed to stay with us till your mother gets home.'

I think of telling her about Mrs Bullfrog and Mr Sweet but a whisper can go around the earth so I don't say a word. She is lobbing her sinker into the middle of the inlet when the train whistles out near Big Tree turnoff. The cold words of the Phantom can chill a tiger's blood. 'My mother *is* home,' I tell her.

The train noses out of the scrub and slows on the bridge. Sometimes the Phantom has to leave the jungle and walk the streets of the town like an ordinary girl. As I run along the bank, Faye calls after me. 'The toffee was an accident! Tell your mother it wasn't my fault!'

Uncle Ticker is parked at our gate in the Bindilla truck, which means Grannie is visiting. Because Uncle Ticker is not a brother's backside, he is waiting in the truck. His ciggie flies out the window. 'What've you done to your hand?'

'Hot toffee,' I tell him, jumping on his butt to stop it smoking.

He winces. 'Sore?'

'Not as bad as before.'

He looks up the drive. 'They've been at it for half an hour. Give her a hurry-up, will you?'

At the back door, I hear Grannie's voice, loud and bossy like she gets when she's ruling the roost with Uncle Ticker. 'Divorce?! You're not the King of England with that Wallis woman. You can't just make your own rules and cast your wife off like an old shoe. I have to live in this town too. Have another kid. That'll get things back on track.'

Then a crash like a falling chair. 'That ponce at the gate might like you running his life but I don't. Why don't you piss off back to Bindilla and mind your own business?'

Grannie barrels out the back door in her bunion shoes, black-bird hat, spotty dress. She beckons me down the drive and leans into my face. Her breath smells of scones, mulberry jam, milky tea.

'Was that you I saw out near Stickynet? With those Daley kids?' I nod. 'What were you thinking of? What if you'd fallen in and drowned? Did your mother know?'

'She was in Muswell.'

'Well, that's when you need to use your head and think for yourself.' She picks up my bandaged hand. 'What's this?'

'Making toffee.'

She looks into my eyes as if she knows exactly how it happened. 'You're too young to be making toffee by yourself.'

'I'm almost six.'

Now she looks as if she's doing sums in her head. 'Five and a bit isn't six. How's school?'

'All right.'

'Thank you.'

'All right, thank you.'

'Come and stay with me next weekend. Give your mother a bit of a rest.'

She stamps down the drive. Uncle Ticker has her door open and the engine running. They forget to wave.

Who is that Wallis woman? What is a divorce? There are prickles inside my nose and my hand throbs. I can't think why I want to cry, because the Phantom is made of rock. I listen at the door with my thousand ears but there are no more yelling voices. I know I should go in but he who sees the Phantom's face dies a horrible death so I sit on the step and wish Grannie was still here ruling our roost so I wouldn't have to use my head and think for myself.

5

Dad puts his foot on the chair next to mine and ties double knots. His hair is slicked down smooth and he smells of my shampoo. He's going to the footy because the Roosters are playing at home. Dunc and Pardie are already there. Mum says she might take me after she's made a sponge but I know she won't; she doesn't like footy.

'Ticker's lost his marbles,' says Dad to his shoe. 'He's shaved every bloody tree off the ridge on Robe Road. I asked Denver bloody Boland if he knows what's going on. You know what he tells me?' Mum's beating eggs so Dad flicks a look at me as if I'll do for the asking. 'Ticker's building a bloody big ditch. Reckons he can drain the swamp right through the range into the lake.'

'Big ideas,' says Mum, putting down the beater.

It's not the right answer. I can tell by the way Dad pulls on his nose and frowns at his fingers. 'Big?' His voice gets louder. 'Try barmy. Try ten bob short of a shilling. Goes off to New Guinea and builds a few bridges for the war effort, comes back thinking he's an engineer. How many years ago is that? Ten?'

'Something like that,' says Mum.

'I worked on the roads in the Top End and dug plenty of dunny holes in the jungle around Darwin and I didn't come back thinking I was the council engineer, did I?' Mum doesn't answer and Dad looks at me. Before I can shake my head, he goes on: 'Anyway, I said to Denver: How'd this get through council? You're the bloody chairman, I said, shouldn't people be given a chance to object? He says it was advertised in the *Mail*. And I say: Yes, in print the size of fly shit. Then I said: What about the orange-bellied parrot? And ya know what he says?'

My eyes go cross-eyed with looking and listening.

'*Orange-bellied what*? That's what he says. I'd get myself elected if I thought it'd do any good but who'd want to work with that group of mugs. Anyway, I told him the orange-belly breeds in Tassie and comes here to winter. Told him they need saltmarsh and samphire and what's going to happen when every swamp's been drained for miles around? You know what he says?'

I uncross my eyes. Mum turns from the stove with her mouth twitching and I wonder what I've missed in my listening because nothing seems funny to me. Then she blinks at me, just one blink—or is it a wink?

'*Can't it find another swamp*? That's what he says. Can you believe it?'

A sound escapes from Mum's mouth. 'Maybe Denver's right,' she says between snuffles that grow into giggles. 'We've got nothing but water around here. Aren't those purple parrots' — more giggles— 'smart enough to find another swamp?'

Dad doesn't laugh. He pulls on his nose and watches Mum as she wipes at her eyes with the tea-towel and her giggles slowly stop.

'Orange,' he says quietly, before heading into the lounge.

'Orange. Pink. Purple.' Mum slides onto the chair next to me. 'Who cares?' She shakes her head and sighs heavily. 'Who's the mad one? How'd you ever know?'

Suddenly Dad's back at the door, rifle in his hands, face smiley smooth. He lifts the gun. 'Think this is funny?'

'Don't be stupid…Mick…'

A shot explodes in my ears and eyes, piddles my pants, the smell of bonfires and Guy Fawkes, rabbits in spotlights, their sad floppy ears. But when I open my eyes, Mum's right there, staring at a hole above our heads where plaster is drifting down like snow. At the door, Dad looks cocky.

Mum reaches to the sink, grabs a saucepan and hurls it at his head. 'Get out!' she screams.

Dad ducks into the laundry porch. When the saucepan bounces off the door, he pokes his head back in. 'Rotten shot.'

Mum throws the saucepan lid. 'Get out and stay out!'

Now she grabs the jam dish. It hits the wall high up and Dad laughs a crazy laugh, and then I see the dish sliding slowly down the wall with a snail trail of apricot jam following behind. It hits the skirting board and topples onto the floor. I think of snail shine on the morning path. Of Chicken McCready jumping on snails and the way their green stomachs ooze out.

When I look back, Dad has gone.

I hide in the leaves of the kurrajong tree. I hide in my reading and writing and sums. I hide in my Sunday-school singing and Mrs Bullfrog's big bosom breathing the hymns, that same secret bosom I've seen at the lake without her pink-strapped brassiere. I hide in the stillness that flattens the sea before the storm comes, in the cloud of black ducks that spreads like an inkblot across the white sky. I hide in Miss Taylor's kind eyes. I hide.

'For once in your life, just do what you're asked and take her with you.'

Dunc says they can't dink me, not carrying the net and bucket. Pardie opens his mouth to speak but Dunc frowns him into silence.

Pardie has grown red fur on his face. In the light from the window, he shines like an angel with a halo. I have stuck my Sunday-school stamp into my Jesus book. It is the Rock of Gethsemane stamp and Mrs Bullfrog gave it to me because I knew it took three days for Jesus to rise again. Dunc doesn't go to Sunday school because it's for Methodists and we're Catholics, but the priest only comes once a month so Mum says, what does it matter, she was a Methodist before she got married. Dad says we're descended from apes and anyone who thinks there's a Heaven or Hell needs their head read. There are a lot of redheads in Burley Point—Jude and Pardie Moon, Mr Sweet and his son Kenny, even Blue Daley is a darkish kind of red, which is why he's called Blue. Redheads are always called Blue.

Mum narrows her eyes at Dunc. 'It won't hurt you for once.'

Who will win? The Demon Dunc or The Phantom Mother? Who will take the Jungle Girl into the Deep Woods where the pygmy people live?

Pardie saves the day. 'It's all right, Mrs Meehan, I'll dink her.'

'We're not taking turns,' warns Dunc as we wait for Mum to make sandwiches. 'She's all yours, the whole way.'

Outside the Institute there is a poster for a film called *Oklahoma*. Pardie says he wouldn't miss it for quids. Dunc rides ahead, skidding around Lanky Evans as he crosses the street. The sea is a bright autumn green, with the boats all riding their moorings; soon it will be the end of the season, no more fishing until next spring. After Stickynet, the wattles are bent over the road in a long tunnel. The sun shines through in dappled patches and Pardie's hay fever makes him sneeze even though there are no flowers. At Big Tree turn-off, the farms are a green rug all around and Dunc on the road far ahead. When we arrive at Five Mile Drain, he's already tying meat onto strings.

I squat on the edge of the canal and watch the water swirling towards the sea. There are skater beetles catching a ride, a spider on a leaf, even a dag of wool from a sheep. Dunc's legs next to mine are brown and scabby. After we've caught nine yabbies—two of them mine—we eat our sandwiches on top of the bank and there's a happy buzz in the milkweed and an old black crow watching from the other bank. When a tractor starts up on the range, Dunc tells Pardie it's probably Uncle Ticker and why don't we leave the yabbies in the bucket and take a look at his ditch?

As we ride beside the lake, three pelicans fly so low over our heads that we can hear wind through their feathers. Pardie says they're flying home to their breeding grounds with their bellies full of fish from the reefs. Dunc says they mate for life and maybe one of them's a young'un and they're coming home from Lake Eyre. Pardie says the fathers sometimes peck the young ones to death, but the mother feeds them with her own blood and after three days they come alive again.

I wonder if Dad's orange-bellied parrots could fly to Lake Eyre for a good feed. If parrots mate for life like pelicans? If parrots peck their babies to death, and if they come alive after three days like Jesus did? There is too much to know.

At the top of the lane that leads to the ridge, Uncle Ticker has fenced a viewing platform but there's not much to see. The tractor has cleared all the trees and there's white rock underneath. Pardie says it's got a long way to go and wouldn't a bulldozer be better? Dunc says a Caterpillar with a double winch and blade is just as good. He says before long they'll be blasting right through the rock. It's hard to see who's driving the tractor—Uncle Ticker or Chicken's uncle who works at Bindilla. The swamp is a purple-green sea far off to the fence line. I think of all the snakes that must live in those reeds and I'll be glad when they're gone, whatever Dad says about parrots. Dunc says when Uncle Ticker's finished he'll have himself another thousand acres so it's not such a hair-brained idea.

Pardie lobs a rock into the ditch. 'Who says it is?'

Dunc lobs a rock too. 'My Dad, for one.'

And suddenly they're both firing off rocks as if it's a fight with no rules and there's nothing but rocks raining down on the ditch until the tractor turns and trundles towards us and we tear into the bush on the other side of the road, crashing through bracken and banksias, wattles and heaths, running fast, me in the middle where it's safest from snakes, running fast to keep up, my legs scratched by branches and slipping on rocks, Pardie laughing and sneezing close behind.

We stop in a small clearing surrounded by black yakkas and wild cherry trees and a giant muddy gum growing beside a big rock. The sound of the tractor is now far off. Dunc says there's a cave around here, millions of years old and full of fish fossils because once it was under the sea. He says an Abo used to live there, and maybe still does. I can hear my heart thumping loud in my ears and I can feel the sea breathing in the grass under my feet. We sneak around looking for the cave, whispering so the Abo won't hear. Everything is warm and quiet like a secret and I have a feeling of being watched by someone like God who knows all my hidden thoughts.

Suddenly there's a loud rustle in the bushes and we turn with a fright in case it's the Abo. It's an emu! Staring at us with crazy bold eyes and, as we stare back, not breathing, not moving, its long neck pokes at the air like a stretched question mark. Then Pardie sneezes, sending it sprinting off in a flap, our laughter chasing it into the scrub far away.

Pardie's freckles are bright against his pale skin, his eyes wide and as crazy as the emu's. 'Let's get out of here.'

Dunc doesn't argue and leads us over logs and dead branches, me in the middle and my mind full of black men with spears, and snakes and emus that could peck out your eyes, all of it mixed up in the panic of following. We are almost clear of the scrub when Dunc stops. There on a fallen tree is a beautiful green and blue bird, twittering and talking in a pretty bird voice. *Georgie Porgie Georgie Porgie,* it says, clear as a bell. One step at a time, Dunc moves forward, the bird still talking: *Georgie Porgie Georgie Porgie.* Closer, Dunc reaches out with his hand and the bird steps onto his fingers and walks up his arm. Dunc says it's a budgerigar which is really a small parrot, sometimes called a lovebird. He says it must have escaped from a cage and might not survive in the wild. He lifts the bird to his face and makes kissy sounds and the bird nuzzles his lips and whistles happily. In the same quiet voice, Dunc asks me if I'd like it for a pet. I'm so surprised that I don't answer but Dunc tucks it inside his shirt anyway. He says I can keep it in the cage he found at the tip and used for the rosella that died. He says I'll have to clean out the cage every day and give it a name. That's easy, I say, Georgie Porgie, that's his name.

When we get to the bikes, Dunc says he'll dink me because it's downhill all the way. I'm surprised for the second time and climb on the bar in front of him. We coast down the hill, gathering speed, Dunc singing 'Rock Around the Clock' and Georgie Porgie squeaking inside his shirt.

At the bottom, Dad's jeep is parked by the side of the road, half-hidden behind a she-oak. His binoculars are trained on Uncle Ticker's tractor. Dunc stops singing and rides past without stopping, pedalling faster, faster. The sky is enormous, blue without one cloud. I won't tell Mum we saw Dad. You can forget everything if you want to.

Dad comes home from the Coorong with a train full of brumbies for bait and there is buck-jumping at the station stockyards.

Aunt Cele and Pardie's mum are sitting on the rail opposite Lizzie and me. Next to Aunt Cele is that Lewis woman who is married to Mr Lewis with the ginger moustache and the war medals on Anzac Day. Lizzie says if they're going to kill the horses for bait they should do it straightaway and not play rodeos with them, they are poor dumb creatures and they don't know what's happening. She says she'd rather go and get a Paddle Pop. Or we could spy on Wanda the Witch. I tell her I want to see my dad ride.

The horses are boxed in the stockyards behind the goods shed. I can smell their horse terror; it is the smell of salty plains and blue skies and men with lassos. The smell shivers through the air in loud snorts and terrified whinnies and mixes with the noise of everyone cheering.

Dunc and Pardie are working the gate with Bullfrog Fraser. First out is a horse with Chicken's brother, Sid, on its back. Sid is older than Chicken but he is soft in the head and hardly has time to look surprised before he's sitting in the dirt looking silly. Next is Pardie's dad. He rides halfway round the yard before he's off too. Then out gallops a black horse with Dad hanging on by a rope, no saddle, no stirrups, no reins. He is the best rider, everyone says. His horse tears around the yard as if it's trying to find a way out. It has a mad frightened look in its eyes and froth falls from its mouth. Then it stops. Dad hangs on. The horse whinnies, lowers its head and kicks up its hind legs. Dad leans back and waves his arm in a circle to balance; the horse rears and paws at the air and then lowers his head and snorts at the dirt, and still Dad stays on.

Everyone goes crazy, whistling and cheering. My heart is giddy with hope for Dad to win. I shout into the rodeo ring, which is really a square but I don't care because my Dad can win, I know he can. Again he gallops past and dust full of sheep poo and cow dung flies up in my face. Right in front, the horse twists and thuds into the fence, making the railings shake, making us jump to the ground just in case. And as I climb back, I see Dad on the ground.

'That's the winning ride or I'm a monkey's uncle,' says Denver Boland into the loudspeaker. 'Good on ya, Mick. Bring on the next rider.'

Dad finds his hat in the dirt and walks to the gate, waving and doing little bows. Then I see he's bowing to the fence where Aunt Cele and Pardie's mum are sitting. Although Aunt Cele has her camera, she's not taking photos. She is laughing with that Lewis woman as if they are best friends, and that Lewis woman is making loud whistles with her fingers stuck in her mouth. The sun shines on her shorts and long legs; it shines on her waving hand and turns her hair into a ginger frizz as if she is a rowdy angel without wings. As if she is the rodeo queen. And Dad is waving to her.

Her. It is her.

Straightaway I jump down from the railing and follow Lizzie through the goods shed where the trains stop to unload. Aunt Cele comes up behind.

'Long time no see. How are you, Sylvie?' She reaches out with long arms and lifts me right off my feet, pulls me around and cuddles me close. 'See your Dad win?'

I snap open her hands and break free of her tricks. 'No,' I say, as I scramble onto the platform. 'I didn't.'

'We did,' says Lizzie, climbing after me.

I push her. It feels good and I push her some more. 'We didn't.'

'Not the best place to play in here,' says Aunt Cele.

On the platform, I am taller than her. 'We always play here.'

She shrugs and smiles but I don't smile back. We watch her lope through the cutting and out the other end of the shed.

'Don't push me,' says Lizzie, pushing me back. 'You were rude to her. Isn't she your auntie?'

'She's not even a cousin. She's nothing to me.'

*

57

Once there was a girl Phantom. She was the twin sister of the seventeenth Phantom and her name was Julie Walker. When the Phantom was injured, she took his place. She had her own costume and mask and gun. She could do everything the Phantom could do. *The female of the species is more deadly than the male,* she told bandits before she shot them dead.

'Don't tell her that!' says Dunc.

'I've already told her,' says Pardie.

6

The invitation is hot and important in my hand. I run on the road. Left. Right. Jump on the grass. Jump off again. I pass Mrs Scott's house next door and wave the invitation but she doesn't see. She is talking to Mrs Winkie. 'You give them your blood and they want more.' Mrs Scott has no blood in her face. She looks like Faye Daley's albino rabbit with blue eyes instead of pink.

Mum is polishing the floor again. 'I've been invited to Colleen Mulligan's party,' I tell her but she's waltzing around the bedroom on her polishing cloths. 'Colleen's having a party,' I tell her again. 'I have to take a present.' But she's off in a cleaning dream and tells me to wait outside till she's finished.

I sit on the back step and show the invitation to Georgie. It has balloons and laughing clown faces that make him whistle and bop all around his cage.

'I have to take a present,' I tell Mum when she shakes out her dusters at the back door.

'But you don't even like her, do you?'

'That doesn't matter.' I follow her inside. 'Everyone's invited.'

'Who's everyone?'

Doesn't she know anything? 'The whole class. Everyone.'

She smells of Wunderwax and Turf cigarettes. 'I'm starting work at Trotter's Cafe next week. Wednesdays and Fridays. It'll be a bit of a change. After school, Mrs Daley will look after you. Understand?'

'What about the present?'

'I'll think of something.'

Something is a pair of nylon knickers, beige, with a bit of lace. 'They're too big,' I tell her on the day of the party. 'They're yours. I saw them in the drawer.'

Mum wraps them in tissue paper and knots them with a blue ribbon. 'She's a big girl. They've never been worn.'

Lizzie's present is smaller. She won't tell me what's inside. 'Wait and see,' she says as her mother drives us to the party.

Colleen lives at the end of Bog Lane, past the soldier-settler farms and the marshy bit that drains into Lake Grey. For miles the wattles are blooming sugary gold. Over the cattle ramp, the driveway to Colleen's house is lined with Christmas-tree pines. As soon as the car stops, Colleen comes running, followed by half the kids in our class. 'Welcome to my party,' she says like a parrot before grabbing my present, then Lizzie's. 'Come and see what I've got.'

Colleen has her own room. She has a bed with iron ends, frilly curtains at the window, even curtains covering the dressing-table legs. Her presents are spread on the bed. A yellow petal bathing cap and a pink plastic manicure set. The new *Secret Seven* book. The new *Archie, Superman* and *Phantom* comics, tied together with a red ribbon. I hope she wants to swap them with Lizzie or me because I now buy my own comics with money from collecting bottles. There's also a velvet headband and gold Jiffy slippers, a new hairbrush with a ballerina on the back, a set of hairgrips with coloured ends, a Violet Crumble that's probably from Chicken.

Colleen holds up Mum's kickers. 'They're…nice.'

Chicken snorts and pokes Roy Kearney. I catch Colleen giving her best friend, Shirley Fry, a raised eyebrow look. While Colleen opens Lizzie's present—Mickey Mouse swap cards—I slide the knickers under her pillow.

We play Pin the Tail, Brandy, Tag and Apple Dip, and then stuff ourselves with fairy bread and lamingtons. We sing 'Happy Birthday' to Colleen who turns pink and can't blow out the candles in one breath. When she cuts the cake, Chicken says the knife has to come out clean or she has to kiss a pig. Mrs Mulligan says it's not pigs, it's a boy, so it will have to be Chicken. Everyone laughs and Chicken's freckles turn red. The knife comes out clean and Colleen looks pleased but Chicken says *Phew* so many times that everyone knows he really wants to kiss Colleen.

Mrs Mulligan hands out slices of cake wrapped in paper serviettes and the cars arrive to take us home. As Lizzie and I are leaving, Colleen comes running, waving Mum's gussies above her head.

'These are too big. I'll have to change them for another size. Can you ask your mother where she got them?'

'I told you,' I say as soon as I walk in. 'I told you they were too big. Now what are we going to do?'

'She might forget,' says Mum.

She doesn't.

'My mother wants to know,' says Colleen next day at school. I take a Phantom leap from the bench under the cypress pine but miss and feel my shin crunch against the timber edge. Looking down, I'm pleased to see a lot of blood.

'She's bleeding!' yells Shirley Fry. 'Someone get Miss Taylor.'

I wince and jump around a lot. 'I think it's broken.'

'Of course it isn't,' says Colleen. 'You can't break a shin.' She goes on and on about shins and splints and how her mother used to be a nurse, but it keeps her mind off gussies.

I tell Mum that I have to stay home the next day because my leg hurts too much to walk to school. She takes off the bandage, sticks on a Band-Aid and says it doesn't look too bad. I am sitting with my leg stuck out in front and she is kneeling in front of me. I think of all the presents she could have got for Colleen except her old gussies, and why didn't she? I think of never having a birthday party like Colleen, not once, not even a cake. She looks up and I feel a frightened kind of power that makes me want to kick her hard in the heart. But her eyes drop back to my leg and she smooths the Band-Aid flat. 'All right,' she says.

The day after, I'm playing near the gate when Colleen steps off the school bus. 'You still haven't told me,' she says, pushing up close with her breakfast breath.

'At Min's in Muswell,' I say, backing away. 'My mother says you should have returned them straightaway. It's too late now.'

At lunchtime, I'm skipping when she says it. 'Anyway, you weren't really wanted. My mother says they only had you because they were trying to save a breaking marriage. She says your father's been playing around for years.'

My feet don't miss a beat. *Swish, skip.* Cicadas scream from the lemon gum tree. Spurts of dust rising like smoke off the melting asphalt. I skip towards Lizzie, who is skipping too. My arms ache and my legs are jelly. I think of Mum at the cafe making ham and cheese, ham and tomato sandwiches, wiping the laminex, counting out clinkers and jelly beans. I think of my dad playing around for years and what does it mean and how can I stop everything from breaking?

After school, I leave my case under the counter and tell Mum I'm going to play in the park with the Daley kids. She says: *Do you want a milkshake don't get dirty be home by five.*

On the swing facing the sea, I swing as high as the cypress pines. I can see the smile of Eastern Beach, the jetty rising and dipping, boats bouncing on their moorings, my father's boat the biggest of them all. The sky falls into the sea and clouds spin out of the trees. I think of days when I play in the park and Dad comes into the bay, cutting too close to the reef and heading too fast for his mooring. And later, when he pushes his crays down the jetty, his laughter sparkles on the sea like daytime stars, but he never sees me.

The Coorong slides by with pelicans and black swans floating upside down, with wattles drowning in the glassy water. On the other side of the bus, there are scrubby brown plains where Dad caught the brumbies for bait; there are dirty brown sheep and a man waving from a red tractor. Soon there is Lake Albert and Alexandrina named after a dead king and queen from England, Great Britain, United Kingdom, the Commonwealth, all the pink countries.

When I wake, there are grey streets and brick walls with no windows. There is a station and a man with no legs sitting on a cart selling newspapers, and Mum says, *Don't stare*; there is a van selling pies in pea soup called a floater, and no, I can't have one. After freshening up in the ladies we catch a train that rattles past houses with white walls and red roofs, row after row with low fences, rosebushes and square lawns, all the same.

Outside the gate, Mum straightens the bow in my hair. 'What'll it be this time? Always living beyond their means. Always something new, bought on the never-never. Why'd I come?'

I don't know.

We walk up the path and Mum knocks on the door. The veranda floor is polished red, the doorstep glistens black. There is a plant with glossy leaves in a pot next to the step. Grandpa Ted opens the door. His face is a shiny plate with piggy eyes and a Santa Claus nose.

'You've left him, haven't you? Well, you can't stay here.'

'I haven't. That's not why I've come.'

Grandpa Ted steps back. My nose is next to his leg. He smells of soap and mothballs and something filthy dirty underneath.

In the lounge room, there's a never-never lounge suite with every chair a different colour. On the wall, three ducks are flying towards the window. I want to be out that window. I want to be a duck on the Coorong or on Uncle Ticker's swamp. But not in the shooting season.

'Well, sit yourself down,' says Grandpa Ted in the kitchen. 'Bess'll be back soon. She'll make us a cuppa.' And as we wait, Grandpa Ted pulls out a chair and sits himself out. 'Divorce is a dirty word. If a man's having a fling there's something missing, that's what I think.'

Mum is looking at the laminex. There are swirly patterns, red and white clouds and a snake creeping out of the corner near me. I trace its scaly path with my finger; I wonder about the King and that Wallis woman and when I reach the doily in the centre near the vase of pink plastic flowers, Mum grabs my hand and puts it on her knee. 'Don't,' she says with a warning squeeze and I know she doesn't like Grandpa's smell either.

'Here's Bess,' says Grandpa Ted.

Grandma Bess has eyes without smiles. She takes biscuits from a tin and puts them on a plate. 'You haven't left him, have you?'

Mum shakes her head and nods at me.

Grandpa Ted takes a biscuit. 'Times are tough. It's no life for a woman trying to manage by herself.'

'Your father was promoted last month,' says Grandma Bess. 'Best thing Ted ever did, getting out of the railways. And Joyce and Bill have just moved into their new house. Lovely, isn't it, Ted?'

Grandpa Ted is spread all over the end of the table next to me. When he breathes, I can see hairs moving in his nose. Joyce is Mum's younger sister, the grumpy bridesmaid in the wedding photo on the mantelpiece. Mum doesn't like her because she's the favourite who never says boo to a goose. Auntie Joyce has two boys who are my cousins but we hardly ever see them because we are not a close family.

Grandma Bess and Grandpa Ted sip their tea and dip their biscuits. I would like another gingernut to dunk in my milk but I'm afraid Mum's hand will reach out and stop me. Outside, a sprinkler swishes round and round. Through the window, I can see a high blue sky, cloud-speckled in one corner above the spotty curtain. I wonder if Lizzie can see the same clouds as me even though they're a whole day away from the city.

Grandma Bess opens the window. 'Hot,' she says. 'A hot September means early summer.' When she sits again, there are water droplets nestled in the fine black hairs above her painted lips.

'A touch of the Dago,' says Dad when he talks about Grandma Bess. He says Dagos have black eyes and hair and skin, and the women have hairy legs and moustaches like men.

I slide off my chair onto the floor and pretend to pull up my socks. Grandma's legs sit beneath the cloth like two extra table legs. Dad is right: they are covered in black hairs. Grandpa Ted's legs are covered in pressed grey trouser pants. He has little feet in shiny shoes, polished patent bright, like Faye Daley's Scottish dancing shoes. Up close, I can see my face in the toes. But Mum's hand is yanking me up and I am glad to be out of there, away from Dago legs.

'You're a big girl now,' says Grandma Bess. 'What are you? Six?' I nod but now she is talking to Mum. 'School must be a blessing. Time to yourself at last.'

They all look at me. Grandpa Ted's piggy eyes, Mum's sad, proud brown ones, Grandma Bess's blanked-out buttons. I turn to the window where the spotty curtain is blowing in the breeze, puffing in and out like the window's heartbeat. I look into the blue sky and past the speckled clouds to the misty part behind. I look all the way back to Burley Point where I belong.

Soon we are gone. Mum pulls me down the path. She says good riddance to bad rubbish. She says why did she think there'd be any help here? There never had been, never would be, and so much for family. She says she was stupid to come, she's got her pride and she's finished biding her time.

7

My father has gone. He has taken his brown skin and flashing eyes, his laughs and shouts and silences. He has taken his beer-man smell, his fishy stink, his whiskers in the basin. Now I sleep with Mum in her bed against the window wall. Dad's smell is in the curtains and the laundry trough, in the lounge room chair; it is in my head.

My father has gone to live with That Trollop Layle Lewis. Mum sent him away because he said he was going to Queensland by himself but she found out he went with that Layle Lewis. She couldn't speak to him, she said to Mrs Winkie in our kitchen, couldn't find the words. She said she told him in a letter that she wrote out many times, crossing out words, starting again.

When Mrs Winkie tried to stroke Mum's hand, she pulled away and said: 'Can you believe it? Everyone knowing…and how many times…'

She looked at me playing on the floor and cried choking, silent sobs that she tried to swallow and, although she turned from me, I could see her shoulders heaving. I could hear mouse squeaks coming from her mouth. I could feel the empty part of her where my father used to be; it was in me too. Mrs Winkie put her big wide arms around my mother; they looked like the elephant and mouse in my storybook but without the trunk and tails.

My father is building a house on the other side of the lagoon where he will live with that Layle Lewis. Already the house has bones. Already he has planted a palm tree that he brought back from his holiday in Queensland. I swing on our gate and wonder, if Mum hadn't given him the letter, would we have the palm tree in our garden? And if we did, where would we have planted it because there's not much room with the pines along the fence and the kurrajong in the corner, and Mum's veggies taking up most of the slope next to the gravel drive. Perhaps she wouldn't have wanted a palm tree in the garden.

Our car bangs to a stop outside the post office. It is the new blue Austin that Dad bought for us before he went to live with that Layle Lewis. Dunc says if he was old enough he could drive it better than Mum. When I climb off the floor, white flowers are pressed against the windscreen, a fence post on the bonnet, blood on Mum's nose. 'You all right?' she says.

Mrs Bloomers is at Mum's window. 'What happened, Nella?' Before Mum can tell her, she pulls me out and prods and pokes and looks into my eyes and then does the same to Mum.

Mrs Bloomers is really Mrs Bloom, Mum's friend from the soldier-settler farm. Before she married, she was a nurse at Muswell Hospital. Sometimes she thinks she still is. Mum says it's a shame she doesn't live closer. Mrs Winkie says Beryl Bloom has tickets on herself.

'Sylvie's fine,' says Mrs Bloomers, wiping blood off Mum's nose with her hankie. 'What happened, Nella?' she asks again.

Mum doesn't seem to know. They walk around the car and Mrs

Bloomers tells Mum she doesn't think there's much harm done and to reverse it out from under the tree. Then they try to prop the rail back on the post but it falls down and Mrs Bloomers laughs and says: 'The council's got more money than sense, putting fence guards around oleanders. Be better off grading the roads.'

Mum peers up and down the street. Reggie Patchett is on his shop veranda having a stickybeak but there's no one else around. Mrs Bloomers says Mum'll have to drive up the hill and report it to Constable Morgan. She says to get some iodine onto her nose as soon as we get home. Then she says: 'I heard about Mick. How are you getting on, Nella? By yourself?'

Mum opens the door and nods me in but the wing window is open and I can hear everything. 'He'll be back. He just needs to get her out of his system. Then he'll be back.'

Why didn't she tell me? And if he's coming back, why is he building a house? Mrs Bloomers opens and closes her mouth. 'You've got a lot on your plate, Nella. Come out to the farm and see me, anytime at all. Have a bit of a break. Come and stay. It'll do you good.'

As we drive off, Mum waves and waves.

On the last day of school, Dunc gets a black eye. Suddenly there's a fight and everyone's running to the far end of the tennis court. Before I'm close enough, Miss Taylor is pushing through a ring of boys, yelling: 'Stop it! Stop it! You're not wild animals! Stop it!'

Then I see Pardie pulling Dunc off Peter Leckie, who has blood on his nose, and Kenny Sweet is holding Peter Leckie's arms behind his back. Miss Taylor says we don't have hooligans at this school and they're to report to Mr Tucker immediately. She pushes them in front of her the whole way across the quadrangle, her skin red and blotchy from so much yelling.

Kenny Sweet is the tallest boy in school. He looks over everyone's head until he finds me. 'Leckie said your old man's shacked up with the town tart.' He says this loud enough for everyone to hear and, in the sudden hush, I want to disappear off that court like a lost tennis ball. I just stand there looking down at the ground, to dirt and worms underneath, to a cave where I could hide, maybe a hidden river flowing far below.

Lining up, everyone is talking too much, too loudly. Miss Taylor blows hard on her whistle and Lizzie whispers behind me: 'It's true, though, isn't it?'

Suddenly my legs are too heavy to walk on. Miss Taylor waits until we're all seated then says, *Sit up straight, arms folded.* She says, *We don't have fights in our school and anyone who wants to start one had better think twice.* She says, *We don't make judgments about other people's lives, because we don't live in their skin, is that clear?*

Yes, Miss Taylor.

Her eyes are an angry blue and she looks hard at everyone but never once at me. She says, *Living in a small town means minding your own business and not spreading idle gossip, otherwise none of us could live together, is that clear?*

Yes, Miss Taylor.

She says to take out our readers and turn to the right page. Then she gives me a tiny, kind smile. And that smile is everything.

The Trollop is still in my father's system. He is living with her in Ron Quigly's bungalow; I've seen his jeep parked out front. Mum knows too. Sometimes I find her peeking through the fence, watching his house grow walls and a silver roof on the other side of the lagoon.

'I'm not stupid,' she tells Mrs Winkie. 'I could go back to school and get my Intermediate. There was nothing wrong with my compositions. I could write. Better than I could talk. I got good marks.'

Mrs Winkie says she has to run along.

'I could have another baby,' says Mum. 'If I wanted to. He'll be back. Then we will.'

I would like Dad back, but I'm not sure about a baby. And no other mothers go to school.

In the morning, Mrs Winkie brings us eggs from her bantam chooks. 'I work harder than you,' says Mum to Mrs Winkie. 'I mow my own lawns.' Then she drags the mower from the shed and mows the front lawn even though she mowed the day before. Mrs Winkie yells at her over the *click-clack* of the blades: 'You're going to run yourself into the ground if you keep this up, Nella. You need to get a grip on yourself.'

Mum keeps on mowing.

Grannie Meehan has invited us to Bindilla to have Christmas with Uncle Ticker, Uncle Pat and Auntie Peggy and our cousins from the city. Only Dunc is going. Mum says Auntie Rose and Auntie Elphie are the only ones she's got any time for and they've both had a falling out with the Old Girl and they're not coming down from the city this year, so why bother?

On Christmas morning, I get a bride doll in a box. She has yellow hair and blue eyes and lashes that flap open with a *clack*. She has a white net skirt with a petticoat and frilly pants and a veil held on with a white-flowered comb. Dunc has a new cricket bat. He puts his face up close to mine and says my bride doll is an *a-bomb-in-a-shun*, you don't know what that means, do you?

'No one will ever marry you.' He looks under my bride doll's dress and pulls her veil over her face. When Uncle Ticker arrives, Dunc drops her on her head on the bed. After they've gone to Bindilla, Mum tells me I've been invited to have Christmas dinner with the Daley kids. If I want to go.

Of course I want to go. Why didn't she tell me before? Did she forget? But if I go, what will Mum do? She is standing at the sink and I cannot see her eyes. Should I go?

'I don't mind. I'm going to get stuck into the floor. It's a day like any other as far as I'm concerned.'

Not for Mrs Daley. For days we've helped her make decorations from strips of coloured paper and now they're draped around her kitchen and across the lounge room walls. Yesterday, Mr Daley cut a limb from a pine tree out near Five Mile Drain and Mrs Daley got the box of decorations from the wardrobe in her room.

I wanted to fix the manger, which had lost its sheep in the bottom of the box, but Faye said I could find the star for the top of the tree. I hurried to get this done because I wanted to hook the coloured balls on the tree's long arms. Faye said she was in charge and I could put the snow on the branches. The snow was cotton wool.

'Not there,' said Faye when I'd finished with the snow and

was trying to clip a shiny bird onto a branch. 'It needs to be done properly.'

'I can do it properly.'

'It's not your tree.'

'That's enough, Faye,' said Mrs Daley from the door.

'It's not. There are tons more decorations to use up.'

'You know what I mean.'

Faye let me do the manger. I found the sheep and pushed them into their sockets and laid the baby Jesus in his cradle bed. I fixed the palm-tree head and found the three wise men. Before I left, Mrs Daley pulled the curtains and switched on the Christmas lights so that I could see how the tree shone in the dark. She didn't tell me I'd been invited for Christmas dinner. Perhaps she did the inviting after I left, though I can't think how and when.

I want to take my bride doll to show Faye. 'That doll is staying here,' says Mum when she's dressed me in my new pink dress and tied a matching ribbon in my hair. 'I don't want it getting dirty.'

'It won't get dirty. I won't put it down.'

'No.' She lifts the kitchen chairs onto the table and sets them upside down around the edge. I wait by the door hoping she will change her mind but she takes a knife from the dresser drawer and kneels down on the floor. Then her arm sweeps out, out and back, out and back, peeling off the polish with each wide-armed reach, sending shavings in the air, onto her hair, the table and chairs.

Did she know my father would be having Christmas with the Daleys? When he walks in with beer bottles clutched to his chest, I see Mrs Daley watching me. But even though I'm sitting at the table, helping Faye fold red table napkins into double Vs, Dad doesn't notice me. He tells Mrs Daley that Layle's old man is on

73

his last legs and if he croaks over Christmas it won't be before time. He says she'll be back the day after Boxing Day. His voice is loud and seems to bounce around the room like a tennis ball thrown hard against a wall. Blue Daley pours them each a glass of beer and they take it into the lounge while I keep on folding Vs.

Mrs Daley says the turkey is almost ready and we'd better get on with opening the gifts. I don't have a gift for anyone. Mum didn't give me any. Should she have? I am no longer sure how much I can trust my mother. She didn't tell me it was wrong to scrape the crust of toast across the butter dish; Mrs Daley told me that. And sometimes she says she can't remember things. Sometimes she says she forgets her own name. What if she's forgotten the presents?

In the lounge, Santa is standing next to the tree but I can tell it's Blue Daley dressed in the costume that Mr Boland wore for the Christmas party at the Institute. It fitted Mr Boland better than Blue Daley; he is too skinny and the pillow for his stomach keeps dropping down. Besides, his eyebrows are reddish-brown and I can see the elastic holding up his beard.

We all crowd in. Blue Daley takes a present from beneath the tree, reads the name, then he tosses it to my father, who tosses it back, and Blue Daley tosses it back again. Mrs Daley says: 'Come on, you two, stop mucking around and get on with it.' But they do the same with every present, back and forth, laughing from too much beer.

I am not sure how Dad can toss the presents and not see me. Then one comes flying at my head. 'Here, catch this,' he says but Faye catches it instead and hands it on to me. It is a new pencil case from Faye. Then my father tosses me another.

74

When I tear off the paper I find a new *Marigold* book inside. *To Sylvie, love from Dad*, says the card but I can see it is Mrs Daley's writing and when I call out thank you like the Daley kids, the present throwing is finished and my father is at the window drinking beer.

I am wondering if I should go home and be with Mum, when Dad looks at me. His eyes are black and shining and as soon as they settle on me they slide right off again. But I know he has seen: I know because he sneaks another look when he thinks I can't see. And then I look away and he looks away and we both look back and pretend we haven't, and look away again. I want him to keep on looking but all through Christmas dinner he eats turkey and pudding and drinks beer; he tells funny stories that I can't understand, but he doesn't look at me again.

I am glad to leave. I thank Mrs Daley and don't look at Dad. I run home along the clay path that edges the lagoon, jumping on the samphire weed to make the blood juice squelch. There is no one anywhere, no one in the streets or in their yards, no cars, no sounds at all except the *glug-glug* of sleepy frogs in the lagoon and the sea breeze rustling through the reeds. No one anywhere, just me. And then I see an eagle, drifting in the sky above my father's new house, rising in a wind draft without a flap of wings, drifting higher and higher, then dropping, rising, hiding in the sun that shines behind the dunes.

I run through the gate and up the gravel drive. I want to tell Dunc about the eagle. I want Mum to be up off the floor. I want to take my bride doll outside and play with her on the lawn.

Where is she? I cannot feel her lying next to me, cannot hear her breathe. The kitchen clock *tick-ticks*; the house fidgets like a dog with fleas, so many sounds I never hear when I'm asleep: a crackle in the kitchen, a creaking in the roof, Georgie snuffling in his cage beneath his sleeping blanket. Then a *tink-clink-clanking* in the street.

Footsteps. Outside the bedroom window, running softly on the path. Could it be my mother? Could it be a robber? I crawl across the bed and look beneath the curtain. The moon is fat and yellow; it sparkles on the leaves of the shiny-leaf tree but I cannot see my mother, or a robber.

Where is Dunc? I slide out of bed and pat my way along the wall, through the kitchen and the lounge to the sunroom door. The moonlight through the louvres shows me Dunc is missing too. To be extra sure, I touch all around in his empty bed. 'Dunc?' My voice squeaks like a baby bird. I say it again. 'Dunc?'

He is not there. Now there's more *tink-clink-clanking* in the street, more running feet. My spit becomes a lump I cannot swallow. I feel my way along the hall to the back door. And Dunc is there! Standing very still. Like he stands in the bushes when he sets his rabbit traps, waiting to see if a rabbit runs right in.

'What's happening?'

High above Shorty's pines, the moon is bright. The gravel shines white; the daisy bush has eyes. Then I see her coming from the shadow of the shed, on fast feather feet. She is wearing her pink satin nightie, the one she chose from the catalogue when she bought my Christmas dress. Her hands are full of paint pots, a garden spade, the old hessian water bag; a roll of rusted wire is under her arm. She hurries down the path next to the

Scotts' fence. Then *tink-clink-clank* from the street.

'What's she doing?'

'Cleaning out the shed.'

'It's night,' I say, 'it's Christmas.'

'I'm going back to bed.'

I grab his hand. 'You can't.'

He shrugs me off. 'I can.'

I look out of the window to the street. Our car is a shadow by the kerb with a black pile next to it. Now Mum brings Dad's broken dartboard, a gerry can, a mop bucket, the rubber boots she uses in the garden. She throws them on the pile and is gone again. Then she's back, pushing my old trike, the one she said Mrs Hammet's little girl could have. Perhaps she has forgotten. I hurry outside and follow her down the path; branches from the trees along the Scotts' fence reach out to touch me as I pass. At the gate, I watch her drag something from the garden, through the fence into the street, something long and sleek that glitters like a snake. The garden hose! She flings it over the car, pulls it down the other side, lies flat on the ground to poke it under, pulls it up again, runs around, pulls it down. Soon the hose is wrapped around our car like a rubber worm.

Now she disappears. Where is she? There. On the lagoon side of the road, a white shape running at the tea-tree. Branches crack and break. She is back, dragging huge limbs and lifting them onto the car, running back, and back again. Why won't she stop? Now the car is covered in a green tree disguise and she hurries past so close that she must see me standing there. But she doesn't. When I follow around the back, I find her dragging the mower. I call out to tell her that she mowed yesterday but she doesn't hear.

From the sunroom steps, I watch her mow the grass up and down, up and down. When will she stop? Mrs Scott's house is all lit up. Should I go in there? Should I go up to Mrs Winkie's? Before I can, a car stops outside our house and someone treads softly through the garden.

'That you, Nella?'

It is Constable Bill Morgan. I cannot see his face behind the dazzle of his torch but I recognise his voice from his talk at school. He shines the light onto Mum but she just keeps on mowing, up and down, up and down. Her nightie is torn and dirty now; her hair looks like a bird's nest spiked with sticks from the tea-tree. I don't want to see: I don't want him to see.

'Now, Nella,' says Bill Morgan, 'I think you've done enough.'

Still she doesn't stop. Close up, he shines the light into her face. Her skin is white, her eyes surprised like the rabbits caught in Charlie Parsons's spotlight. But she just blinks and mows around and past him.

'Stop it, Nella.' Now his voice is loud and bossy. 'Or I'll have to stop you.'

Mum doesn't stop. And when she mows past again, he grabs her arms and pulls them hard behind her back. The mower handle drops to the ground and she tries to reach for it but Bill Morgan holds her tight. She kicks and tries to jab him with her elbows, and her legs run on the spot like the Roadrunner screeching to a halt at the canyon edge.

I want her to kick him hard. I want her to win. But he is too big. 'That's enough,' he says. And quick as a lick, he gives her a slap. Her head bounces back. I cry out but it must be a silent cry because no one looks at me. Mum stops fighting and droops like her carnations do when she needs to water them.

'I'm sorry, Nella,' says Bill Morgan.

I don't think he is. I tell him. 'You shouldn't hit my mother.'

'Sorry, Nella,' he says again. 'Didn't know the kid was here.'

Neither does my mother. Her eyes stare straight ahead like my bride doll's eyes. Bill Morgan takes her hand and she walks beside him easily, as if he's asked her for the foxtrot at the Fancy Dress when all the parents dance. As I follow after them, the torchlight rakes the sunroom louvres and I see Dunc staring out.

At our gate, there are people gawking. Mrs Scott and Mrs Winkie. Merle McCready. Wanda the Witch. 'Never was a strong one,' says Merle McCready. 'Some are and some aren't, that's the way it is.'

When Bill Morgan has Mum in the car, he comes back and talks to Mrs Winkie. She says, 'I should have seen it coming.' Then she holds my hand. 'He's taking her to Muswell to see the doctor. We'll get Duncan and you can sleep with us tonight. Tomorrow I'll take you out to Grannie Meehan's.'

The car drives off. From the back seat, Mum waves to everyone as if she is the Queen. No one waves back, not even me.

8

'When's Mum coming home?'

'That's a good question.' Grannie puts her knobbly fingers on mine and loops the wool over the needle. 'Like this. Down the bunny hole—round the bunny hole—out the bunny hole.' She knits the whole line and starts the next line too. 'See,' she says, handing it back, 'it's coming along nicely.'

It doesn't look nice to me. And I don't like the colour, a watery blue. Uncle Ticker puts his paper down and stokes the fire, which Grannie made him light because the summer night is cold. Sparks fly up like stars, falling onto the carpet. He stubs around with his slipper. 'Coming along fine,' he says, bending over my knitting.

'Keep your voice down, Ticker. You're not talking to the cows.'

Uncle Ticker gives me a wink. He's always doing this. He looks like Dad, but with smiley eyes and less hair. He rustles his paper to a new page. 'Tongues have gone through the roof. Maybe we shouldn't have sold that hundred head.'

'What about skirts?'

'Thicks or thins?'

My eyes are droopy and my knitting is slow. I should move back from the fire but I like sitting at Grannie's feet with their voices drifting over my head. When I drop a stitch and make a hole, Grannie says, *Time for bed, clean your teeth, and school tomorrow.*

'Yell out when you're in bed and I'll come and tuck you in.'

Uncle Ticker gives me another wink. I take my time closing the door and hear Grannie say: 'I've tucked in more kids than I've had hot dinners, you'd think there'd be some end to it. As soon as you're down the aisle, I'm off. London first. Ireland. Switzerland. Norway. Italy. Home through America. You won't see me for dust.'

Uncle Ticker says: 'Pork belly's skyrocketed. Maybe we should have a look at pigs.'

Grannie says: 'Filthy things.'

Because Mum's still in hospital, I have to catch the bus to school with the other farm kids. Now Dunc has gone too. Grannie has sent him to school in the city and I won't see him until he comes home for the May holidays. Before he left, he told me he would run away. He said he would come back to Burley Point and live by himself in the Abo cave and go to Muswell High with Pardie. Every day I pray to Jesus on the cross that Dunc will come soon.

I wait by the side of the road. There is silence everywhere. In the boobiallas and brackens and yakkas, in the willowy weed with the bright yellow flower. The sky is silent too, with high white clouds like the sky inside Uncle Ticker's glass dome that you shake and a snowstorm falls on Big Ben. Except here everything is summer dry and the hills behind Bindilla are speckled with sheep as dirty brown as the ground.

On the school bus, I sit close to Mr Kelly but still the big boys up the back yell that I have done the smell. 'Who did the stink?' says Peter Leckie. 'Was it you?' he asks everyone, seat by seat. 'Was it you?'

Colleen Mulligan and Shirley Fry whisper and point at me. Then Peter Leckie says: 'Hey, you in Grade Two, you in the pink bum-fluff cardigan, can you smell anything?' The air is sour with boy fart smells but I don't say anything. 'A dog always smells its own smell first. It was you, wasn't it?' My cheeks heat up and I shake my head but still the big boys laugh and jeer.

Mr Kelly says: 'Tone it down in the back, or I'll stop the bus and put the lot of you off.' He never does.

Outside there are spoggies on telephone lines and an eagle hawk circling low. There are fences and farmhouses where I wish there was jungle, and tom-toms to send my message: *Phantom…I need you…*And the Phantom would come on his white stallion. He'd freeze Peter Leckie's blood, Colleen's and Shirley's too. He'd bring Mum home from Parkside Hospital. Dunc would go to school in Muswell. And Layle Lewis would fall off the end of the jetty and drown.

'What are you doing?' From under the table, Grannie's legs look like pink sausages stuffed in brown shoes. 'A day like this you should be playing outside. And where are the chair cushions?'

'In my Skull Cave.'

'Be careful of that tablecloth. It's lace. Made by your great-grandmother, the French one. I should have packed it away long ago.'

She stands on tiptoe at the sideboard. Then, 'Shite!', and a book thumps to the floor next to me, papers spilling all over the carpet.

It's the Bible. The old one with our names inside the red cover.

Grannie kneels and grunts and reaches all around. 'Anything under there?'

'Rosie,' she says when I crawl out with a photo of a fat baby sitting in a clamshell. 'Born twelve months before your father. Died twelve months after.' She sits with a sigh. 'I had her photo taken, had all of them taken. Took her to Bert Ferguson in the Mount. He'd just taken on a new man from one of those countries, Latvia or Hungary or somewhere. Wary of him I was, with his bowing and hand-kissing. When he brought out the clamshell, I thought he was mad, never seen one that big before or since.' Grannie slants the photo for me to see. 'I had her dressed in a pink dress and bonnet. He took it all off. Sat her stark naked in that shell. Looks like a mermaid, doesn't she?'

I'm not sure what a baby mermaid looks like but I nod and she shuffles through the photos and finds a baby with a bald head sitting on a bunny rug. 'Brendan. Born twelve months after Rosie.' She stares at Brendan for a long time. The windmill behind the house creaks and squawks. 'He died too.' She slips the photos into the Bible and slaps the cover down hard. 'Well, you can't spend your life sitting in a clamshell. And you can't spend it grieving.' She springs to her feet. 'Come on. This wind'll blow the dogs off their chains. Time to make yourself useful. Start with getting a blanket over your bird or he'll screech himself stupid.'

Outside, the world has turned purple and dizzy. The sky is full of dirty grey clouds with a strange yellow light peeping through underneath. The pine trees are bending and swishing their top branches at each other. 'I'll drop the pegs,' says Grannie, looking over her shoulder, keeping an eye on the weather. 'You pick 'em up. It's going to rain cows and hogs.'

I run around her feet, scooping pegs into my skirt. The wind is so strong it almost lifts me into the air. There is nothing to hold on to, everything moves, the ground seems to sway, a loose sheet of iron bangs on the chook-house roof, the dogs are barking and running in circles, jangling their chains. I smell salt and seaweed blowing in off the sea. There's a flash and a loud crack that shoots right inside me, into my head and chest and legs. I stop and crouch down to catch my breath and, although the wind is blowing noise all about, I can hear other sounds too, a maggie high in the pines, a calf crying out for its mother, even a frog in the pond. It feels like the wind is singing. And suddenly I want to sing too.

'Yeeeeeeeeeee!' I scream and the wind blows Grannie's dress right over her head. I see her stocking tops, her step-ins, even her bloomer legs! My scream turns into giggles and, as I run around picking up pegs, I see she's untangling clothes and throwing pegs, laughing too.

There's another bright flash, then a crack right over our heads. Pine needles fall to the ground in a shower. 'Run!' yells Grannie as the first heavy drops fall. I follow her onto the side veranda. Grannie puffs and wheezes and takes pins from the back of her head and sticks them in her mouth while she rewinds her hair.

'If I could paint,' says Grannie, 'that's what I'd paint.'

I follow her gaze under the pines, down the slope of strawberry clover, all the way to the lake. Although it's still raining, it's not as heavy as before; the sky behind is streaked pink and purple, and a flock of black swans is flying low. If I had my crayons I'd draw it too.

I'm about to tell Grannie this when she says: 'I'm not sure

about the meek inheriting the earth. Meek's not something I'd lay claim to—ask anyone and they'd probably say the same—but for better or worse, I've inherited a good patch of earth.'

'What's meek?'

'You're pretty meek. Your mother pretends to be, but isn't. I was meek when I married Black Pat, but had to get over it pretty quick smart.' It sounds as if I should get over it pretty quick smart too. 'If your father had a bit more meekness in him, he might have held on to his inheritance instead of going off half-cocked.' She looks down at me. 'Don't let me hear you say that. Understand?'

I nod, but I'm already saying it in my head: half-cocked half-cocked. I wonder if you can be meek and half-cocked at the same time.

We make a run for the back door. 'There're worse things than meekness,' says Grannie kicking her shoes off on the mat.

Chicken's Uncle Corker is lying half under the tractor. He pushes himself up, dusts off his hands and takes out his ciggies. 'The cable's off again. No prize for guessing who.'

Uncle Ticker says, *Fucking bastard*, looks over his shoulder at me climbing on a rubble pile and lowers his voice, but still I hear *fucking parrots* and *fucking bee in his bonnet* and *fucking bastard* again. I take a running leap off the pile. 'Maybe a guard dog's the way to go?' says Uncle Ticker as I climb on the tractor treads. He tells me to be careful around the machinery and that he's got to give Corker a hand winding the cable back onto the winch. He says he'll be a while and can I find something to do that doesn't involve breaking a leg?

I run up the channel. Now it has walls on both sides and a wide river bed where one day water will flow to the lake. The walls are pockmarked with holes from gelignite blasting through the stone: Uncle Ticker told me this last time. He said sandstone was hard to rip but good for steep walls. He showed me where tree roots were fossils in the stone and he stroked those roots because they were thousands, millions, billions of years old. When I find the spot, the roots are now high above my head. At the top of the cutting, there are a few straggly trees like hair on a hill and those trees make me think of that day with Pardie and Dunc and the emu. I press against the channel wall, feeling the warm stone, and wonder if Dunc has run away from school already. Could he be living in the Abo cave in the bush above the cutting? How could I find out?

When Uncle Ticker yells, I run back down the channel. The cable is fixed to the tractor and the ripper is tearing into the earth.

Uncle Ticker beckons me to the Blitz. 'While we're here,' he says, 'we'll check the cattle in the top paddock.' He bumps the truck up the slope. 'I need you to spot any calves wandering around by themselves. Think you can do that?' Closer to the herd, he bangs on the door of the truck with one hand and beeps the horn with the other. 'Come aahn, get a move on.' He drives slowly to avoid tussock bumps, and counts as we go. 'Twenty-three. Twenty-four. Did we count that one? Come aahn, you silly old cow, out of the way or you'll have the Blitz up your bum.'

Mostly the calves are close to their mothers, the black and whites with their Angus mothers, the red and whites with the Herefords. Here the gum trees have thick trunks with peeling bark splashed pink and grey. Under one of the trees, I see a black bundle curled in the shadows.

'There! There's one by itself.'

Uncle Ticker lifts the calf onto its legs. It has a white flash on its head and wild, frightened eyes; it wobbles about and sits down again. Uncle Ticker takes off his hat and studies the cows all about. Because we've stopped, they've stopped too and they wait and watch as we watch them.

I can see right down the slope to Bindilla's red roof. I can see the shearing shed, the shearers' quarters and the machinery shed, the lake beyond, the sandhills on the other side, the lighthouse on Seal Island—although I can't see the jetty, or Lizzie. Or Mum or Dad. Because she's still in Parkside. And he is *worse than useless*.

At school, Lizzie said Mum didn't have all her cups in the cupboard. When I asked Grannie about the cups, she said: 'I wouldn't listen to anything Lizzie Campbell says. She's got spuds in her ears and her hair could do with a good wash.'

It is true about Lizzie's hair.

I didn't tell Grannie about Colleen and Shirley, how when they see me at school, they hop like kangaroos, calling out about roos loose in the top paddock. I know roos and cups are the same.

Uncle Ticker says: 'All right, Sylv, I reckon it's a twin. Now we've got to find a mother with a calf the same size, same length of cord. See this'—he lifts the calf and shows me a bit of shrivelled skin hanging off its belly—'if we can match this up, it'll tell us when it was born. Reckon you can spot one like that?'

For a long time we drive through the cows, beeping the horn and banging the door. 'If we don't find its mother, it'll die,' says Uncle Ticker. 'And there goes five quid. No point trying to handfeed them this early, they need the colostrum in their mother's milk.'

'What's colostrum?'

'The good stuff in the mother's milk just after the young'un's born.' He slows near a mother with a black calf. 'Whaddya reckon? Same white flash on the head? Same size cord. Could be the one?'

He swings the Blitz at the cow. She bellows at us with mad eyes and trundles off, calf following. 'Go aahn!' Uncle Ticker yells after her. 'Get back to your other calf, you apology for a mother, you've got two and you darn well know it. Go aahn, get back there and feed it.'

The cow bellows some more and Uncle Ticker bellows back. When we reach the calf under the tree, it stands on wobbly legs and stumbles forward.

'That's its mother, all right,' says Uncle Ticker. 'Now feed it, you stupid thing.' But as soon as the calf gets close, the cow backs off. 'Feed it!' yells Uncle Ticker.

The cow stares at us with surly eyes. Again the wobbly calf sidles up. But as it noses under its mother, she kicks out hard and knocks it right off its feet.

'You effing…cow!' yells Uncle Ticker.

I want to kick that cow hard in her big balloon belly. I want to break her legs and leave her there with nobody to look after her, and I don't want the calf to keep pushing in where it's not wanted. But the calf is so hungry that every time it gets kicked, it picks itself up and tries again.

'I'll show you,' says Uncle Ticker, driving the Blitz forward, forcing the cow and her calves to run down the slope, the wobbly calf stumbling and crying behind. Soon they are separated from the herd and heading for the stockyards near the bottom fence. 'I'll box them in the corner,' says Uncle Ticker. 'Think you can open the gate and hold it, while I drive 'em through?'

When the cow and her calves are squashed near the fence, I run for the gate. I have to climb onto the bottom rung to reach the wire loop and, as I drag the gate open, Uncle Ticker skirts behind the cow.

'Stay there. Don't let them pass.'

The cow comes at the gate with a crazy look in her eyes and I'm afraid she's going to trample right over the gate, over me holding it open, but I yell and scream like Uncle Ticker and at the last moment she turns and lumbers into the yards with the calves following.

'Good work,' says Uncle Ticker, closing the gate. 'Now you sit up there on the fence while I show her who's boss around here.'

From the top rung, I watch him being the boss. He lets himself into the yard with the cow, a small yard, gated off from the others. Over his arm, he carries a collar and chain. First he grabs the wobbly calf and drags it into another yard, closes the gate and leaves it there. Now he makes clucking noises at the cow. He gets up close and rubs her rump. She snorts and fidgets and blinks her long lashes at him and, when she's rubbing her head against the fence and really enjoying herself, he grabs her calf and drags it into the yard with the other calf. The mother bundles over to the gate and bellows at Uncle Ticker. She swings her head in angry arcs, her cries are terrible; they are the cries of maggies protecting their nests, the cries of foxes in the night. They make me want to hide in the lily patch behind the fishpond, where I go when I miss Mum too much.

Uncle Ticker opens the gate and the calves run out. And now I see he's collared them together with a short chain so that wherever one goes the other must follow. The strong calf pulls the wobbly one under the mother and straightaway it's sucking for all its worth. The mother gives it a kick but she hits the wrong one and somehow seems to know, so doesn't kick again. She gives Uncle Ticker a maggoty look. He just laughs. 'You'll learn,' he says as he climbs up next to me. 'You've got plenty of milk to feed both.'

The wobbly calf sucks noisily. There are cauliflower clouds in the sky and the day shines like clean window glass. Uncle Ticker's hand on the rail is as red-brown as a Hereford cow. 'You know what? I reckon we'll give that calf a name. Whaddya say?'

I try to think of cow names. After a while, Uncle Ticker jumps off the fence, holds out his arms and lifts me down with a wide swing before settling me on the ground. As we drive back, he says: 'How about Sylvie? It's a good name. And it means I won't forget you found her. Whaddya say?'

I don't say anything because the window-glass day has thick-ened with tears and I have to blink them away.

PART TWO

9

Mum has come home with short hair and no words. There is silence everywhere like static on the wireless. She keeps the blinds pulled down and the curtains closed. 'Who's that?' she says when we hear footsteps on the path. She creeps to the window and peers out. 'What's she want?'

Mrs Winkie wants to stomp through our house, as she did the day before, and the day before that. 'Come on, duck,' she calls as she pulls up the blinds, 'you'll turn into a mole.' She fills the kettle and stirs the stew she's bought for our tea as if she's in her own kitchen. Mum watches with fidgety eyes. Mrs Winkie tells Lizzie and me to lift a hand to help.

'What's wrong with your mother?' asks Lizzie at the wood pile. I tell her Mum's eyes hurt and she has to stay out of the sun. Lizzie says that's not what her mother says. 'She's cracked. Just cracked.'

Lizzie's hair is tied with blue ribbons in bunches above her ears. I think of heifers in the Muswell Show, the way their prize ribbons dangle over their foreheads and they gaze at you with fat happy faces, the same way Lizzie looks at me because Mum has cracked.

'You're a stupid cow,' I tell her.

In the kitchen, Mum lights a ciggie. 'I ache all over,' she says.

'We're stronger than we think,' says Mrs Winkie between licks of her stirring spoon. 'You'd better believe it, Nella.'

Lizzie and I play on my bed where I keep my dolls: she doesn't know I sleep with Mum and I don't tell her. In the kitchen Mrs Winkie says: 'You've got to get out more, Nella. It's not healthy hiding away, working yourself into the ground.' Mum says she knows what they're saying about her. Mrs Winkie says, 'Half of them would leave their husbands tomorrow if they had your guts.'

'He's told everyone I'm crazy,' says Mum, 'I know he has.' A chair scrapes. It must be Mrs Winkie because Mum takes care never to scratch the lino. 'You know what he did the other night? And the night before? Waits till it gets dark and comes sneaking around, tossing gravel on the roof, trying to scare me, trying to send me crazy. That's what he wants: he wants me to go mad.'

Mum's voice is high and crazy-sounding and I look at Lizzie to see if she's listening but she's undressing Marilyn and doesn't seem to have the same ears as me. Mrs Winkie is quiet for a long time then she says: 'Are you sure, Nella?' I hear the doubt in her voice as if Mum really is mad and I think: Why didn't I hear the gravel on the roof? Wouldn't I wake up? Mrs Winkie says: 'Be careful saying things like that, Nella, you never know what others might make of it.'

'I have to get a photographer,' says Mum. She lowers her voice but I walk to the dressing table where I can hear. 'I have to set the two of them up in bed to get proof. That's what the law says. He's agreed, through his solicitor, to do it in a hotel in the Mount but if he could prove I was out of my mind, he'd be able to do the suing and say it was my fault, not his playing around. That's what he wants.'

It doesn't make sense to take photographs of Dad in bed with that Trollop. Who would want to do that? Would Aunt Cele? Suddenly

I think of passing Dad in the street and how he never looks at me. How when I try to find his eyes, he turns his head away: he looks at the footpath and his feet; he lifts his head and looks at clouds racing overhead, at fat white summer clouds, at rain clouds from the south. To him, I am not even a mosquito or a scarab beetle.

In the kitchen, cups rattle and clink, a chair scrapes again. 'It's a dirty business,' says Mrs Winkie. Later, when she leaves, Mum pulls down the blinds and turns into a mole.

In books, everything makes sense. From Lizzie's *Arthur Mee Encyclopaedia*, I know about *The Crumpling of the Earth* and *The Story of Rubber* and *Columbus in His Hour of Despair*. It is a cold night outside but Mum and I sit close to the stove in our nighties, ready for bed. In Mum's *Women's Weekly,* a film star called Grace Kelly has married a prince. I wonder if there are any princes in Australia that I could marry.

Mum is reading her *True Confessions.* On the cover, a man and woman are looking into each other's eyes. She has yellow hair, blue eyes and red lips. He has black hair, brown eyes and pink lips. *Why My Husband Will Never Trust Me Again. The Other Woman. Threesome Tragedy. Hollywood Hounds.* Are the *Hollywood Hounds* dogs or men? I've read enough covers of Mum's *True Confessions* to know they are probably men. At least in the *Secret Seven* they have adventures called scrapes.

In the May holidays, Dunc comes home from the city with a surly face. When Pardie arrives to swap comics, Dunc locks me out of the sunroom. I kick at his door until my foot hurts then I spy from Dad's old room.

They're on Dunc's bed with their backs to the wall and I can read over their heads—*Archie*s and *Batman, Roy Rogers*—no new *Phantom*s. Soon I get bored and sit on the back step and talk to Georgie Porgie. Pardie comes out and asks how it was on the farm. Georgie slides along his perch and makes kissy sounds at Pardie, who puts his lips to the cage and kisses him back. It sends Georgie berserk; he kisses his mirror, attacks his cuttlefish and gives his bell a good rattling. When Dunc appears, Pardie and I are laughing our heads off.

'What's so funny?'

'None of your business.'

Dunc's mouth drops open. 'Are you cheekin' me?'

Pardie grabs him by the arm. 'Come on, we've got better things to do than hang around here.'

As soon as they've gone, I think of Faye Daley saying my father has a new dog. A scared sort of feeling shivers right through me and I dare myself to walk past his house, maybe even sneak up the driveway and spy on his new dog. I've never been before. What if I'm seen? I swallow my fright and leave without telling Mum.

His house is still not finished. There are bricks and timber lengths in the drive, a cement mixer, a big pile of rubbish. It is easy to get to the shed without being seen: it is full of crayfish pots, glass buoys, marker flags, his jeep parked in front. The house has a flat roof and three big windows with a view over the lagoon to our house on the other side. Already there is a veggie garden on the slope below the palm tree. I creep around the side of the house and hide behind a creeper trellis.

Dad and the Trollop are right there! Sitting on the back veranda, legs hanging over the edge, no shoes. She has red polished toenails; her feet are huge. They look like dead puffer fish. Mossie is as cute as Faye said. He has golden fur, fluffy ears and wriggles himself inside out trying to catch a reel on a string that Dad jiggles in front of him. 'Good boy, Mossie, good boy. Clever boy!'

What a dumb name for a Cocker. If I was allowed a dog instead of a bird I'd call him Sunny or Scamp, maybe Sammy. And I'd have a smart dog like Blue at Bindilla, or a real dog like the Phantom's Devil.

Then Dad starts singing to Mossie, or the Trollop, maybe to both of them, maybe to himself. It's more of a hum than a song, with soft words, but straightaway I recognise my favourite tune from the Top 40 about the doggie in the window with the waggely tail. There is a sound in that song that sticks in my chest and I decide to find another song for my favourite, one that has nothing to do with dogs. Then Dad jiggles the reel too close to the edge and suddenly Mossie's upside down on the ground. Dad and Layle laugh as if it's the funniest thing they've ever seen. As if it's a laugh no one else can share. Layle's hand is on Dad's knee. As if it belongs there. Dad leans over, scoops Mossie up and settles him back on the veranda. Layle says something about dogs and men with big feet. She giggles and rubs against Dad's ear. Now Dad's hand is on her knee and she is all peaches and cream.

Next door, without warning, Mrs Jones turns on her sprinkler and it spits over the fence. I shift to escape the drips and Mossie's ears prick up, so I stand rock-still, hardly breathing, because dogs have ESP. And right then Dunc—*Dunc!*—walks out the back door. Eating an apple. Her apple! He sits on the veranda edge, almost touching her. What a traitor! But at least Mossie forgets me and leaps all over Dunc. I decide I'll tell Mum that he was here. But then she'll know I was here too. Faye told me, I'll say. Or Pardie. There are plenty of ways.

I slide quietly along the trellis into the veggie patch. I rip off a whole row of runner beans and scatter them in the street where they will be squashed by cars. They are nothing to me.

Nobby Carter's bed is pushed against the window and his head shines like a baby's skull without a tuft of hair. He is Betty Carter's father and older than Grandpa Ted in the city. I had another grandfather called Black Pat, who was Dad's father. There are photos of Dad's grandfather, Old Pat, and Black Pat on the dining room wall at Bindilla. Old Pat has a fat moustache and smiley eyes. Black Pat is all black hair and beard and black eyes. When Dad was a boy he pulled up the ladder and left him down the well. He says he didn't sit down for a week. I like Old Pat best because Black Pat has whipping eyes that follow wherever I move in the room, as if he'd like to whip me too.

Nobby Carter is reading a magazine in bed, a magazine full of girly pictures with boobies hanging out of bather tops, some with bottoms poked in the air. He lets the magazine drop and Lizzie and I spring back. Across the road, Lizzie's mother opens a window and looks out. We crouch down until she's gone then take another look and see that Nobby's hand is wide-awake beneath the blanket, jumping up and down like Chicken when he throws a fit at school and twitches on the ground. Suddenly Nobby's hand stops moving and he lies so still that Lizzie widens her eyes at me: *Is he dead?*

What if he is? What if he isn't found until he's stiff and smelly like Lizzie's cat when it died behind the school toilet block? Who should we tell?

We tell Mum. She says she's not impressed. She says he isn't dead. She tells Lizzie her mother wants her at home and hands me the peg bag. She wrestles with a sheet, drags it over the line and steps sideways as I pass pegs. Clouds race overhead and sheets flap in my face. I beg her to go and see. She says she wouldn't waste her time.

Mum hates wasting time. She lumps the clothes basket onto her hip and tells me she's just done the floors and to wait on the back step while she butters Saos for lunch. She says I can take some to Dunc and Pardie. I study the pines beyond Shorty's fence but there are no bouncing boughs. In the pittosporum hedge, insects buzz like the bar at Hannigan's. In his cage, Georgie pecks at his cuttlefish. In the dirt next to the step, the earth is freshly turned: Dunc's rosella from the bush is buried there. *It's your fault,* yells Dunc inside my head, *he died because you didn't look after him while I was at school.*

It's no one's fault, says Mum, *birds like that aren't meant to be caged. You know that, Duncan. I can't think why you gave it to her to look after.*

I can't think either. I don't want to think. I can't walk and eat my biscuits while carrying Dunc and Pardie's so I lift my skirt and put them in my knickers and, although they scratch a bit, I can eat and stamp my feet to scare away snakes in case they've forgotten it's winter and they're meant to be asleep in their holes.

99

At the big pine, Dunc yells down. 'Bring 'em up to us!'

He doesn't think I can. But this tree has withered skin and knobs close to the ground where Shorty has lopped off limbs. I use them as a ladder until I reach the first big branch. 'Where are you?'

The branches shiver. 'Shit, she's coming up.'

Soon my head is level with their branch. *Don't look down.* They have built a platform from old fence palings and are lying on a mattress they must have dragged from the tip. I pull myself onto their branch and prop against the trunk. When I reach inside my knickers, Dunc's mouth turns upside down.

'In *there*?' He gags and chokes and shows off in front of Pardie. 'We don't want them if they've been in *there*, do we, Pard?'

Pardie grins at me behind Dunc's head.

'Get out of here,' says Dunc, flicking pages in a magazine. 'We've got better things to do than eat your stinky biscuits. And I know you dobbed to Mum about me going to Dad's. See if I care. I go there all the time, don't I, Pard?'

Pardie nods and looks away because I am a dobber. I prop against the tree trunk and stuff their Saos in my mouth. They read Dunc's magazine and pretend they can't see me eating. The magazine has booby girls with bare bottoms and lipstick smiles.

'Nobby Carter's got a magazine like that.'

Dunc looks up with wary eyes.

'Mum won't be impressed,' I say.

'Mum won't know.' He tucks the magazine down his jumper and climbs to his feet. 'Come on, Pard, we're getting out of here.'

As they push past, I slide onto their mattress and lie flat on my belly. From a lower branch, Dunc reaches up and shakes the platform hard, singing: 'I said shake baby shake—'

'She'll fall,' says Pardie, but still Dunc doesn't stop.

'M-u-u-u-m!' I scream.

Dunc looks through the branches to see if Mum's coming, then slides down the trunk as fast as a circus monkey.

'What about her?' calls Pardie.

'She got up. She can get down.'

Pardie makes a sorry face at me and follows Dunc down the tree. A gust of wind rushes past and makes the platform sway. I yell down. 'Half-cocked! Half-cocked! Half-cocked! Half-cocked!'

'I'll show you who's half-cocked,' says Dunc, turning back.

'Half-cocked! Half-cocked!'

There is dust up my nose and there are crumbs in my pants. Again the wind shivers the platform. Turning, I reach down with my feet, then I reach further, but somehow I am dropping and a scream is dropping with me, loud in my ears, someone else's scream, someone not me.

'I'm not going back,' Dunc tells Mum, traps on his shoulder, straddling his bike. 'Grannie can do law herself. I'm going on the land. I don't need school for that.'

'You're not old enough to leave school.'

'Try and stop me.'

Mum looks up from her staking. She has forgotten to wear lipstick and her face has faded. 'Duncan, you're thirteen, you've got another year to go. By then you might have changed your mind. You don't have to decide now.'

He gouges his front tyre into the gravel. 'I've already decided.'

'Don't do that.' Mum reaches for his handlebars but Dunc

twists them away. Her hand hangs helplessly in the air. 'If you do law, you'll be made.'

'I'm not doing law. Uncle Ticker says I can work for him.'

'You've asked him?'

'Yesterday. Outside the post office.'

'What do you think your father would say if he knew that?'

'I know what he'd say. *Workin' on the land's a mug's game. Who'd want to be stickin' their arm up a cow's arse and cleanin' up flyblown sheep? There's no point anyway, the government gets it. You're better off sittin' on your bum.*'

'You've seen him?'

'He said he didn't want to leave. He said you kicked him out.'

'You wouldn't understand.'

He turns to me on the back step. 'Show me.' He grabs my arm with the plaster cast and reads: *Sylvie Meehan. Age 7. Burley Point, South Aust. Australia. The World. The Universe.* 'Dumb,' he says. 'And you're not seven until next month.' Then he turns back to Mum. 'Why isn't she at boarding school?'

'Sylvie? She's far too young.'

'You sent me away but you don't send her.'

'I didn't send you away.'

'You sent Dad away. You sent me. But you don't send her.'

Dunc rams his pedals and skids down the drive. His traps rattle and clank along the lagoon path. Mum stares after him for so long that my teeth ache. Then she rakes all around in big arching sweeps until everything is smooth and neat.

10

It is the law, so Mum said she'd get Constable Bill Morgan to put Dunc on the train if he didn't go back to school himself. Now she's gone to the city because Dunc has been getting into fights and stabbing his compass into his desk, which is destruction of school property and Mum will have to pay.

'We're going to Mick and Layle's to play cards,' says Mrs Daley. 'You kids take your pillows. You can sleep on the floor if you get tired.'

Mum wouldn't want me anywhere near that Trollop. Doesn't Mrs Daley know? In the back of the Daleys' ute, I think of the Phantom riding past on Flicker, plucking me out of the ute and carrying me off to live in the Skull Cave in the Deep Woods. I think of how miracles can happen: how Mum might change her mind and let Dad come back to live with us and everything will be the same as before. I think of the whale that came into the bay and how we watched from the jetty and the whale had a baby stuck to its side like a big barnacle with a million silver bubbles floating behind. Then we arrive at Dad's house and I still haven't thought of how to escape from the Trollop.

We step over planks and bricks in the drive, and Mrs Daley says, 'Will he ever finish it?' Off the back veranda, there is a big square kitchen with a view over the lagoon. At the table in the centre, Dad is shuffling cards with Pardie's dad and mum, Augie, and Jude. As soon as we walk in, I look for Dad's eyes but he doesn't look back at me. Instead, he laughs at my plaster arm and says, 'Who brought George Bracken?'

Augie and Blue Daley laugh too. 'It's a lovely dressing-gown,' says Mrs Daley, ruffling my hair.

My dressing-gown is red tartan with a gold-tasselled cord. The Daley kids have blue chenille. What is wrong with tartan? And who is George Bracken?

Layle says she's going to fry up some black duck that Mick shot. I decide I won't speak to her the whole time we're there, that is my plan. When she asks if we'd like to play cards in the bedroom, I don't look at her. Faye asks if we can first see the sunken bath and we sit around the edge and dangle our legs over the rim. Faye says how fab it is, but all I can see is Layle's big bra under the basin and my father's overalls scrunched up next to it. Mum would never leave clothes on the floor and I wonder if Dad would rather come back to live with us because Mum is better than the Trollop at keeping things clean and looking after him.

In the bedroom there's a wardrobe with sliding mirror doors, a cow-hide mat on the floor, paint patches on the walls. I decide I won't sit on that bed; instead I perch on the edge, but it has a slippery green spread and I keep sliding off. Faye knows all the card games. She says we're playing Snap and begins shuffling.

'Your Dad's right. Boxers do wear dressing-gowns like that.'

'Once I saw a picture of George Bracken in the ring,' says Dawn. 'He wore red shorts and a satiny gown, not tartan.'

'Her father ought to know.' Faye puts the cards down slowly and sneaks a look before turning them over. She wins every time.

'Deal,' says Dad in the kitchen. 'We haven't got all night.'

Dot curls in a ball on the bed as if she wants to go to sleep. A grey speckled moth walks down the wall close to my feet. 'Concentrate,' says Faye, 'or don't play.'

'All right,'—I slide off the bed and curl into my pillow on the cow rug—'I won't.'

The moth flops onto the floor and skittles towards me. My father has kicked his slippers off under the table. He has a hole in the toe of his sock. Augie is leaning back, his chair balanced on two legs. He says: 'See in the local rag your brother's got another medal. Those who fought at Kokoda. Something they should've got sooner but didn't due to some kind of enquiry.'

With a little hop and flutter, the moth climbs onto the rug. Its wings are papery grey with black spots. Two long feelers flick at the air. Faye calls down. 'I'll let you shuffle.'

'No.'

'You can play whatever game you want.'

'No.'

'They can weigh Ticker down with medals,' says Dad, 'but with your flat feet, Augie, you were one of the lucky ones. No one with any sense would've gone if they could've stayed put.'

'You're stupid,' says Faye to me.

'Leave her alone,' says Dawn.

'You should've got a medal for pushin' Bert Leak's kid into the drink and saving him from that bullet,' says Augie.

'Don't try and make a hero out of me,' says Dad. 'Albie Fisher's the one who should've got a medal. Ten quid and how many kids did he keep out of the firin' line by sayin' he needed them on the chicory flats? And you won't hear me blamin' Derm Murphy for buildin' a dairy the day it all began. Never milked a single cow, white feathers dumped at his gate by the bucketful, but he didn't end up with six kids dead in Borneo.'

The moth stands high on its front legs and stares at me with hard black eyes. It is close enough to squash into moth dust. I could pull off its wings like Chicken does to blowflies in the shelter shed.

'You know how many died in Darwin?' says Dad, and I see Layle kick him under the table. Dad kicks her back. 'Let him answer.'

'A couple of hundred,' says Augie, 'that's what they said.'

'Try a bloody thousand. Maybe more. A total cover-up. That's why I told 'em what to do with their medal. When they tried to give me a stripe, I gave it right back. I said, stick your promotion up your—'

'—Khyber Pass,' says Layle.

Faye says, 'You can lie on the bed. It's more comfortable.'

'I'm comfortable here.'

'And don't get me started on that bloody ditch Ticker's digging.'

'No, don't,' says Layle. 'Come on kids. The duck's ready.'

We sit on a cloth on the floor and eat with our fingers as if it's a picnic. Then I get lucky. 'I've got the wishbone! I get a wish.'

'Only if you get the big bit.' And before I've even got a good grip, Faye has a finger inside the bone. 'Ready?'

The wishbone snaps but I've got the big piece! 'What'll I wish for?' I say, waving it under Faye's nose and thinking of a new bike, a yoyo, Derwent pencils like Lizzie's.

'Wish for a win in your next bout,' says Blue Daley, snorting into his beer as if he's said the funniest thing. Faye laughs too.

Then Dad and Augie. Layle says they're all stupid. Her voice sounds silky and kind and I forget my own plan and look at her for a quick second. Then I remember she is to blame for everything and I hope her throat will be squeezed tight by her own fingers. That is my wish.

I find the photograph at the back of the dresser drawer, in a brown envelope. Dad and the Trollop. Sitting up in bed. Dad has angry eyes and shadow cheeks. The Trollop holding a bedspread up to her chin. It is too much to look. I bury the photo under pencils and pens, lacker bands, the ball of string I was looking for.

When Dunc comes home for the September holidays, I show him the photo of Dad and the Trollop in bed. He looks at everything I couldn't bear to see. He says: 'You know what this means?' I shake my head, listening for Mum in the garden. 'It means they're divorced.'

'What's divorced?'

He looks at me as if I'm too stupid to believe. 'It means Dad lives with Layle. That he likes Layle better than Mum. That Mum kicked him out. It's more than a year since he's gone. That's how long divorce takes.'

'Mum might change her mind. She might let him come back.'

Dunc waves the photo at me. 'They are DI-VORCE-D! It is forever. They can't get back together again. That's what divorce is.' He turns to the stove. 'You know what I think of this?' He rips the photo in two. Then in four. Then in four again. He tosses the pieces into the fire and Dad is gone forever because that's what divorce is.

I am crying silently inside so that Dunc won't see. He says he's going to meet up with Pardie.

'You said you'd run away.'

'I did,' he says at the door, 'but the cops brought me back.'

Why didn't Mum tell me? What else don't I know?

'It's not as bad for you. You hardly knew him. I was twelve when he left. How do you think it is for me?'

After he's gone, I wonder if Dunc cries silently too. But how would I know, how would anyone know, if our crying has no tears?

Chicken McCready is walking past our gate. I take my time with the latch because I don't want to talk to him. He has green teeth and smelly breath and sits behind me in class with candles hanging out of his nose. And I hate the handkerchief he wears knotted over his head even though it's ages since he had chicken pox and his grandma shaved off his hair.

When he turns the corner I lie in the dandelions like a star and listen to my heart beating in my ears. I think of Chicken throwing fits at school and how his tongue has to be found before he swallows it. And how he's always hanging around and drawing his own hopscotch next to ours and talking to himself as he jumps from square to square, saying exactly what we're saying in a girly voice. And slithering out of the tea-tree when we're in our cubby. There's a shiver in the rushes and we know it's him. If we ignore him long enough, he goes home and plays in the old cars that sit on blocks near his back fence. They were his father's cars before he disappeared. That was after Chicken's mother ran off with the Rawleigh's man. But I don't think Chicken's father ran off with someone like his mother did. Like my father did.

I would like to run off too. But I can't think of anyone to run off with, or where I'd go. I look at the sky and think I'd like to be an eagle flying high above Burley Point. And if I were an eagle with an eagle eye, could I fly high enough to see the Coorong, and Dunc in the city? Could I sweep down and rescue him in my eagle feet? Could I see Betty Cuthbert being the Golden Streak in the games in Melbourne? Could I fly above Ten Mile Rocks and see my father in the *Henrietta* pulling pots? And if a storm came up, and his boat sank on the reef, would I tell anyone or leave him there to rot? Like Mum would.

'Sylvieeeeee. I want you to go to Mr Sweet's. There's a note on the table. You'll need to hurry or he'll be closed.'

I need to go to the dunny. Green light snakes through cracks and holes in the corrugated iron. Nasturtium stems snake through too and wave their green heads at me as if they are lost in the dark. I pull down my pants, sit on the stinky pan and keep my nose closed. From the box where Mum keeps her crosswords, I find one half done. Four down is *Arc*. I pencil in *Curve*. Eight across is *Waver*. I don't know that, so I check the dictionary with the loose pages. *Vacillate*. It fits, and connects with five down: *Wed*. I know that too. I know more words than anyone in my class and now I have to remember to make mistakes in the spelling tests so that Chicken won't say I've swallowed the dictionary. Mum knows more words than me but she still gets them wrong. Six down is not *Marry*. I scratch it out and write *Match* over the top. Then I can't stand the stink so I leave the rest for her.

Two forequarter chops, says Mum's bird writing. I sit on the step and fold the coins inside the note. Georgie is hunched on his perch, feathers fluffed around him, not even a twitter. For the first time I think he might like to be out of his cage, flying free in the bush where we found him. What if I opened the door and let him out?

'You had six down wrong,' I tell Mum as she runs from the pump, bucket slopping. 'It wasn't *Marry,* it was *Match.* It didn't fit with *Vacillate.*'

'Vas-ssss-ilate,' she says, throwing the water in a rainbow arch between the cauliflowers.

'It's spelt with a *c* in the dictionary.'

'It's pronounced with an *s,* like *face.*'

From the well, I hear the squeak-suck of the pump and the glug of water running into her bucket. I hear loud party voices coming from Shorty's shed and his wireless blaring out about someone *pushing up along the inside by a length gone out wide followed by a half head before the turn strides out on the straight.* Can't she hear? Can't she tell my father's laugh from all the others? Doesn't she know Layle is there? Close enough to see her running around the garden? Doesn't she care?

Now she's back. Tears itch behind my eyes and I don't know why. 'You get everything wrong!' I yell at her. 'Everything.'

She drips water onto her seedling box, slowly, drop by drop. 'Don't be cheeky.'

'I don't want you for a mother.'

I jump up and run down the drive, across the road and onto the lagoon path. I feel hot and mean and the prickles behind my eyes have dried as stiff as the white weed on the lagoon.

I wish it was winter and the lagoon was full of oily brown water, deep enough to pole our raft into the middle. I wish I could see an eagle. And as I make the wish, I see one coming off the dunes. It drifts without a wing beat, rising high in the sky, but even far away I can see the frill of feathers on the end of each wide wing. Then it spirals into the sun and disappears and I'm not really sure I saw it at all, and the whole way to Sweet's shop, I watch the sky and wish I was Julie Walker and lived in the Deep Woods with my own falcon called Fraka and a dog called Devil. And, although I make all these wishes, by the time I arrive at Sweet's all I've seen are two maggies and a silver eye.

Just my luck. When I open the door, Chicken is there. Wearing his handkerchief hat. Smelly as a rat, though no candles today.

As the bell jangles, Mr Sweet says: 'How're you doing, young Sylvie? About to shut up shop but I've been waitin' for you.' I know he hasn't. I ease along the counter, as far from Chicken as I can. 'Be with you in a half, when I've fixed up young McCready here.'

Mr Sweet lifts his meat cleaver and brings it down on his chopping block, chops through a bone, chops off chops. Chicken and I watch. While he's chopping, Mr Sweet hums 'Heartbreak Hotel' as if he is Elvis. When he's finished, he hooks up the front of the dead sheep that's left over from his chopping and sends it sliding along a rail above his head. It knocks into four dead friends who are hanging by their legs at the back of the shop.

Mr Sweet is not very sweet. He has a grumpy face full of fat freckles that join up like a map with white bits underneath where the sea should be. His hair is faded orange with comb marks in the Brylcreem. There isn't much space between his eyebrows and hair so it looks as if someone sat on his head and squashed it flat. 'You tell your Gran she won't get better mutton than this,' he tells Chicken. 'Tell her I'll eat my own head if it's tough.' He wraps the chops in white paper and ties string around the middle, then twists it back the other way and snaps it fast with his fingers. 'Three bob,' he says, slapping the parcel down hard, making me jump.

While Chicken fishes in his pocket for the money, a blowie buzzes past Mr Sweet's nose. 'You let that in?' he asks me, but it sounds like he's telling rather than asking so I don't answer. Mr Sweet swats at the blowie with his swatter, misses it on the chopping block and sends up sawdust from the floor as he jumps about after it. Eventually it hides in the window and Mr Sweet leaves it there with the other blowies to buzz itself to death.

'Well?' he says to Chicken. 'Spent it at the cafe, have we?'

Chicken turns out both pockets and looks confused, as if the money might be in his ear, as if he's on stage with the magician who came to the Institute and pulled eggs and pigeons from the air. 'It's here somewhere, it has to be. She gave me a note. Maybe I lost it.'

Mr Sweet says: 'The only thing you've lost is your brains. Come here.' He leans over the counter and pulls off Chicken's handkerchief hat. Sure enough, the ten-bob note is underneath. Mr Sweet pings the register and takes out the change, is about to hand it to Chicken when he stops and reaches for his pen. He pulls Chicken over the counter by the front of his shirt and holds him there while he writes on his forehead. Part of me feels sorry for Chicken, whose ears are burning red. 'There,' says Mr Sweet when he's finished, 'no way you'll be spendin' the change. In case it's what you had in mind.'

Chicken's face is fiery red. He turns to the door and I see Mr Sweet has written 'seven bob' in big blue letters right across his head. Mrs Bullfrog comes in then and I can't look at her without seeing her in the bushes with Mr Sweet, her big boobies, and Mr Sweet is so busy smiling and smoothing down his hair that he gets my chops quickly and hardly speaks to me.

Halfway home, I find Chicken dawdling on the road. He is playing in a puddle, a small one left over from last night's summer rain, hardly big enough to splash about in. I'm about to hurry past when I see Chicken's still got seven bob written on his head. And as there's no one around to see me talking to him, I stop and say: 'You could rub that off.'

Chicken looks at me as if the Queen has stopped to speak to him, so all he says is: 'What?' and 'Why?'

'If it wasn't written on your head, you could spend some of it on lollies and your Grannie wouldn't know.'

He looks at me for a long time, just standing there in his puddle. I can see that under his handkerchief hat, under the seven bob, Chicken has blue eyes just like the blue of Mr Sweet's biro. And I see they're nice eyes with soft brown lashes that curl up like my bride doll's do, and his mouth is soft too, and sad at the edges. I think of his mum running off with the Rawleigh's man and then his dad disappearing, and for the first time I wonder if he knows where they live. Does he ever visit them? Are they divorced? Does Chicken cry silently, like me?

The whole time I'm thinking this, Chicken just stands there looking at me as if I've said something so awful and strange and wrong—so not like what the Queen would say—that he can hardly bear it. But still I go on. 'You could spend sixpence and I could find a pen and write six and six on your head. She'd never know.'

Chicken is not good at sums. But, although he looks at me and looks away and back again, I know he can add up that one. He kicks at the water and a splash hits my leg. It is warm, like a cat's tongue. It dribbles down my shin to my ankle and disappears into my sandal. After a long time, he says: 'I don't like lollies.'

It's not true. I've seen him at the cafe selling bottles to get money and straightaway heading for the lolly counter. And suddenly I want to be the one in the puddle. I want it to swallow me up and suck me down into the mud where Chicken's blue eyes can't find me. But I just shrug and say, 'Suit yourself,' and walk away.

I'm on the lagoon path when I start to run, lumping the meat on my hip, nearly dropping it. Tears rise in my throat. I can see the party people in Shorty's shed and Mum's sheets flapping on the line but the tears are bigger than me, everything is bigger without end and no hope for anything. Before the path reaches the road, I push through the reeds to the lagoon. There is a tree bent low and I throw myself over a branch, roll my stomach backwards and forwards on the soft paper bark. I have the feeling of Mr Sweet's knife slicing into my stomach and how deep can his knife go and can it slice out everything? When I look up, I see my father's house wobbling about on the other side of the lagoon and I hate him and his house and her living with him there, her ginger hair and long legs. With my hate I peel bark off the branch, long pieces that leave pink underneath. In no time at all, the branch is stripped bare. The new bark is pale pink, pale as Mum's new dancing dress that she's keeping for best. I'm still crying, but not as much now. And I can feel this quiet place inside that wasn't there before, as if it was filled to the brim and is now emptied out.

When I return to the path, Chicken has gone.

11

'Your mother is the most common woman in Burley Point.'
Colleen Mulligan says this to me in a parrot voice on the first day
of school, sounding just like her mother might sound. She blurts it
out as if she's been saving it up all the long Christmas holiday and
couldn't wait to find me as soon as the bus pulled in.

At first I just stand there with an empty head, staring at her. I
can't think of my mother as a common woman; I don't know what
it means. Then I think: She's got it wrong; she must mean the
Trollop. And in a muddle of thoughts, I remember Bridie Maguire
who stumbles home drunk every night from the pub. I could
believe Bridie was common if Mum hadn't told me she was once
a mother with a little girl who died from drinking poison that
Bridie left too low on a shelf. By the time I've thought about all
this, Colleen has run off with Shirley, and Lizzie has gone to play
with them too, leaving me alone beneath the classroom window,
eyes pricking, hands shaking.

Divorce. That's what she means. Divorce makes you common.
I know this from the way my whole body turns hot with something cold and fearful underneath. I see Colleen far away near the
fence with the others and want to pretend it never happened. At
the same time, I want to run home to Mum and hide in our house
and never go outside again, ever. To stop myself from shaking and

running, I take my library book from my case and hide in the *Secret Seven* world. Soon I am the girl who runs away from home and cuts her hair short to become a stable-boy.

I am in Grade Three with Mrs Tucker as my teacher in the portable building with the Grade Fours. She is stricter than Miss Taylor and has a rule of never any talking or you go straight to Mr Tucker for the cuts. No one talks, not even Chicken.

The year has hardly started when she has to go to hospital. Mrs Gregory, who lives on a soldier-settler farm and used to be a teacher, takes Mr Tucker's Grades Five, Six and Seven, so that he can be with Mrs Tucker while she has her operation. It is serious, everyone says; she might die.

Our new teacher looks like a younger sort of Grandpa Ted, red face, brown sweater, shiny shoes on little feet. At assembly, Jimmie Lewis gives the bass drum a few quick biffs, Miss Taylor lifts her hand and we belt out the anthem. *God save our gracious Queen...* Then hands on hearts. *I am an Australian. I love my country. I salute her flag. I honour the Queen. I promise to obey her laws.*

The new teacher gives a blast on his whistle and waits for us to stop fidgeting. In the row behind, Chicken laughs but it sounds like a fart and forces everyone in the front row to suck in our cheeks and widen our eyes to keep our laughter inside.

'Stand—At—Ease! I'm Mr Allen. Like it or lump it, Grade Three and Four, I'm what you've got while Mrs Tucker's in hospital. Do the right thing and we won't have any problems. Anyone want to argue with that?'

No one does. There's a long silence while we think about the difference between Mr Allen and Mr Tucker at school assembly. About the way Mr Tucker sometimes plays his violin for us. The way he wears his Bombers hat and scarf on cold days.

'Atten-shun!' barks Mr Allen, and the boys on the drums let rip. 'Left right left right no talking left right.'

Mr Allen waits at the door, whistle in his mouth. As Chicken marches past, Mr Allen clips him over the ears. Inside, he patrols the aisles with a heavy tread, tweaks Roy's ear half off his head, slaps a ruler hard against Shirley Fry's desk, makes her jump right off her chair. He tears a page from Lizzie's book, says it isn't good enough, start again. He laughs at Chicken's drawing and holds it up for everyone to see, but when we laugh a little, he shouts that *he'll laugh his head off if he wants and we'll get along just fine if we speak when spoken to and not before, or after, or in between, and do we have that clear?*

Yes, Mr Allen.

He is everywhere. At my elbow, making my ears prickle and burn. In the playground, pushing in to play football with the boys. On the day Colleen's away and Lizzie lets me join in the skipping, he holds our rope and turns too fast, laughing as we get muddled and stumble out.

Next morning, I tell Mum my stomach hurts and I can't go to school. She says she'll give me a dose of castor oil. I notice how she doesn't wear rings like Colleen Mulligan's mother and I'm sure that doesn't help with being common; even Mrs Winkie wears a gold band when she's not really married because she's a widow. I can't tell Mum about Colleen saying she's common, so instead I tell her I don't like the new teacher. She comes out of her bubble and blinks at me. 'What's wrong with him?'

'He smells like Grandpa Ted.'

Mum leans on the table and puts her face in her hands. 'I've found your report card from last year. You love school, you know you do.'

When the jungle sleeps the Phantom wakes. The quickest way to the back beach is over the track past Dad's house. In the summer mist, my breath is a cloud. After a night of drizzly rain, the lagoon is squashy around the edges and the ground squeaks where I walk on it. At Dad's side gate, I see Mossie gnawing a bone on the veranda. Right then Layle walks out the back door.

I run into the jungle behind the houses where there is no sound except firetails and finches chirruping in the mist. Soon I am climbing into the boobialla, using my school case to bash through branches speckled with moss, through spider webs spangled with watery beads, through wattles dripping dew. Soon I am standing on top of the world with only the sound of surf on the back beach and water trickling off leaves. Burley Point is a pastel drawing before me: the foreshore pines finger-rubbed green, the lagoon an egg-white cloud in the middle, our house half-hidden behind the kurrajong, the Scotts' between us and Lizzie's, Chicken's across the street, Shorty's behind ours, a ribbon of smoke from Mrs Major's chimney, and the red roof of the school behind Shorty's pines.

All at once, I wish I was sitting at my desk next to Lizzie, shooting my hand up: *Ask me. Ask me.* Way up here above the town, it doesn't seem to matter what Colleen and the others say about Mum or me. And I can't even remember why the new teacher's smell reminds me of Grandpa Ted except a thought of grey trouser legs. That thought makes me turn away from the town to the back beach where a man is fishing off the rocks, standing too close to the edge, the dangerous part where the swell can turn into waves without warning.

It's Pardie! I can tell by his blue cap.

Shoving my shoes and socks in my case, I leap off the dune, running and tripping and rolling to a stop at the bottom. While Pardie is casting out and concentrating, I leave my case on the beach and creep onto the rocks. The water is icy but I'm close behind him now and my heart is warm with joy at the sight of him. His hair is long under his cap and his freckles are honey spots you could lick. In his bucket, there's a pinkie and a good-sized flattie.

He turns with a grin. 'Whaddya doing creeping up on me?'

'Wagging,' I tell him.

'That's pretty dumb.'

'You're wagging. So who's the dumb one?'

He arches the rod over his shoulder and flicks, letting the line fizz out before it plops over the reef into the deep. Straightaway he decides it's not right, reels it in and does it again.

'I'm older. You'd better bugger off. It's dangerous here.'

'You're here.'

'I know what I'm doing.'

There is a sudden feeling of everything changed and Dunc in the city and no one to talk to about Colleen, and being teased, and Mr Allen. I blurt: 'It's not your beach. Or reef. Or sea. Or sky. Or anything.' I slosh away from him through rock pools full of sea slugs and starfish and trapped spotty tiddlers. One pool is as big as a lake; you could drown in that lake and be washed out to sea and who cares what Pardie Moon says.

'Sylvie-ie-ie-ie!'

I am not listening; I am walking on feet with no bones. But when I look up from my sloshing, I see Pardie running towards me, mouth shouting, arms pointing. He is too late: all around the sea roars into a wave and rises out of the deep, so huge and blue that I am stiff with fear and slow thoughts. Yet still I hear the sound of my terror, the silence of sharks, a drenching heaviness. Then suddenly I can breathe again. The wave has gone and Pardie's arms are hanging over my shoulders, his hands holding clumps of weed, holding them as if his fingers will break; and I realise that Pardie is the weight pressing me into the reef, saving me from the sea sucking us backwards as if we are pebbles. I grab at weed too, our fingers fishbone-white, holding on for our lives. Then the rush of water has gone and we are left on the reef like stranded fish.

'Hurry!' says Pardie, helping me up. 'The tide's coming in. We've gotta get outta here.'

Running and hopping, I follow across the rocks, the sea lapping behind, its wicked tricks. Back on the beach, we collapse against the kelp and shiver into our fright. Gulls shriek at the sight of us. Pardie bunches his jumper and wrings water onto the sand. His freckles are so bright they must have been washed clean by the sea.

'I could've drowned,' I say through rattling teeth. 'You saved me, Pardie.' Then I remember his fish. 'Where's your rod? Your bucket?'

'On its way to the South Pole, where do you think? You should've listened when I told you to get outta here. That was my best rod. It's your fault. All of it.'

I grab my case and run along the beach. I run from knowing that I am the fault of everything.

At Stickynet, I leave the beach and push through the tea-tree to Cele's place. I think of Grannie saying Cele has to have rocks in her head to squat in a humpy in the dunes when she could live in the city and be part of the society set with a bank manager husband instead of travelling to every tin-pot town in the state with that no-hoper photographer, and now that's fizzled out what's she got?

She's got the best magpie. Before I'm even out of the scrub, Fred hears me coming, 'Faack orf. Faack orf,' he squawks from his cage.

With Fred carrying on, there's no need to knock and I'm already in the door when I see my father at Cele's big table, head bent over a paper. *Why didn't I see his jeep?* Too late, he flicks a look at me.

'Drowned rat at your door,' he tells Cele, going back to his paper.

'Sylvie-ie-ie,' sings Cele from the kitchen. 'Well timed. I've made spider biscuits.' She gives me her big dimply smile and for no reason that smile makes my eyes sting. 'Day off or wagging?' she says, running her fingers through my stiff hair. She doesn't seem to care which so I don't reply. 'Come on, I'll find you something dry.'

Cele has the best house. The roof beams used to be telephone poles and a pelican skeleton hangs over her bed. She has a drift-wood chair that she made herself, and there are photos in frames on the walls and stacked on the floor, photos from her exhibition in the Mount. Nobby Carter looks like an old turkey gobbler; Jude Moon a bleached out Bambi; Bridie Maguire with eyes like black cherries. Cele buttons me into her shirt and I notice a photo of Dunc and me has sad cherry eyes too. What is wrong with Cele, finding sad eyes everywhere? She drapes my clothes next to the stove and asks if I want something to eat.

I want to leave but I am trapped at the table with my father and no clothes. Cele's biscuits are bumpy yellow lumps, some with spider legs and others without.

'Eat the ones without legs first,' says Cele.

Dad sniggers behind his paper. 'I wouldn't if I were you.'

'They're good for you,' says Cele, flicking her tea-towel at him. 'All Bran and curry powder. Not too much sugar.'

They are revolting. When she returns to the kitchen, Dad looks at me, looks into my eyes, then opens his mouth and pretends to choke. I nibble spider crumbs and a feeling of gladness creeps over me. When Cele returns with a beer for Dad, she pushes the plate towards me. 'More?'

'My sandwich,' I say, opening my case. Dad widens his eyes at me, sharing the secret of Cele's spiders.

Cele asks about school and when I tell her about Mr Allen, she says new teachers can be a pain, she hated most of hers.

'I've got my report,' I tell her as I find my sandwich.

She reads it right through. 'Your daughter's a brain, Mick.' She slides the booklet across the table. 'Look how well she's done.'

Dad sets his paper down and has a swig of beer. 'Remember how smart I was? Didn't do me much good.' Cele stares at him. 'What?' he says, jutting his jaw.

'I'm thinking it's not about you. I'm thinking you need more than brains.'

'Like?'

'Like it's what you do with what you've got that counts.' She pours beer from Dad's bottle into a glass for herself and licks off the froth. 'Use your brains, Sylvie. Do something with them. Not like us.'

'Speak for yourself,' says Dad.

'I am.'

'There's not one thing I've done my whole life that I regret.'

Cele shakes her head. 'That's so much piffle and rot. Everyone regrets something—'

'That's what I'm telling you. I don't.'

Dad flicks the pages of his paper like a fan. Cele just stares. He still hasn't read my report. He hasn't looked at me again. I chew on my sandwich crust with the gladness seeping out of me. Parrots screech past the window and Fred tells them to 'Faack orf—faack orf'.

'For God's sake, Mick,' says Cele at last, 'you've got to regret an argument with a brother that's gone on for twenty years!'

The paper drops. 'Don't mention that bastard.'

Dad and Uncle Ticker don't speak because the hurt is too deep: Cele told me this before. Mum says it's a pig-headed kind of hurt and the Meehans are famous for it. Cele looks at me and shakes her head. 'All because of a stupid squabble over a few hundred acres of land.' She rocks back in her chair. 'At least on the surface of it.'

'What else?' says Dad, jutting his chin.

'There's always something else,' says Cele with a sad kind of sigh. 'Always the same old things hiding underneath.'

'Don't talk in riddles,' says Dad, hiding in his paper again.

'That's the point,' says Cele. 'Life is a riddle.' Dad looks over his paper and taps his head as if Cele has a screw loose. 'Mick, I'm six years older than you—'

Dad grins. 'Easy to see who's got the wrinkles.'

Cele pokes out her tongue at him. 'I remember how you used to follow Grandpa Pat around like a bad smell. When you were learning to walk, he used to tie you to a lead and you toddled along beside him like a puppy. And when he got sick—I must have been about ten so you were what?—four?—you wouldn't leave him... not for a minute...'

'So?'

'So'—she rocks forward and takes a sip of her beer—'when he died, you wouldn't come out from under his bed. Not for three days. And after Brendan—'

'That's enough.'

Again Dad hides in his paper. I remember Grannie telling me about Rosie and Brendan, her babies who died. But what's that got to do with Dad? When he lowers his paper to have some beer, Cele is still staring. 'What?' he says with a big innocent grin.

Then I notice Cele's eyes are soft and glassy. And behind Dad's silly smile, I can see a sad clown with droopy eyes; but just as quickly the sadness is gone and I wonder if I saw it at all because now he's wearing his clown face and I don't like that face at all.

'No,' says Cele, pushing back her chair, 'I don't think you let yourself think about any of it, let alone regret it.'

Dad's beer is close to my report. Suddenly I don't care if he reads it or not. I don't care if he walks past me in the street and looks up at the clouds, not at me, as if there's a hole in the sky with no birds. I bump up from the table and ask Cele if my clothes are dry.

'Almost,' she says, handing me the scrap bucket to feed Fred.

Fred's cage is as big as a shed. I empty the bucket of food scraps through the side flap. He is not very grateful. 'Faack orf,' he tells me, flapping crazily. 'Faack orf.'

Fred was a baby when Cele found him with a bent wing. As he flaps amongst the scraps, I think he must have more brains than most maggies because he's smart enough to learn how to talk, yet he's stuck in a cage telling everyone to 'Faack off'. What sort of life is that for a maggie?

The path is covered with sand from the dunes and I make no sound crossing the porch. Dad is still at the table. My report is in front of him: I can't remember if I left it open or closed.

Before I'm halfway across the road, Mum comes pushing out the gate. 'What's wrong with your hair? Where've you been?' And then she's hitting me, right there in the street. 'How dare you.' *Hit. Hit.* 'Don't you think?' *Hit. Hit.* 'I've got enough.' *Hit. Hit.* 'To worry about?' *Hit. Hit.* 'Without.' *Hit.* 'You.' *Hit.* 'Too?'

At first I just stand there holding up my case but her arms are everywhere, hitting and puffing, and I'm bending and ducking. She's never hit me before, not like this. Between hits, I can see Lizzie watching from under our tree and I know she's told Mum that I wagged. I see Mrs Shorty on a ladder, clipping her hedge, turning to look. But I don't see Mrs Bloomers' car stop at our gate until she's running towards us, grabbing Mum and pulling her off.

'Stop it, Nella. Stop it. What's happened?'

Mum clasps her arms across her chest as if to keep them from hitting. 'She wasn't at school,' she tells Mrs Bloomers. 'I was worried sick. Anything could've happened.' Her shoulders are shaking and I can see bones pushing through the skin at her neck. She looks as if she might break. 'She's all I've got. All I've got.'

12

When the telephone rings, Mr Bloom turns off the wireless, making the newsreader squawk. He hands Mum the receiver and kisses Mrs Bloomers on top of her head. He tries to kiss Penny and Poppit but they cover their faces with their hands and duck their heads, so he pretends to be a bear and creeps up behind them. When he catches them with a kiss on the back of their necks, they scream and wipe off his kisses. Mr Bloom laughs and takes his hat from the peg on the wall. When he opens the door, cold air creeps in, making me shiver and hug myself warm.

We are staying with the Blooms on their farm called Clovelly because Mum needs a rest. Mum is still on the phone, listening, not saying anything. Penny and Poppit are fighting over the soldier in the Cornflakes packet, snatching and hiding it, teasing each other. Mrs Bloomers tells them to *Stop It*. Penny and Poppit make faces and mouth words behind her back. The kettle hisses. Penny's cat slicks down its coat. Mum replaces the receiver and sinks against the wall.

'Everything's gone. Everything.' Clutching her knees, she slides down the wall and curls in a ball on the floor, rocking, rocking.

Mrs Bloomers stops buttering the sandwich bread. Penny and Poppit stop their bickering. Even the cat stops licking and looks up as Mrs Bloomers brings a cup of tea and lowers herself onto the floor next to Mum.

'Drink this,' she says, holding the cup under Mum's nose. 'Drink this, Nella. And tell me what's happened. Come on, tell me, what is it?'

'All gone,' says Mum, rocking. 'Nothing left. Nothing.'

From the table, Penny and Poppit stare down, their mouths two soggy cereal holes gaping at our mothers on the floor. Outside, the gum trees are wearing swirling skirts of fairy mist. The mist comes closer and peers through the heat-streaked windowpane.

'What'll I do?' says Mum. 'What'll I do?'

'Tell me, Nella,' says Mrs Bloomers. 'Tell me.'

Suddenly Mum sits up with a straight back, head cocked as if she's listening to something far off, maybe as far as Bindilla, which is not far down the road, maybe as far off as Burley Point. We listen too. The cuckoo comes out of the clock and cuckoos seven times. Outside, the tractor coughs and splutters into life.

'Morgan's his mate,' says Mum. 'Of course he'd say it was an old house, needed rewiring, no need to investigate.' And suddenly her mouth is full of words. 'They're drinking mates. He's covering up for him.' She looks at us with wild eyes. 'The divorce has come through. He hated the judge giving me the house. He's been biding his time, waiting for us to be out of the place. Give him that, at least he didn't torch it with us in it.'

Mrs Bloomers heaves her bottom off the floor. She takes Mum's cup and puts it on the table. Then she lifts Mum under her arms. Mum is a rag doll, her arms and legs flop and bend. Mrs Bloomers sits next to Mum and moves Mum's hand to her cup of tea. 'Come on,' she says to Penny and Poppit. 'Clean your teeth.

Get a new handkerchief. Where are your lunch boxes? Hurry up or you'll miss the bus.' I start to follow. 'Not you, Sylvie, your mother needs you here.'

I want to tell her it's my day to be blackboard monitor, the day I get to clean off the old date and write the new one with yellow chalk. But Mum is staring into her tea, gone off into her bubble again. I climb back onto my chair. The cornflakes soldier is sticky with jam.

In the back of the Blooms' black Buick, I am safe from old-man gum trees with peeling skin and twisty limbs that grab at me as I walk the long track to and from the school bus. I am safe from snakes, from having to watch my feet in case there's one under a branch or a piece of bark. The tyres roll and crunch, breaking backs, killing snakes. I try not to think of Penny telling me of snakes thrown up under cars, clinging to the axles, slithering inside through the engine, crazy mad creatures that attack the driver and stab the passengers with needle-fork tongues until the car runs off the road and crashes into a tree and everyone is killed. *Except the ssssnake*, Penny hisses when she's walking next to me. *The ssssnake alwayssss getsss away.*

We drive across the cattle ramp and onto the main road, bucking over corrugations, past the soldier-settler farms where Mrs Bloomers says their rough-cleared land is hardly good enough to scratch a living from. When we pass Bindilla, I peer out the window, hoping to catch sight of Grannie down near the chook run. But dust follows the car like a horse's tail, hiding everything in sight.

In front, Mum is telling Mrs Bloomers what Grannie said: 'Stay with him and I'll support you all you can. Leave him and I won't lift a finger to help.' Mrs Bloomers says: 'She's full of hot air, Nella. And you don't know if he had anything to do with this or not. You're just guessing.'

Our house has gone. No walls, no roof, a blackened square, like the picture of the Hiroshima bomb that Miss Taylor showed us in the old newspaper with the heading, *All Living Things Seared To Death*. We stand in the yard, Mum and me and Mrs Bloomers, staring in the sun.

'Nothing,' says Mum. 'Nothing left. Nothing.'

Nothing is the stink of gunpowder and burnt meat on Guy Fawkes night when the council has a bonfire beside the lagoon; it is the smell of fairy dresses, shrivelling and frizzling. There is nothing but the hole where our house used to be. I walk up the sunroom steps where there used to be a door.

Dunc's eggs!

All at once I am glad that Mum made me leave Georgie Porgie with Lizzie to look after. I kick at a blackened bit where there used to be a wall. Fine black ash sifts up in tiny mushroom clouds.

'What about Dunc's eggs?'

'Everything's gone,' snaps Mum. 'You've got eyes, can't you see? We've got nothing but what we stand up in. Nothing.' She glares down at me as if I have lit the fire, as if it's my fault. She is wrapped in her fake fur coat even though the day is warm. It is not fur pretending to be a fox with tiny feet and toenails, like Mrs Winkie's got, more a shorn brown skin, a pale, scared bear. I turn from her frightened face. *It is not my fault.*

The path next to the Scotts' fence is covered with blobs of broken glass, blue and green, red and mauve and clear. I collect them in my skirt until I have a belly full of coloured glass, heavy as Denver Boland's beer gut, heavy as my heart.

'The leadlight windows,' says Mum, 'Melted in the heat.'

I collect more glass. I spread the pieces on the path and group them together in their matching colours.

'Nothing insured,' says Mum. 'I didn't renew it. Didn't have the money.'

'We'll get a fund going,' says Mrs Bloomers. 'You've got to stop worrying, Nella, you'll make yourself worse.'

I have five piles of lead glass winking in the sun. From each, I choose pieces to take back to the farm. 'I don't want that rubbish in the car,' says Mrs Bloomers, stepping over me.

Maggies in the pines are singing up a storm. The smell of the Hiroshima bomb is up my nose. I want the coloured glass to melt back into windows, our house to rise up from the dirt. I want Mum to yell and curse like Mrs Winkie does when she burns the toast. But Mum is walking down the path ahead of me, a hunched brown bear still saying, 'Nothing. Nothing.' And there is nothing in my throat except dry spit, and nothing in my head except crackling fumes and spitting flames swallowing our house with fiery tongues while people run in the street and fetch buckets, and everything is too late, everything is blowing up in our faces as we sleep in our beds on the Bloomers' farm, safe from fathers and fires. *At least he didn't torch it with us inside.* And everyone watches with red eyes and the heat pushes them back and what can they do? What can anyone do?

I lift my foot and scatter the glass. I kick it off the path and under bushes into the blackened dirt. Then I jump on any bits left; I smash them into a million pieces. When every single blob is broken, I follow down the path.

Mrs Bloomers is holding Mum's arm, leading her to the car. As we climb in, Sid McCready comes rolling down the road. Because he has a screw loose, he talks like a big baby. 'Hey, watch out!' he yells. 'Sid is coming.' As if we didn't know. He is panting when he gets to us, his head all Brylcreemed black and shiny by Grandma McCready, who still looks after Sid although he is a man. 'Next time,' he says with shining eyes, 'there'll be a fire with Guy Fawkes and rockets and bangers and crackers...Mick says next time I can let off the rockets...'

Mum turns from the car. 'What did you say, Sid?'

'He didn't say anything,' says Mrs Bloomers, trying to get Mum in.

I wind down my window. Now Sid is chanting: 'Pardie Moon and Mick and the moon—'

Mrs Bloomers says: 'Off you go, Sid, there's a dear. Don't hang around here.' As she climbs in, she says: 'He's harmless really. But you never can tell.'

I can tell. Mum can tell. Even Sid McCready with a screw loose can tell.

The car rolls down the hill and gathers speed. Mrs Bloomers is talking, talking, but Mum and I aren't listening. We are looking across the lagoon at my father's house where he is standing on a ladder, painting his guttering blue.

13

Mum says she hates the smell of other people's stuff, and we'll make do with what we had at the farm. She hides the box under the seat that folds down to make our bed then looks at the kerosene heater and says they're dangerous things and we might as well go to bed and read. But when the wind squalls in from the sea and rocks the van like a baby's pram, she blows out the lamp and cuddles me close, and we are safe and warm in our caravan world.

I wake to her scream: 'God, the roof's sprung a leak!' She bumps about in the dark and lights the lamp, grabs the bucket, the piss-pot too, and sets them on the floor to catch the drips. 'God,' she says, 'what'll I do?'

God must have suggested the tarpaulin in the shed. Mum pulls on her dressing-gown and grabs the torch. 'Stay here,' she says as she opens the door. The light from her torch streaks past the window like a lighthouse on a wet night, searching and safe, despite the storm all about. Then she's back at the door with the tarpaulin in her arms, her hair plastered to her head, and her face potato-white.

'Put on your raincoat!' she screams. 'And your rubber boots. I need you to help.'

The rain in my face smells of seaweed and salt and the dead

cat they found under the post office hedge. Mum has leaned the workmen's ladder against the caravan, and is pointing to a pile of bricks that she's carried from where our new house is being built. 'You need to pass these up. Understand?'

She struggles up the ladder with the tarpaulin flapping behind. At the top, she tries to spread it out but the wind picks up an end and slaps it about. As I climb up, I drop the first brick and she screams, 'Brick!' and 'Brick!' and 'Brick!' again. When she has the tarpaulin half-anchored, she moves the ladder and climbs up again to reach across the roof and bully it into place. 'Brick!' she screams, and 'Brick!' and 'Brick!' again, until soon the van is wearing a canvas hat held down with brick hatpins.

Inside, we strip off our clothes. Mum puts on the kettle and dries my hair, refills our hot-water bottles and belches out the steam. Back in bed, we listen to the wind as it bickers and brawls, to the silence of thunder far over the sea. I wonder if the blocks beneath our wheels will hold and what will happen if they loosen while we sleep and the caravan rolls down the drive and hurtles through the tea-tree into the lagoon? Will it float like a ship or sink beneath the choppy waves? And if it bobs to the other side, will Dad rescue us or leave us there to drown? And what if he comes in the night and burns down our van? It is raining again, heavy like hail. Maybe everything is too wet to burn.

In my dream a log truck is driving at me and I try to run but my feet won't move and I'll be squashed flat. I thrash awake and my nightie is a sweaty tangle, Mum's arm wrapped too tight around me. When I get free, my heart is a jungle drum—*boom—boom—boom. Go into the jungle and call: the Phantom will hear.* Soon the dream fades into a smudge of half-remembered things.

The wind has stopped battering. In the listening silence, Mum begins to cough.

'They know he did it,' says Mum. 'Or they wouldn't be so keen to reach into their pockets to build us something new. You can't tell me they don't know.'

I tell her I don't want to live in Wanda the Witch's house and why do we have to? She clutches a hot-water bottle to her chest and asks how do I think it makes her feel, living off handouts and knowing every Tom, Dick and Harry will want her undying gratitude as soon as the new house is finished? And she's not Wanda the Witch, she's Mrs Major to you. And we're lucky Mrs Major's in Melbourne for a few months helping her daughter who's had a baby, because otherwise where would we live? And have I ever thought about anyone except myself for one single minute?

Mrs Tucker is back at school with one kidney: everyone has two but one is enough to keep you living. Lizzie puts her ruler exactly down the centre of our desk and says not to touch her half. When Mrs Tucker looks up, Lizzie blinks at her with innocent eyes but as soon as she looks away, Lizzie inches her ruler further over. I push it back. She inches it over.

Colleen has made a Gang of Four against me with Faye, Lizzie and Shirley Fry. When I come near, they run off screaming: 'Wi-i-i-i-tch!' At playtime, I go to the seat under the pine tree with my book, or sometimes I play with Chicken and Roy Kearney, but then the gang yells, 'Boy lover!' Roy says to ignore them because they are jealous.

Roy has nice even teeth and freckles on his nose like tiny spots of gold. He's almost as smart as me in class, and his father has a racehorse like Dad once had. He lives in a big house out past the oval with white painted rails and a special galloping track. Sometimes he has a horsy boy smell, but there is also a nice shampoo scent in his hair, clean and fresh as open windows. I am not a boy lover but if I was, Roy would be the one.

One playtime when Miss Taylor is on yard duty, and I am playing Brandy with Chicken and Roy, she comes over and asks how I like Grade Three. She says she's heard I'm still top of my class and sometimes doing Grade Four work. Colleen and the gang run past but when they see Miss Taylor their running slows to a guilty slink. Miss Taylor follows them with her eyes and says softly: 'You know, Sylvie, there are some people in Burley Point who think your mother is a very brave woman.' She pauses, then adds: 'I think you're pretty brave too.'

I don't know how to understand this and my face pinks up. The Phantom is brave and so is Julie Walker; Superman and Wonder Woman are brave, and also the boy in the city who rescued his baby sister from their house when it was on fire. Miss Taylor smiles at me and walks away. But her smile stays with me for a long time, even when I go home to have lunch with Mum because Wanda's house is next to the school and it is easier. Lizzie goes home for lunch too and runs past Wanda's house without stopping, probably because Colleen Mulligan said she should. I snap off a dead rose stick in the front garden and whap it around my head. If it was a witch's wand, I'd turn Lizzie into a lizard that gets squashed on the road and dries out like an old shoe, and I'd do the same to Colleen too.

Inside, Mum is on her knees, washing the kitchen floor. 'I

should be in bed,' she says with a cough.

'Why aren't you?'

'Why do you think?' She pulls herself up by the table leg. 'It doesn't wash itself, you know. Clothes don't wash themselves. Food doesn't appear on the table like magic.'

My sandwich has. I eat it while she's emptying the bucket. On the table there's an envelope with photos of Dunc and me inside. Cele's photos. 'Why'd she give you those?' I ask when she returns.

'They're copies; the others were burnt in the fire.' She puts her face in her hands and starts crying slow tears. 'I'm going to bed. Don't be late home.'

Before returning to school, I creep into the bedroom. Mum is a tiny mound beneath the eiderdown, hardly there at all.

Dad came in the night and burned our house down. I want to spit the words out so that Dunc will know what really happened. How long will I have to be the keeper of the secret? We stand where the fence used to be, watching Shirley Fry's father and Mousie Tibbet, the carpenter from West End, hammer an asbestos sheet onto the frame of our new house.

When Dunc came home for the holidays, Mum told him the fire was an electrical fault. She said she didn't tell him in a letter because she didn't want to worry him. She said I was not to say anything about Sid because with his screw loose, how did we know it was true? So did Dad light the fire, or didn't he? I was too frightened to ask.

Dunc doesn't seem as upset as I thought he'd be. He says the house would've gone up like a bomb because everything in it was combustible. He says fires need oxygen, fuel and energy to get started; it was a theory invented by a French man but anyone with half a brain could've worked it out. He says he'll start a new egg collection straightaway because he'll be fourteen in a few months and when he's working he won't have time for collecting eggs. I look at him closely to see if he's telling the truth. He is taller than before and has grown soft fur on his face like a day-old chicken. I wish I could see right under his skin, under his blood and veins and bones, right inside his brain, so that I would know what he's really thinking, his secret thoughts about everything.

That night he says Wanda's house is an accident waiting to happen. He says the saggy ceiling above our beds in the sunroom will probably fall in and I'll cop the worst because the saggiest bit is above my bed. He says the rainwater tank is half under the house: can't I hear the water lapping? He says the floor's probably rotten and our beds might fall through while we sleep. He tells me he'll soon have a farm of his own and he'll run five hundred head. It is hard to sleep with worrying about the water under the floor.

When Mum's at work, Pardie comes around and Dunc belts out 'Bye Bye Blackbird' and 'The Sheik of Araby' on Wanda's pianola. Pardie gives Dunc a box with ten eggs for his new collection. There's a hopping dolly bird, a singing honeyeater, even a western whipbird. Before he returns to school, he finds a blue wing's egg out near Bunny Brennan's soak. It is his rarest and best egg.

I have kept the secret of our house.

The Phantom Julie Walker would not let her mother spoonfeed her dessert, not when she's just turned eight. With one flick of her head, she'd twist the spoon from the offender's grip. She'd spit custard into the baddie's face. She'd use the spoon as a deadly weapon and stab the baddie between the eyes until she begged for mercy.

'Just a little bit more,' says Mum.

I button my lips against the spoon. I am the only girl in Grade Three not invited to Colleen Mulligan's birthday party. When she gave out the invitations, I pretended I was deaf and blind and couldn't hear everyone talking in excited voices.

Why don't I have birthday parties like Colleen and Faye, and sometimes Lizzie? Why does Mum feed me dessert when I can do it myself? Why did Dad burn our house down? Why do we pretend he didn't? Nothing makes sense. And then a terrible thought: What if there are no answers to anything?

Miss Taylor is wrong: I am not brave in any way. I open my mouth and swallow the custard and cream.

On the train, Nobby Carter wipes his seat with his handkerchief and mutters about never knowing who's been sitting where. He says he's going to the Mount to have his eyes checked out. Mum says we're going to Muswell for me to have my tonsils out. On the bay, the waves are cutting up a chop, the dinghies buck-jumping on their moorings. At Stickynet, the train lets out a warning shriek; I press my nose to the window and watch waters from Lake Grey being tricked into the sea, sticks and leaves battered like dead birds against the pylons of the bridge. Then I see Pardie fishing in the inlet. And Kenny and Peter Leckie creeping along the bank towards him when they should be at school in Muswell.

I tell Mum I've seen Pardie. 'Girly-boy,' says Nobby Carter from across the aisle.

'What's a girly-boy?' I whisper to Mum.

She shakes her head at me. The train gathers speed and my eyes grab trees, a sign, a beer-bottle flash by the side of the track. I wonder about Pardie—sometimes he fluffs his hair with his fingers, the way Mum fluffs at her perm—is that what Nobby means? When I look again there's a tractor in a paddock ploughed black for chicory. Cloud shadows chasing sheep down a green slope. A dam slushy with reeds. Soon we're passing backyards and dunnies and clotheslines heavy with whites, and the train slides into the station at Muswell.

Mum and I walk up the hill. At the town hall, she coughs and holds her chest and we read the poster for *The African Queen*. Mum says Humphrey Bogart's all right but Katharine Hepburn's not much. In the hospital foyer, she has another coughing fit. 'That's a graveyard cough if I ever heard one,' says the nurse at the desk. 'You all right, Mrs Meehan?'

Mum says she is. Liar, liar, your pants are on fire. But it is not a proper lie: people don't really want to know if you're sick. Or that fathers burn houses.

The nurse leads us down a corridor and pushes through swing doors into a room with three empty beds and a high window with cloudy bubble glass. Although it's still morning, Mum opens my school case and hands me my pyjamas. As I pull on the bottoms, she says: 'Hurry up. I don't want to miss the train.'

The train? 'Aren't you staying?'

'I'll be back in a week, it's not long.'

'You'll be fine,' says the nurse, tucking me into bed. 'You'll go to sleep and wake up and be eating jelly and ice-cream in no time. It's your mother who needs to rest.' She smiles a big-toothed smile, rattles the curtains and leaves. The doors clunk closed.

I don't know how to understand this. If I'm in hospital, shouldn't Mum stay with me? But if she's sick, who will look after her?

'Besides, I've got to move into the new house. There's a lot to do.' She puts my case in the bedside drawer and coughs again.

How can she move into the house if she's sick? And if she's not sick, why can't she move into the house, and still come to see me? Everything is a muddle. The scratchy sheets, the rubber floor, the cold walls.

'I'll see you Friday then.'

Her shoes squeak in the corridor. Then a cough outside the window glass.

'She's got dollar signs for eyes,' says Grannie to someone on the phone, 'but he's left it so late, the pickings are thin on the vine.'

Uncle Ticker is engaged to a shopgirl from Muswell called Josie. *Shopgirl*, Grannie says so often that at first I think that's her name. Josie Shopgirl. Like Don Coffin the Undertaker. Grannie says the families are getting together on the weekend. She hoots into the phone, says that'll be an eye-opener, no prisoners taken, hoots again and hangs up.

'When's Mum coming home?'

Grannie says pneumonia can be tricky, she'll phone the hospital tomorrow. If she gets time.

She doesn't. Next day, Uncle Ticker drives into Muswell and brings Josie back to Bindilla. She is very pretty—Grannie didn't mention that—with white-blonde hair and blue eyes that squint up at Uncle Ticker when she smiles. She was a beauty queen— Miss Muswell and then Miss Something Else—Grannie didn't mention that either.

Josie helps Grannie with afternoon tea. She tells me to have a rest because I'm recuperating. I recuperate on a cane chair on the veranda while Josie sets out the cups and Grannie pours. Afterwards, Uncle Ticker says he's taking Josie for a drive to show her the cutting.

'Take Sylvie too,' says Grannie.

Uncle Ticker's mouth opens. Josie touches his knee. 'Lovely,' she says, squinting up at him.

Through a sea of yellow turnip weed, we drive towards the lake, Josie in front, me in the back, the Blitz bumping over ruts and rocks, bouncing so high that Uncle Ticker laughs and tells me to hold on to my head or I might lose it. At the lake, he stops to show us a flock of black duck fluttering to rest in the shallows. He tells Josie that when Old Pat first came to Bindilla the duck rose off the lake in their millions, clouding the sun and darkening the day. He says he knows that from Old Pat's diary, which is mostly pretty boring.

We're about to drive off when he peers along the shore. 'Emus,' he points, and when Josie and I follow his finger, we see two big birds loping around the lake, long rubber necks poking out in front, tail feathers flopping behind like pillows tied to their backs.

'Silly buggers,' says Uncle Ticker, driving off fast. 'That's the bad patch. If they're not careful, they'll get themselves bogged.'

When we reach the shore, the emus are struggling in the mud, trying to lift stuck legs, crying out for help, flapping useless wings. 'Stay here,' he says, grabbing a rope from under the seat and running towards them.

Josie follows like she knows what she's doing. As Uncle Ticker treads carefully along the water's edge, one emu breaks free from the mud and runs for the tea-tree, then Josie scrambles under the fence with Uncle Ticker yelling at her to stay where she is, all of it happening too fast.

Then I see Uncle Ticker is stuck too! I jump down and run to the lake with a cry of mud in my mouth. There are bees buzzing in the turnip weed, too many, too loud, and I think: What if he goes too? Now the emu is a feathered boat, sitting on the mud, making mournful squeaks. Josie grabs my arm and we watch Uncle Ticker pull at his ankle with both hands. His boot slops out with a glug too far away to hear, but that sound is a shout, a cheer. As Uncle Ticker edges to the shore, Josie's fingers dig into my arm. On solid ground, Uncle Ticker coils the rope and tries to lasso the sinking bird, every throw too long, or too short, or in between. He gives up and runs for the Blitz.

'Don't watch!' he yells as he passes.

Now the bird is tired, accepting. Suddenly a shot and the emu's neck crumples. Swans and pelicans and a cloud of black duck fly up, honking and squawking at the fright of us. Josie's arm is on my shoulder; we watch the birds flutter to rest on the lake, far from us.

'You're a couple of disobedient dames,' says Uncle Ticker as we head back, his voice like a Yank in a movie. 'Didn't I tell you to stay in the truck? You coulda gotcha selves shot.'

In the Blitz, Josie leans against Uncle Ticker and says: 'I was so scared—' and, 'I didn't know what to do—'

Uncle Ticker winks at me in the back. 'She won't get rid of me that easily. Will she, Sylvie?'

I don't really know what to say to that. I look at the waves in Josie's hair and think of sunlight on sand. How Mum puts vinegar in the rinse water to make my hair shiny.

'But I smell like a turnip,' I tell her.

'It'll wear off,' Mum says.

Uncle Ticker says. 'Never go near the lake, Sylvie. Understand?'

The Blitz bounces me up to the roof, but there is no more laughing.

Now the cutting has stone walls sloping down to a V at the bottom. 'It's a wonderful achievement, Tim,' says Josie.

I think: Who's Tim? Then I remember Timothy is Uncle Ticker's real name. At the same time, I notice he's lowering his face towards Josie as if he's going to kiss her, but I'm breathing down their necks so Josie tilts her head back and says why don't I climb over the seat and join them in the front where I'll have a better view of the cutting? When I'm between them, we look at the scar on the hill and the swamp stretching away to the treeline, and after a while, Josie says: 'How about I kiss Uncle Ticker, then you can too?'

I'm not that interested in kissing Uncle Ticker but I lean forward and let them kiss over my head. Then Uncle Ticker gives me a quick peck on the cheek and Josie says: 'Now I'll kiss you.'

Me? She pecks me on the cheek. 'Now you.' So I give her a peck too. 'Now,' she says, 'I'll kiss Uncle Ticker.'

This takes a lot longer.

Soon I'm sick of all this pecking and kissing. I tell them I need to go behind a bush and Josie moves over to let me out. I take a long time sitting behind a patch of boobiallas and when I come back, Josie has a red face and Uncle Ticker's wiping lipstick off his mouth.

'Better get going,' says Uncle Ticker, 'if we're to pick up the Old Girl and get to your place on time.'

Josie's place is behind a high cypress hedge on the outskirts of Muswell. It has a tiled veranda and rosebushes around a circular lawn that would be good for playing cricket, that's how big it is. As we walk inside, Grannie tells me to close my mouth and breathe through my nose because that's why I've had my tonsils out.

Josie has two brothers. The older one has thin hair, a wispy moustache, and works in a bank. Colin is about sixteen, with white-blond hair, a big nose and pimples. Josie's father pours sherry into little glasses and lemonade for me. The bubbles get up my nose and make me cough and Grannie snatches my glass off the table and wipes where it's been. Josie's mother tells Colin to show me his eggs.

'Eggs?' he says, wrinkling up that nose.

'Yes,' she says with a warning stare.

I follow him down the hall to a room with red velvet curtains and shelves of books to the ceiling. 'Don't touch anything,' he grumps before leaving me there.

I've never seen so many eggs. They're in cabinets with glass lids, on a shelf below the books, three whole walls of them. Emu eggs in different sizes, glossy black, others bottle green. I would like to steal some for Dunc but I can't think how I could hide them in the car because Grannie sees everything. And I'm too scared. Later I hear voices down the corridor, Uncle Ticker's laugh. I notice he laughs a lot more when Josie's around. I wait for Colin to return, for dinner to be over, for Mum to come home from the hospital.

Driving back to Bindilla, Grannie says: 'Why did you mention Mick?'

'They know I've got a brother,' says Uncle Ticker.

'They don't know there's bad blood.'

'Of course they do. They wanted to invite him. I had to tell them.'

'Be interesting to know your version.'

Outside the night is black and cold. Shadow trees and farm-house lights loom out of the dark and disappear again. After miles of silence, Grannie says: 'That woman has more front than John Martins. I'll get through the wedding but you won't find me palling up with her. The way she carries on, anyone would think she was getting married, not the daughter.'

At Bindilla, she bustles me into bed. 'Come on, it's cold enough to freeze udders on cows.' She pulls the curtains, stirring up a gust of icy air. 'Weddings,' she says. 'All that frippery. And a lifetime to regret it. Well, let's hope he doesn't.' She tucks me in and pulls the quilt up to my chin. 'Say what they like about your father, at least he's honest. And if someone's honest, you can forgive a lot.'

Doesn't she know about our house, the fire? I curl in a ball beneath the quilt and think of emus stuck in mud. I don't have a father. He is the space on the form that I leave blank when Mrs Tucker asks us to fill in *Father's Name*. He is the spider's web I break through every morning at the gate. He is dead flowers from the kurrajong that I kick off the path when they are squashed and brown.

14

It's hardly big enough to swing a cat in—that's what Mum says when we move in. There are two bedrooms, a kitchen and bathroom, with a porch in between. There's no water connected so we carry buckets from the rainwater tank and still use the dunny in the old laundry shed that backs onto Shorty's fence.

There wasn't enough money to build the front veranda so Mum has blocked off the door with the dressing table from her new maple bedroom suite. She sold the car to buy furniture. She said beds come before cars; from now on we can walk.

The dressing table across the door stops us stepping into a three foot drop and killing ourselves in the process. So much for charity. She says this while she's lugging buckets from the tank, while she's painting undercoat on the bathroom walls. Also when she's on her knees, polishing the lino in the bedroom that should be a lounge, but what good's a lounge if we don't have visitors? That's what she says, so we have two bedrooms instead. The smaller one is for Dunc when he comes home for the holidays.

'Why can't I sleep in Dunc's room when he's not here? I'm eight. Lizzie has her own bed. Everyone does.'

'It saves time,' says Mum, puffing and polishing. 'I only have to make one bed.'

'I can make a bed, Lizzie makes hers.'

'It's less work only washing one set of sheets.'

'I could wash them.'

'Don't be stupid.'

I reach out with my foot and kick her hard in the head. I hate sleeping with you, I tell her. How do I know anything if our arms and legs are always mixed up and muddled? How do I know who I am if I'm always lost in your smell? Then I blink and she's still on the floor, polishing, polishing. 'You're the stupid one,' I say, leaving her there.

At the woodpile, I lift the axe and smash it into a Mallee root. I smash and bash and make as much noise as I can but still she doesn't come after me. Soon my bones get heavy, my arms droop; I drive the axe into a log and give up.

Then I'm sick again. A car door slams in the street and Mum shoots across the floor, climbs over the bed and peeks out.

'Bloody hell! They could've let me know.'

In no time her apron and house dress are stuffed away in the wardrobe and she's wearing the new dress with the swirly skirt from the catalogue.

I sneak a look too. A blue car and silver caravan are parked out front. Grandpa Ted's trying to close our side gate, lifting it half off its hinges when it hasn't been closed for years. Grandma Bess has new purple hair. As they walk below the window, I can see every strand of Grandpa Ted's oiled white hair, the red skin of his scalp beneath; I can see the big lumpy pimple with the whisker on Grandma Bess's pink powdered cheek.

'You could have let me know,' says Mum at the back door. 'I've got Sylvie home from school with bronchitis.'

'Didn't know ourselves,' says Grandma Bess. 'We're not staying. We're heading over to Melbourne in our new van. Aren't we, Ted?'

I can't see Grandpa Ted but his grunts are inside my head, in the bed. Mum says she'll make a cup of tea.

'What on earth are you doing?' says Grandma Bess.

'We've only just moved in. The sink's not connected yet.'

'Well, you don't need anything too big, not with just the two of you. And Duncan almost old enough to leave school.'

'He's not leaving school. The Old Girl's paying for him to do law.'

'Law?'

Silence. Then Grandma Bess at the bedroom door. 'Sylvie dear, how are you?'

She doesn't look at me; her eyes are peeking into the spare room, checking out Mum's wardrobes, the pink curtains, the satin quilt. I close my eyes and pretend I'm too sick to speak. When I open them, she's back in the kitchen.

'Didn't she have bronchitis last year?

Mum is now sitting where I can see her. 'They took her tonsils out but it's made no difference. She's got a weak chest. Like me.'

'Auntie Jose had pneumonia. Lucky you didn't get that.'

Mum doesn't look lucky. She peers into her tea and everyone speaks at once and I can't hear any of it, and then Mum says: 'I need more work, to make ends meet. More hours at the cafe would help.'

'What about him?' says Grandma Bess.

'It's like getting blood out of a stone.'

'We told your sister she could do worse than marry a plumber. Bill's got his head screwed on the right way, hasn't he, Ted?'

Mum's head is not screwed on at all. It bobs into her cup and out again. It turns to me in the bedroom; her eyes are brown currant holes in a white cake face.

'The Meehans always thought they were too good for us,' says Grandma Bess. 'Didn't they, Ted?'

Mum's head jerks up. 'You thought he was Christmas. You couldn't get me down the aisle fast enough.'

I cover my head with the quilt and breathe in pink air and stay safe from everything, until I hear chairs sliding back and the sound of Grandpa Ted's voice, loud and cheery. 'See you've been making jam. Could do with a jar or two if it's going begging.'

Don't give him any! But already, Mum's wrapping jam jars in the pink pages of the *Border Mail*, one after another, too many.

Go, go! I tell them as they walk down the side path and struggle with the gate. *Go and leave us alone and never come back.*

As Mum changes out of her dress, she talks to the wardrobe. 'Don't see them for dust for over a year and then they breeze in just wanting to have a good squiz. Did they ever offer an ounce of help when I needed it? Have they ever been to see Dunc at school? No, not once.'

'Why didn't you tell them you had pneumonia?'

'What's the point?' She turns to the window and wraps her arms across her chest. 'If you knew what he did to me—'

There's a creature on the ceiling, a shadowy lump that is the shape of Grandpa Ted, reaching down with greedy arms, reaching down for Mum, for me. Can't she see?

'Good riddance to bad rubbish.' In the kitchen, cups clatter into the sink. Mum sits at the table; her head drops into her hands and her shoulders shake and heave.

When Dunc comes home in September, his eyes skip from the towels on the ironing board to the boxes stacked against the wall. 'I'm not sleeping here. It's a girly room. What's all this pink?'

Mum lumps his case onto the bed and begins sorting his clothes, not answering him. When she leaves, I cringe near the door and see all Mum's pink when I didn't really see it before— even the gum-tree picture on the wall is a kind of pink.

In just one term Dunc has grown pimples on his chin and a dark fur moustache on his top lip. I can't stop looking at that moustache. It is the same as Dad's but not stiff hair that needs shaving, not the same as men with dark cheeks and beards. It is too weird that Dunc could be a man.

He catches me looking. 'Whaddya gawking at?'

I cross quickly to the boxes. 'Pardie left some comics. He said he'll come over later.'

Dunc flicks through the pile and then shoves them back at me. 'Read the lotta them.' He turns to the window. Under his shirt, his shoulder blades are bony wings. He smells different too, like a warm horse, like a smoky tree might smell. Suddenly I think he might be blinking into the lace curtain the way I used to blink into *The Magic Pudding* at the hospital so no one could see me sniffling. What is wrong with him?

'Kenny Sweet's left school,' I tell him. 'He works in his father's shop.'

Dunc spins round. 'You think I give a fuck about Kenny

Sweet?' I feel the punch of the rude word as he passes. 'Anyway,' he calls from the porch, 'I'm leaving school too.'

He is late home for tea. He pokes his vegetables around his plate and says he's sick of eating rabbit, isn't there anything else? 'And I'm not sleeping in that room,' he says when he's finished playing with the rabbit. 'I'd rather sleep in the shed.'

'Don't be silly,' says Mum.

'I'm not a girl.' He flicks a look at me. 'Let her sleep there.'

'Let me, let me!' I jump up and down and bang my feet on the floor, then I think of Dunc having to sleep with Mum in the double bed and just the thought of it makes me laugh, loud and crazy as Sid McCready.

'Shut your fucking face,' says Dunc, grabbing my wrist across the table and giving me a Chinese burn.

I give a good bellow and Mum bellows too. 'Stop that!' Her face is white with two red spots on her cheeks. 'And don't bring that language into this house.'

Dunc drops my wrist and pushes back his chair. 'I won't,' he says as he heads for the bedroom, 'and I won't be sleeping here either. Now. Or ever.'

Mum scrapes the plates and I rub my wrist and we strain to hear what Dunc is doing. I wish I hadn't laughed like a ninny. Then Dunc is back with his school bag, a shirt sleeve hanging out.

'Where do you think you're going with that?'

'Pardie's.'

'No you're not.' But he's already outside. There's a skid of tyres on gravel and Mum leaps across the kitchen. 'Duncan! Come back here!'

Silence. Mum returns and throws plates around in the sink,

her face pink and stiff. In the kurrajong, spoggies are settling for the night, skittering about on our roof before chirruping into the tree. There are faint shouts from kids playing near the lagoon; I think I can hear Chicken shouting. It is getting too late to be out playing.

Dunc returns next morning after Mum's gone to work. I find him in the bedroom packing clothes into the big case he takes to the city—shirts, shoes, the *Biggles* book he borrowed from Mrs Major's house. He's packing his school books too, shoving everything in; it's a mess. 'Where are you going?'

He doesn't answer and I have to ask again. Still he doesn't look up. 'To live with Dad,' he says.

My heart thumps in my ears. 'You can't,' I say.

'Watch me,' he says.

I watch him pack his toothbrush bag, then his cricket bat squashed in on top. The thumping is deafening. 'You can't,' I say again.

'I can.' He pushes down the lid and buckles the straps. 'I can have my own room. My own dog. I can leave school. I can do whatever I want.'

Words fall out of my mouth. 'He burned down our house.' I tell him this twice and when he still doesn't look up, I say it again. 'Dad burned down our house. Everyone knows.'

'Don't be stupid. It was an electrical fault.'

'Morgan's his mate. Ask Mum. Sid McCready was there.'

He stands the case on the floor and looks up. 'Sid's mad. And you're a liar.'

'Ask Pardie, ask anyone. Everyone knows.'

He touches a pimple with careful fingers as if it might pop. I see doubt smudging his smirk. 'He wouldn't.'

'He did. He didn't want Mum to have it. Everyone knows.'

He stares at me as if he's looking right through me into a fire with raging flames and angry heat and Dad skulking around with petrol and matches, as if he's thinking, how do you burn down your own house? Then he balls a fist into his palm—*thwack-thwack*— and pushes past me without another word.

'Half-cocked, half-cocked!' I yell as he rides off, but he doesn't even bother to look back.

I slump on the step with all the power of my words emptied out, wanting him to come back and give me a Chinese burn, the pain of it. Later I see he's forgotten to take his case and I pack everything away so Mum won't know. When she comes home, I tell her he's sleeping at Pardie's and she grumbles about Jude not checking with her and tomorrow she'll have a thing or two to say.

Early next morning, Pardie arrives at our door looking for Dunc, his face a worried kind of white, his eyes not meeting mine.

'Well, if he didn't stay with you, where did he stay?' says Mum. Pardie scuttles off like a rabbit with Mum calling after him, 'Tell him he's not staying anywhere tonight. Tell him I want him home here, right now!'

In the laundry shed, Mum scrunches up newspapers to get the fire going under the copper, twisting and scrunching as if she's wringing rabbits' necks, Dunc's neck. 'I'll kill him. Where did he go? That's what I want to know.'

My mouth is dry and scared but I make myself say it. 'He said he was going to live at Dad's.' And straightaway: 'But I didn't believe him. I thought he'd gone to Pardie's.'

She stands with a flounce. 'Well, you can just go and get him.'

'Me? I'm not going there.'

'Well, I'm not talking to *her*. Am I?'

I'm halfway down the drive when I get worried and come back, wondering how to tell her, how to say it. He made me, I'll say. He tortured me with Chinese burns till I cracked, that's what I'll tell her. She's bluing sheets in the trough. 'I told him…that… Dad burned down our house.'

She lights another ciggie and squints through the smoke, and her words are not as bad as I'd feared. 'Well, why shouldn't he know?'

Layle says Dunc didn't sleep at their place. There's a worried crease between her bushy brows and I have to look away quickly so she won't see my worry too. Where did he go? Would he run away like he did from school?

Dad comes to our house when the pub closes. Mum stands on the porch and her eyes skitter all over the place as if she can't bear to look at him. She tells him she has a bad feeling. Then her eyes shift to me in the kitchen, back to him and then back to me again. I think: If she tells him, I'll say Dunc forced it out of me with the power of his mind. I'll say he's been practising to be a magician and can see what you're thinking. Why not? I'll say. Mrs Scott knows things from tea-leaves.

'I can't hang around here all night. Serves him right if he has to sleep under a boobialla.'

'The least you can do is go and look. Or I'll get Bill Morgan?'

Dad grumbles off. 'He'll get a good thrashing when I find him.'

After he's gone, Mrs Winkie yoo-hoos down the path with jars for Mum's marmalade. 'Dunc still not back?'

'Mick's gone to have a look. I've told him to let Bill Morgan know but he's probably got a skinful too. Useless, the two of them.'

Later in bed, I close my eyes and see exploding stars and red vein things that wriggle in the blackness then disappear and I am still awake wondering if Dunc might have gone to Seal Island with Mr Hammet to change the lighthouse cylinder. Has Mum thought of that? And while Mr Hammet was winching the cylinder up the cliff, Dunc might have hurt his ankle in a penguin burrow and be lying there right now unable to get up and, no matter how loud he screams, Mr Hammet can't hear because of the shrieking gulls and terns and mutton-birds.

I am still awake when Dad comes back. 'No one's seen him,' he says from the porch, the light above his head buzzing with midges. 'Though I wouldn't trust that Pardie Moon as far as I could kick him. Shorty and Augie had a drive around too, looked in the goods shed, under the lifeboat cover, flashed car lights through the scrub out near the lake in case he's hiding there. He could be bloody anywhere. Bill says we'll do a proper search tomorrow. Serve the little bugger right. He'll high-tail it home when it gets cold enough.'

Mum's voice is a squeak. 'What if he doesn't?'

'Well, he'll learn, won't he? Like we all bloody have to.' He looks into the darkness beyond the doorway where I am a spot in the bed. 'What the hell got into him? That's what Bill wants to know.'

I press the sheet into my mouth, taste blood on my lip. Then he's gone and Mum hasn't told him, and I can breathe again.

I am still awake when she comes to bed. The mattress sighs as she climbs in. I want to tell her that I'm sure Dunc will come home in the morning, wet from searching the swampy reaches of Lake Grey for swan's nests floating in the reeds, and from wading out to the islands where the pelicans make their nests. I want to tell her that he's probably there right now, on his own little island, safe from snakes and other things. But I don't say anything.

On the lagoon, a fence of men nose about like tadpoles in a brown puddle, poking spades and hoes and garden rakes into the water. Some are wearing waders that come up to their chests even though the water is hardly higher than their knees.

Dunc has been gone two days.

Bill Morgan has been all over town, searching, questioning. Mary Campbell had to show him the spot on the jetty where she said she saw Dunc arguing with Sid McCready. Bill Morgan asked Sid if he had a fight with Dunc. Mary says he asked over and over until Sid cried and covered his ears. Bill Morgan borrowed a dinghy and poked about under the jetty where the kelp clings to the pylons with long leathery arms. Later, fathers and fishermen searched all the way to West End but there was nothing to find except skeletons of seals and squid and banjo sharks.

I sit in the kurrajong tree and think about Dunc, and about Chicken's dad and where he might be, and his mum with the Rawleigh's man, and then I remember Mr Smythe, who walked off the end of the jetty and drowned and how sometimes his old dog just sits there and has to be dragged home and tied up. A car passes and I keep very still in case they look up. In case they can read minds and everyone finds out that I told Dunc about Dad and the fire.

Later, Lizzie and I are playing sevens against her wall, when Kenny Sweet and the new boy, who's just moved into the Sneddens' house, jump the fence. 'So what's happening?' says Kenny. 'They found him?'

I hate Kenny's red flaky skin, the yellow glints in his eyes. And why isn't he working in his dad's shop? 'We're talking to you,' he says, grabbing my ball.

'Bill Morgan's started a search,' I say.

'Constable Morgan to you. Bet he's at Bunny Brennan's soak. He's got a cubby there. Uses it for watching blue wings.'

'You should tell someone,' says the new boy. He takes off his glasses and huffs on them.

'Naah,' says Kenny. 'Why spoil it for him?' With a flick of his wrist, he tosses the new boy a cricket ball and they toss and catch, toss and catch, all the way down the road.

I tear home and tell Mum. She runs to the gate and searches the street, flicks a look at Dad's house, the streaky sky. The noise inside her head is mine. *Where is he? It is too long.* Then Aunt Cele pedals up and Mum says: 'I'm beside myself. They've done Lake Grey. Now they're doing the Back Beach again. Salmon Hole… he could be…'

'He'll be back. He's a boy, just being a bugger. I ran away once when I was a kid. I knew coming back meant the strap, so I dragged it out until I was so darn hungry, the strap started to look good.'

When Cele rides off, Mum picks up a Mallee root for the

stove. She tells me to wait at the gate, for Dad, or Bill Morgan, or anyone—someone—to tell about blue wings and the cubby at Bunny's soak. A Peewee magpie calls to its mother from Shorty's pines. For a long time I watch two wood ducks floating on the lagoon, so still and unmoving that they could be fake ducks like shooters use. Then I shout: '*Shooo-oo-oot!*' and they take off along the surface before coming to rest far away from me and my shouting mouth.

When Dad drives up, I tell him before he's even through the gate. 'He might be at Bunny's soak, watching for blue wings.'

'And he might be bloody dead or drowned. You thought of that?' He's inside with Mum for hardly any time before he's striding back. 'If he's there,' he says, climbing into his jeep, revving and reversing, 'you're in line for a bloody good thrashing. Spreading those bloody lies.'

'You're not the only one thinking it,' says Mum when I rush inside and ask why she told him. 'Why shouldn't he know?'

But why did it have to be me if everyone was thinking it? Why didn't everyone say it? Why didn't Bill Morgan? Why didn't she?

Later Mrs Winkie comes with pea soup. It is raining outside and her hair is covered in grey mist. Then Cele comes with Pardie's mum and they're wet too. Mum stands with her back to the stove while we squash around the table. When Dad returns, Bill Morgan has his arm around him as if he's worse for wear. He sits Dad on the spare chair.

'Not good, Nella,' he says. 'Found a bower of branches at Bunny's soak where he might've slept last night. But no sign of his bike. Or him.'

Mum's eyes are eager, excited. 'Well, where'd he go from there? That's what we need to find out.'

'Too wet now, and too dark. We'll have to wait till morning.' Bill Morgan turns to Dad in the chair. 'There's something else…'

Dad lifts his head. 'We found his sock next to the soak.'

Bill Morgan's voice is gentle, careful. 'We'll get some divers down from the Mount. You know what I'm saying, Nella?'

Mum shakes her head. 'He's a good swimmer. You haven't looked properly.' And when no one speaks, she says it again, louder. 'You haven't looked properly!'

'We have to check,' says Bill Morgan.

'No!' she says loudly, making me jump. She looks from Bill Morgan to Dad, to Cele and Jude, to Mrs Winkie, back to me. 'No!'

I am deaf, I cannot hear Mum's scream, the splash of Dunc in Bunny's soak, the sound of leaves falling from the silver wattle tree.

They have taken Mum away. Dad turns from me. 'Get the Old Girl to look after her. I can't stand the sight of her.'

15

At assembly, there is a minute's silence for the tragedy of a past student. Mr Tucker was waiting for me when the school bus pulled in. He told me how sorry everyone was and said Dunc was a very smart boy with a big future and he simply couldn't believe it. *Couldn't believe it!* He said anytime I needed to talk to Mrs Tucker, I could, anytime. I couldn't think of anything to tell her.

In the quiet of the assembly, I look at my feet. They are a blur in the silence of everyone's thoughts. After the minute, Mr Tucker plays a tune on his violin in memory of Dunc. He says it is a song about wings, and the bow scratches the strings in a sad and beautiful way. I keep looking at my feet and thinking of blue wings and birds' nests. I do not believe Dunc has drowned. He has run away. He will come home when he is ready. He is hiding somewhere, waiting to be found.

When it's recess, everyone is playing with the new hula hoops. I am almost at the dunnies when Mr Tucker's corn patch erupts with arms and legs and screaming heads. Boys from Grade Six and Seven form a wall around me. Their eyes glint and their faces wear red blotches of blame.

'Your brother's floating around in a soak,' says Dessie, the boy from the farm near Bindilla. 'He's never gunna be found. Whaddya think about that?' Someone says Old Man Tucker's coming and to get away from his corn patch. 'Never, ever,' says Dessie, nosing up to me.

I sit on the dunny for a long time. Leaves have blown under the door and there is a paint blob on the floor shaped like a frog. I think of the Banjo Frog that Chicken brought to school and the *bonk-bonk* sound of frogs in the lagoon saying *never-bonk-never-bonk-never*. Noise rushes through the dunny wall, the sound of water and gurgling at the trough. Then Mr Tucker's kind teacher voice: *Not much of a place to play, lads. How about the Bombers, Dessie? Think they've got a chance?*

Mum still hasn't come home. It is a new year and Elvis is in the Army. I am in Grade Four and Mrs Tucker is still my teacher.

Miss Taylor is engaged to Joe Marciano. His grandfather was an Itie who jumped ship in Burley Point and became a fisherman. Joe looks like Tony Curtis, almost as handsome, and he has started a co-op so the fishermen will make more money. He is not really a New Australian because his family has been here a long time.

Miss Taylor is wearing a diamond ring on her engagement finger, which is on the left hand. Her ring is called a cluster. When she's on yard duty, she lets us look at it and I think how good it would be if I could be her bridesmaid, or maybe a flower girl.

After school, I ask Grannie when Dunc is going to be found. She thumps at the pastry on the table then takes a hankie from her cuff and blows her nose hard. 'I suppose there's no law against hoping. But we have to accept that he's died, even if he hasn't been found. I know it's hard but that's just a fact of life. We've got to accept it.' She upturns a plate on the dough and cuts around its shape. 'And don't go anywhere near our dam,' she says, 'or I'll have your guts for garters. Understand?'

'When can I go home?'

'That's a good question.' Her shoulders lift and sink. She says I can have a scrap of dough if I'm hungry. She says life doesn't stop for anyone and I can change into my old clothes and go and play. 'Your father's coming for tea,' she says as I turn to leave. 'Ticker's going out.' I hover nearby, picking at the dough. 'Well,' she says impatiently, 'what're you going to do with yourself?' And when I say I don't know, she says: 'Well, what would you do if you were at home?'

'Play with Lizzie. Or the Daley kids.'

'Play with Blue. If Ticker hasn't taken him, you can let him off the chain. Watch your feet and don't go in the long grass in case of snakes. You can feed the fish, but don't give them too much.'

Blue has gone. His chain lies under the pines like a silver snake. On the lawn, the sprinkler hisses round like a buzzy wasp. The Phantom Julie Walker runs under the waterfall without getting wet, finds the fish food beneath the flat rock and sprinkles two pinches. She sees a fish floating, but cannot rescue it because the pond is a jungle waterhole filled with hungry crocs, nosing close to the surface, snapping their terrible jaws.

The Phantom lies on a branch, high in the old mulberry tree, and looks up at blue chinks of sky between branches and leaves. She listens to the screech of monkeys, the whispers of pygmy people. She thinks of her brother lost in the jungle. This country is riddled with sinkholes and soaks: could he be in a secret cave far beneath the surface, living on fish and rats and birds? Could he be living in the Abo cave in the bush above Uncle Ticker's new cutting? With help from the pygmy people, she will find him.

Suddenly the jungle is filled with the throb of drums. Tiny drums, giant drums, coming from all directions. A message travels over hills and valleys, over the great swamp, into the Deep Woods. *Sylvie—your—bath—is—ready.* Boom. Boom. *Sylvie—your—bath—is—ready.*

I sit at the end away from the chip heater and the stain where the tap drips. What if Grannie thinks I killed that fish because I gave it too much food? She shampoos my hair, scratching at my scalp with hard fingers. Those fingers could stab a charging rhinoceros between the eyes and bring it crashing to the ground without a single blow.

'There was a dead fish in the pond,' I tell her.

She pours water over my head and doesn't answer so I have to tell her again. 'There was a dead fish in the pond.'

'It must have been one of the old ones.'

'It wasn't my fault.'

'Fish die. It's no one's fault.' When I step out of the bath, she dries my hair and points to my pyjamas on the floor. 'Dress yourself. Then you can look at my stamp album until your father gets here.' She bundles up my dirty clothes. 'Stamp-collecting would be a good hobby for you. If you could get interested.'

Dad cuts a potato in two and moves it around his plate with his fork. He looks at the froth on the top of his beer glass and reads the green label on the bottle. He looks at Grannie but he doesn't look at me.

With my ears turned into eyes, I listen to the smell of him. It is cold and beery; it is a southerly wind off the sea before a storm.

'That Pardie Moon knows more than he's letting on.'

Grannie looks over her glasses. Her nose is a pincushion of pores. 'Pardie Moon?'

'Yes, Pardie bloody Moon.'

'About what?'

Under the table, Dad's foot knocks mine. Does he know that is the touch of me? 'About Dunc. They were thick as thieves.'

'Have you asked him?'

'Course I've bloody asked him. He scuttles off like a rabbit. Moping around with a long face. Wagging school. I told Augie he needs a good hiding.'

'Missing Dunc. Like all of us.'

In the silence, I slice my potato and spear it with my fork. I can hear the sound of chewing and swallowing in my ears.

'So how's the sharking season?'

'Swell up like a puffer fish if I'm stupid enough to nick the sperm bag and get a squirt.'

'You'd be better off on the land.'

'I won't work alongside him, so you can stop right there.'

'Work never killed anyone. It's the best way to get through.'

'What would you know?'

'I've buried a husband and two children, that's what I know.'

'Babies aren't the same as thirteen-year-old boys.'

Grannie looks at me as if I should close my ears. 'Brendan wasn't a baby.'

'He wasn't thirteen, days off fourteen.'

There is a howl in his voice that I don't think Grannie can hear. 'We still have to keep on living.' She looks at me again. There is a whistling sound outside. It could be an owl. 'That's the choice we make. All of us. Every day. Hold on or let go.'

'What kind of choice is that?' Dad's chair scrapes back with a clatter. 'And who chooses?' He grabs his hat from the dresser. 'Who decides?' His face has crumpled into long folds and he looks at Grannie and me as if we are worse than worms, as if I am to blame. 'Layle says thanks for the invite.'

'I'm not having that woman here.'

'We got married. Get used to it.'

The door slams. The calendar with the picture of a Massey Ferguson tractor falls to the floor. 'Stay off the sauce!' yells Grannie. 'It won't help anything. Never has and never will.'

Grannie returns the calendar to its hook behind the door. Blue barks from his kennel under the pines. The kelpies, in their cage behind the old stables, bark at Blue. Dad roars into the echo of the night. He roars over the cattle ramp and onto the main road. In my listening eyes, his headlights sweep past boobiallas and she-oaks speckled with sleeping birds. He roars past Bunny Brennan's soak without once turning to look, past the Tantanoola turn-off and Big Tree turn-off and the waiting sea behind the dunes. He slows at Stickynet and weaves through quiet streets to his house, where Layle and Mossie wait for him. And there is nothing for me.

'He was the most beautiful baby,' says Grannie, watching me eat my apple pie, not eating hers. She takes off her glasses and rubs at her eyes. 'And good. Always so good. Never stepped a foot out of line.'

Grannie tells Uncle Ticker it's a bit rich inviting all and sundry to watch water dribbling through a drain when her grandson's been missing, presumed drowned, for no decent time. Couldn't he wait a few months? Uncle Ticker says the swamp's full to the brim with the best autumn rains they've had for years and he's had it planned long before anyone disappeared, so no, he couldn't.

Josie arrives early in her red coat. At the cutting, the Muswell Mayor and a whole bunch of others—even a photographer from the *Muswell Times*—are all rugged up against the cold. Chicken's uncle has the grader ready next to a mound of earth, the swamp water banked up behind. The Mayor makes a speech, a history lesson about the land in the early days being drained by men from the city, and this is a day for progress and prosperity for everyone.

I stop listening and look down the long channel. Now it slices right through the range with high walls and a fringe of green on top of the ridge. For a second I think there's someone leaning over the lookout fence and for no reason I think it might be my father but it's probably not because when I squint up my eyes like binoculars, it's too far away to see. Then I feel a shock right through me like being hit by lightning, if you were still alive to know it. What if I really did see someone? What if it was Dunc and he really is living in the Abo cave in the scrub behind the lookout? I need to go there. But how would I find it? Grannie and Uncle Ticker wouldn't take me; they'd think I was crazy.

Pardie! And then another thought: What if Pardie knows Dunc is hiding there? What if he's always wagging school so he can sneak out to the cave with food for Dunc? An icy wind shivers across the swamp and I think of winter coming, how cold it will be living in a cave, and suddenly I'm muddled about whether I want Dunc to be living there or not. But where else could he be?

The Mayor has finished his speech and everyone is clapping, clapping. Uncle Ticker helps Grannie onto the grader and climbs on himself. The tractor smokes and roars and reverses. The last mound of earth is pushed free and water dribbles through the opening, a trickle then a rush. As people crowd forward, someone says it'll be a hoot if Ticker's got his levels wrong and the lake drains backwards into the swamp. It doesn't. The Mayor helps Grannie down from the tractor and water rushes towards the lake in a long dirty stream. Everyone is clapping and cheering. Suddenly I ache with the cold of everything. There is no one on the ridge: I must have imagined it.

Mum comes home soon after my birthday. She doesn't bring a present. Her hair is short again and scrappy around the ears. Every morning I wake up with a jolt like I've heard someone closing a door. Like it could be Dunc? Mum is always awake, listening. Every morning, I remember Dunc has gone. Is she remembering too?

Lizzie and I find the best bed base at the tip and drag it home, springs jingling like sleigh bells must jingle in the snow. Mum is at the wood pile. Her head jerks up. 'What's that?'

'A bed,' I say, resting my end on the ground. 'For our cubby.'

'I thought it was traps.'

Behind me, Lizzie sniggers. *Rabbit traps*, I want to tell her. *She thought it was Dunc's traps rattling. What's so funny about that?* But my mouth is full up with rabbit fur and I don't say anything. Yanking my end of the bed, I force Lizzie to follow me. As we cross the road towards the lagoon, Aunt Cele shoots around the corner.

'Nella!' she calls, braking to a stop, panting for breath. 'I could smell your marmalade. As far back as Nobby Carter's. I'll do you a swap. Some of my muntrie jam. For a jar of your marmalade.' She laughs as if it's not much of a swap. 'Good bed!' she calls to Lizzie and me and, from her bike basket, she holds up a timber lamp. 'Only needs a shade,' she tells Mum. 'Jude'll fix it. She can fix anything.'

'How's Pardie?' asks Mum.

I have not seen Pardie since I've been home from Bindilla. One day after school, I went to his house but no one was there, not Augie or Jude, not Pardie or his dog, Rastas. He is a mystery.

'All over the place. Won't get a job. Worries Jude to death. Understandable, I guess...' Her voice trails off and Mum brings the axe down hard on a log. 'I think of you all the time, Nella.' She lowers her voice, but I can still hear. 'And Sylvie. How is she?'

Mum doesn't drop her voice at all. 'Nine going on ninety. Always got her head in a book.'

I pull Lizzie into the tea-tree. The lagoon is full to the brim and soggy beneath the weed. In our cubby, we lie on the bed and sing 'A Pub With No Beer', every verse. I like the way singing fills you up inside and you can't feel anything except your bursting heart. Before going home, we tie cotton thread across the branches so we'll know if Chicken's been nosing around.

Back on the road, Lizzie says, in a hurry, as if she's been saving it up: 'Your brother's dead. He's not floating around. He's drowned. Everyone says.'

'I know.'

She stares at me with surprise and no pity. And I stare at her with my emptiness growing into an ache and I can't wait for her to take her face away from me. When she leaves, my ache is without mercy. I will not believe what she says, what anyone says.

In the kitchen, Mum is bottling her marmalade. My face in the glass jars is pop-eyed, fish-mouthed. I breathe in the smell of oranges and sugar and spice and everything nice. When Mum has finished, the jars are filled to the brim, shining and golden like a piece of the sun dropped onto the table. She says the biggest jar is for Cele. She says Dunc liked her marmalade better than anyone.

It is the first time she has spoken his name since she's come home with her short hair and slow way of talking. I don't really know what to say. Except I like her marmalade too.

When she's watering the garden, I go to the spare room and look for Dunc's things. The room is cold and empty of him. Then my eyes settle on the tea chest in the corner. Inside I find his school clothes folded neatly, further down his boots and shoes, then two small cardboard boxes full of cotton wool and eggs. And more. Two *Phantom* comics I've never seen. His pencil case. An old tobacco tin with *Imperial Ruby* and a picture of a Union Jack stamped on the lid. Inside: his pocket knife and three cat's-eye marbles.

His skull ring! I slide it onto my middle finger and press the metal bits behind until it fits. I'll have to keep it well hidden. It's not really stealing. He gave it to me, I'll say if I'm asked.

I burrow through the comics. I'm on the floor with an old

Phantom when she looks in. 'What do you think you're doing?'

'Reading.'

'No'—she snatches the comic out of my hand—'you're not! Who said you could just come in here and do what you like?'

Kneeling on the floor, she bundles it all up, comics, shoes, clothes, all of him. She folds his shirts, neatly, grey short pants, the blue sweater Grannie knitted with the big white 'D' on the front. As she stands, the comics slide out of her grasp. Her mouth trembles. 'Now look what you've done!'

She smells of marmalade and garden dirt. My chest hurts. It is too heavy to hold. Can't she see the weight of it? When everything's packed away, her red eyes stare into mine. 'I don't want you in here. I want everything left as it was. Understand?'

Behind my back, I rub Dunc's ring: it is silvery cold and full of Phantom power.

16

Mum stands with her back to the stove, shivering, her pale pink dressing-gown hanging open like a loose skin. She asks me if I know what day it is. September the fifteenth?

My toast has no taste. I haven't remembered. Mum is frantic and fidgety like she's got ants in her pants. Like her eyes want to bore right through me and blame me for it being a year since Dunc disappeared, for making him run away. She says how can we remember properly if there's no grave, no resting place? It's the not knowing, she says, not knowing where he is that makes it so hard.

My heart flutters with hope. 'You mean…he might be hiding somewhere?'

'Hiding?' She frowns for so long that I think her brain might be working too slowly, like it has since she's been home from the hospital. Then her face clears and she snaps at me as if I'm crazy and she's only just realised. 'Why would he be hiding? If he was alive, he'd come home. How could he be hiding?'

Because he's run away and might not want to come home. Because he's still upset with me. Because he might like living wild like an Abo. And because he might have gone far away and will only come back when he's ready, and he's not ready yet. I want to shout all of this at her, loud-mouthed and strong, so that she will stop believing

Dunc has drowned. Can't she see? I want to hurl the words at her head like she used to hurl saucepans at Dad. But I am scared of shouting and throwing, and her face is all furrows again, so I hide in my toast and she shuffles off to the dunny. Then I get dressed and hang around reading in the kurrajong tree while Mum hides inside, cleaning, cleaning.

Pardie must know something. After weeks and months of him avoiding me, I was riding my bike along back beach road when I turned a corner and he was there, Rastas running beside him, no escape. I told him I needed him to take me to the Abo cave in case Dunc was hiding there—it all came out in a babble. Pardie kept walking, not even looking at me, but I pedalled beside him, faster, faster, asking if he was taking food to Dunc, if he was keeping the secret? Without warning, Pardie leapt off the road and ran into the tea-tree, whistling Rastas after him. Why would he do that if he didn't know where Dunc was hiding? If he didn't know something? For days I thought about telling Mum; now I'm glad I didn't. She has given up hoping. But I haven't.

In the afternoon of Dunc's anniversary, Mum sends me to the cafe for cigarettes. On the way home, I'm passing the pub when Dad stumbles out. 'Lilies,' he says, steadying himself against the door before easing onto the veranda. 'Always bloody lilies on the gate. How many times do you reckon?'

He stinks. Of beer and smoke and rain. Of mutton-birds thudding into their burrows full up with fish from far out at sea.

'Lilies on the gate,' he says again.

I remember Grannie telling me they tie lilies on the gate at Bindilla whenever anyone dies. Did they do it when Dunc disappeared? Is that what Dad means?

He peers into my face with his mutton-bird breath and dark sunken eyes, puzzled, trying to focus. My chest thumps at his closeness, but I can tell he hasn't the foggiest idea who I am. In my hurry to get away, the front wheel of my bike knocks the seat on the veranda, lifting it out from the wall. He looks at that seat, confused, as if it moved by itself, as if there's no sense to things moving. Close up, his eyes are pirate patches; they are Mum's eyes and my eyes too, all of them filled with the awfulness of remembering.

He is nothing to me. I tell myself this as I push my bike up the hill. *It is his fault, all of it.* I tell myself this again and again. I come down the other side at a run, trying to hold back, wrestling my bike to a stop at the bottom. My eyes have started to leak. Dunc always fixed punctures for me, the tube in the bucket, bubbles marking the hole, glueing the patch. Should I ask Chicken or Roy to help? Can I do it myself?

I'm ready to cross the road when Dad's jeep crawls past, stopping up ahead where anyone coming around the corner could crash right into him. Then he just sits there. As if he's waiting for someone. Could that someone be me?

I cross the road quickly. At the same time, he lurches out of the jeep and stumbles around in circles as if he's lost something right there in the gravel and dirt. The sun is setting, the light as bright as a searchlight; his hat is tipped back, his face, pants, shirt, boots, all of him lit up like a beacon. Then he drops down as if he's kneeling to pray—but he wouldn't, would he?—not with his feeling for apes?

As he leans forward, his hat topples off; his forehead sinks onto the dirt. I want to run off and pretend I don't know him. I want to leave him there to grovel in his own shadow. But tiny groans come from the road. Squeaks. Moans. Like a kicked dog might make as he crawls away from a boot.

I look down at the mound of him. I don't know what to do. Faye Daley could come out of her house any minute and see him. A car could come, he could be run over, anyone could come. And right then, Layle does come. Striding around the corner, swinging her shopping basket. The first time I've ever been glad to see her. 'Mick!' she yells. 'What the hell are ya doing?' Then she's running. 'Come on, get up, I'll drive you home. Get up.'

Hands under his arms, she tries to help him up. 'No-o-o-o-o!' he bellows. It is the wail made by calves at cattle sales when they're taken from their mothers. The wail of someone fallen deep down in a well. But somehow Layle lifts him out of the well, jams his hat on his head and moves him to the jeep while he's gabbing at her. 'I looked away for a minute…just a minute…and when I looked back he'd just disappeared…there one minute and gone the next, how can you explain that? I couldn't find him…I tried…I tell you I tried—'

'Shhhh,' says Layle, as if she's talking to a baby. 'It's not your fault, you know that, and it's a long time ago. Come on, get in.'

And somehow he's in the jeep and she's brushing dirt off his face, slamming the door, grabbing her basket from the road and climbing in the driver's side. Another glance at me. 'It's okay, Sylvie, you can go home now.'

Then they've gone, and the sun has gone, and the road shines white in the fading light. But it's not okay. How could he have looked away for a minute, and then looked back? Dunc was gone three days before they found his sock at the soak. And it hasn't been a long time ago since he disappeared. It's only been one year. So what was Dad talking about? How could he have been there?

Then Pardie goes too. Mrs Winkie tells Mum he'll turn into a juvenile delinquent in the city—if he's not one already—what with his loafing around and not getting a job and wearing bodgie clothes. She says those bodgies and widgies should be sent off to the Nullarbor on a rail gang; that'd soon put a stop to their rocking and rolling. She bites on her Anzac biscuit and crumbs fall onto her chin. Given half a chance, she says she'd be out there marching with the Ban the Bombers because what happened in Hiroshima was just plain wrong. And as for that Khrushchev and his Sputniks; if the Yanks are stupid enough to make it a race, good luck to them. She's never had much time for Yanks, not since the war, when she saw those soldiers on R and R in the city, turning heads with their fancy talk then leaving our girls in the family way to fend for themselves; don't get her started.

Mum sips her tea and sucks on her ciggie, both at the same time. She looks dizzy-eyed, as if Sputniks are spinning close to her ears and she can't think properly.

I think about Pardie at the school fete, just before he left town. Mum didn't come to the fete even though I won first prize for Grade Five flower arranging. Colleen said it was favouritism because Mrs Denver Boland was the judge and my sweet peas came from her garden. So what? They had to come from some-where. She didn't know Mrs Denver taught me to arrange them on her sunroom table and that the spiky thing in the bottom of the vase belonged to her too.

In the shelter shed, Roy had set up his gramophone and when Lizzie and I arrived, Pardie was dancing with Lizzie's sister, Mary, rocking and swinging and whirly-gigging, better than anyone. Mr Allen was back because Mrs Tucker was sick again, but I'm in Mr Tucker's class so I didn't care. Mr Allen was watching and clapping along with everyone else to 'Party Doll', and Lizzie and I tried to jive along too but we couldn't get the steps right and just ended up giggling and doing Elvis wiggles. Then I saw Pardie watching us and there was something about those eyes picking me out like a spotlight that made me stop dancing.

Next thing, Mr Allen's gone back to the city and Pardie's left town without Rastas, or his *Loving You* LP. Only a pile of comics on our back step. Not even a goodbye.

I hide in the kurrajong tree. Bridie Maguire stumbles past, tripping all over the road from too many shandies in the pub. I drop itchy pods onto her head but she has the luck of drunks and lurches away from every one of them. I hide from Lizzie, who walks arm in arm with Faye Daley under my tree, their long-legged shadows leading them down the road. I hide from Mum at the back door, her strangled scream. 'Sylvie! Where are you?' Another scream. 'Sylvie!'

On my leg I have a school sore with a thick brown scab. I pick at the scab and loosen it; I pick around the edge and let the blood ooze out. Smoke from the stove curls through the tree. It smells of black crows and turnip weed. Mum runs at the clothesline, pulls off sheets and tucks them under her chin, folds them in four and then four more. Blood trickles down my shin and drips onto the bark.

Mrs Winkie persuades Mum to go to the Institute on Sunday to hear Billy Graham.

'Billy who?'

'The evangelist. It'll do you good.'

We put on our best dresses. Mum wears gloves, stockings, high heels and a little pink hat, the whole bit. Her hair has grown back and she's had a fluffy perm: she looks like a pink carnation on long-stemmed sandal shoes. Mrs Winkie has saved us seats. On the back of her head she wears a feathered hat that looks like a green lorikeet.

It is standing room only with everyone squashed onto the blue chairs where yesterday Lizzie and I saw *Pillow Talk* and *Ma and Pa Kettle*. The Daleys are there, but no Uncle Ticker or Grannie: Catholics are not meant to come but I'm half-Methodist because of Mum. Next to me is Mrs Bullfrog Fraser, but no Bullfrog. Chicken and Roy are in the front row with Sid and Grandma McCready. When Lizzie gives Chicken a wave, her mother slaps her hand down and says it's the same as being in church and keep that in mind.

On the stage, a huge poster of Billy Graham hangs over the screen. He is not like old Father Brennan or the Methodist minister. He has lovely golden-brown curly hair, sparkling blue eyes, perfect white teeth, a real movie star smile. Mrs Bullfrog shifts and sighs but we don't have long to wait: soon a minister from the Mount leads us in the Lord's Prayer, then Billy's voice comes preaching out of the speakers.

'And this great crowd here today is due to the spiritual hunger of thousands of people in this age of despair and discouragement. Nations are arming themselves to the teeth with hydrogen bombs, shaking their fists at each other, and it seems the world is about to come to an end...'

It's the first American voice I've heard, except in the movies and singers like Elvis and Jerry Lee. But Billy Graham's voice is different, strong and syrupy like honey bees feeding off wattles on a spring day. There's not even a cough or shuffle.

'Many of you have come here with spiritual hunger and thirst. Many are here with burdens that cannot be lifted, problems that seemingly are too great to master. And you're searching for an answer.'

It feels as if he's speaking just to me. Maybe it's the same for Mrs Bullfrog because when I sneak a look, her mouth's hanging open as if she's died and gone to Heaven. Mum has shiny eyes as if she's trying not to cry. Even Lizzie is staring at Billy's poster in the same way that she drools over her *Love Me Tender* poster of Elvis on her bedroom wall.

'I tell you there's going to be a resurrection and all of those loved ones of yours who have died in the past in Christ, they're going to be raised. And there's going to be a glorious and grand reunion that day.'

There are tears trickling down Mum's cheeks. Is she wondering if Dunc is going to be raised? And if he died in Christ, and what if he didn't? What if he believed in apes like Dad? I will not worry about this because I know that he is alive and one day he will be found. The music wells up and Billy Graham's voice is reaching out and filling me with something big and fluttering.

180

'Now Christ doesn't promise to take your troubles away…but he promises a new dimension to your life, new strength, a new power…if you are willing to receive him.'

A ripple seems to run right through the Institute and Billy Graham says: 'By this open acknowledgment today, you're saying I receive Christ openly in front of everyone as my saviour and my Lord. You get up and come quickly from everywhere.'

Beside me, Mum stands and I do too, without even thinking. But Mrs Winkie hisses at Mum: 'You don't have to go, Nella, not if you already believe.' And Mum sits down again. But Lizzie is pushing along the row and I'm following. I look around and see everyone's shuffling up to the front and I've got Mrs Bullfrog pushing behind me, so I squeeze past Mum and Mrs Winkie and join everyone else in the aisle with Billy saying: 'Hundreds are coming from everywhere. There's plenty of time, just take your time. What a glorious moment this is.' As I shuffle forward, it seems as if I'm drawn along on strings until I reach the stage and the minister from the Mount blesses me. I feel it's a magic moment, a great wave, and I know that Dunc will be found, I just know. I float back to my seat with everyone smiling and some people crying, some standing right there and cuddling each other and, although Lizzie and I don't do any of that, I feel everything will be fine from now on because God is on my side: Dunc will come home, Mum will go out more and be the same as other mothers, I will stop picking my shin.

'It's a private thing,' says Mum on the way home. 'You can believe without making a spectacle of yourself.'

*

'I'm almost ten, I don't need you to wash me.'

She bends over the bath until her nose is almost touching my leg. 'It was getting better. What've you done to it?'

She yanks my ankle out of the water and plants it on the edge of the bath. 'Don't,' I say, trying to yank it back.

'Have you been touching this?'

I pat it with the flannel. 'I'm touching it now.'

'Get out.' Her voice has that poker sound that warns me not to press her. She tells me it's probably infected and asks if I'm pleased with myself. She says how do I think she's going to get time off work to take me to a doctor?

In bed, my fingers pick at the plaster strip that she's stuck on the wound. That's what she calls it. *The Wound*. As if I'm a soldier, as if I'm at war. I think of Mr Patchett kicking Chicken's old dog off his shop veranda: how he did this after he stood next to me at Billy Graham and was blessed. I think of being a saviour in Christ and the glorious and grand reunion day. So why hasn't Dunc been found? And when is it going to happen?

And why don't I feel special anymore? Why do I feel as if I've drifted away from myself and can't feel anything? I rub and rub on my skull ring; I rub until it is hot on my finger. Then I give up and lift the plaster from my shin. I pick all around the edge. I feel the rip of skin.

On the train Mum tries not to look at me because I'm the reason she'll miss a day's pay and money doesn't grow on trees. My wound is definitely infected, that's what she says. All the ointment in the world won't fix it. And what's wrong with me?

At Muswell, she pulls me along Main Street and into the doctor's surgery where we flick through magazines. When it's our turn, instead of old Dr Jeffries there's a new doctor with a wispy moustache; he's perched on the corner of his desk as if he knows Mum already.

'How are you, Nella?'

'Getting there,' says Mum, smiling at him. The name on his door is Dr Richard Sorenson. And her smile is the same shy, flirty smile that Roy sometimes gives me. Then I notice her new Sunray pleated skirt, her best twin-set, her strand of Mikimotos. 'It's about Sylvie's leg,' she begins and, before I can even open my mouth, she tells him it started out as a school sore, that I fell out of a tree and grazed it some more and the scab came off and it just won't heal. The whole time she's telling him this, her eyes are warning me not to speak.

Dr Sorenson tells me to climb up on the bed. He has short clipped nails and smells of soap and mints. Before I have time to wince, he rips off the plaster. 'Goodness,' he says, 'how did it get like this?'

For a moment, I wonder myself. It looks like someone else's leg. Again Mum goes on about what she's done to dress it. She doesn't mention I've had it on and off for almost two years, or that she's tried tying mittens on me at night but I still get them off.

'Odd shape,' he says as he swabs it. Then he tells Mum to come and watch because she'll have to dress it herself every second day.

Mum looks as if she likes standing next to him. I can hear him breathing through his moustache, her breathing too, as soft as when she's sleeping next to me. I cough loudly and he tells me to sit still.

'I want it left alone,' says Dr Sorenson when he's finished, looking straight at me. 'Understand?'

'What about school?' I say in a fluster.

'Hop down,' he says. I limp across the carpet. 'If you can walk, you can go to school,' he says, smirking at Mum.

Mum nods and crosses her knees like the women in the waiting-room magazines. And sure enough, when he hands her the prescription, she gives him another flirty smile. As soon as we're on the footpath, she lights up a ciggie and stands there sucking for her life. At first I think she's trying to decide how to fill in time until the train arrives. Then I see her staring at a car parked in the gutter, a spiffy red MG Sports with silver-spoke wheels and a black canvas hood.

It's his! I know it is. Straightaway, I see him driving around town with the hood down, flashing around corners and speeding along Muswell Road. Mum's sitting next to him, laughing her head off, her perm a mass of wild curls blowing about in the breeze. Worse, I'm standing alone on the footpath, not knowing what to do.

'Whose car is that?' I ask.

'How would I know?' She stubs out her ciggie with the toe of her high pink sandal. 'And why are you wearing that ring all the time? Don't think I haven't seen.'

PART THREE

17

After a while I forget things. The colour of Dunc's hair, his eyebrows and ears: unless I look at a photo, I can't remember him having any ears at all. Mum forgets worse than I do. She says she's got huge blanks because of what they did to her in the hospital; you can forget a lot with electricity but some things you never forget. She says no one knows what it's like to have a lost child, it's supposed to get easier but it doesn't, and she never stops thinking.

After Dunc's second anniversary, and then his third, I try to believe what everyone else believes: that he fell into Bunny's soak; that he floated into underground rivers and caves, which is why he couldn't be found by the divers. So what happened to his bike, I wonder? Did that fall in the soak with him? Not very likely. So I always come back to believing he's alive somewhere, he has to be. And one day he'll come home. When he's ready. When he's forgiven me. And Dad. Who I will never forgive.

There's a hard little lump inside my chest, in the cave of my heart where I keep all this hidden. When Dunc was here he used to tell me about the black men who once lived in caves all around Burley Point, the Coorong, all through the Bindilla Range. He said they lived under rocky overhangs and in wurlies made from bark and branches. There are scratchy old photos in a book at Bindilla of men with spears and women in wurlies. Uncle Ticker said these photos are Old Pat's guilty secret because he and the other early settlers killed off the Boandik people with flu and smallpox and sometimes poisoned flour.

In Grade Six, I know every English king and queen from William the Conqueror to our Elizabeth, but I don't know anything about the Boandik. There are no books about them in the school library, none in the Lending Library that comes once a month; there are only Uncle Ticker's whispered words and Old Pat's guilty secret. I wonder if Dunc is my guilty secret and if there is the same kind of whispering around town. *Where is he hiding hiding crying crying dying dying?*

There is a grave in the tea-tree outside the cemetery fence where Long Tom Dobbin, the last of the Boandik people, is buried. Dunc said he was a tracker who helped the police find lost children, runaways, escaped prisoners. He could read a footprint in the sand as if he was reading a story book. A bent blade of grass or a broken twig could tell him if a person was injured or limping, if they were carrying something, if they were thirsty or had recently eaten. If Long Tom Dobbin had been alive when Dunc disappeared, he'd have found him easily.

Long Tom Dobbin was buried outside the cemetery fence because he was an Aborigine. Uncle Ticker is fighting the Council to have his body moved and rightfully recognised.

'At least he has a resting place,' says Mum, which is her way of saying Uncle Ticker would be better off fighting to find Dunc than trying to bury a black man with white people. And if she had the money, she'd have a plaque erected for Dunc on the side of the road near Bunny's soak. Why hasn't anyone thought of that? she says. Why hasn't his father?

Mum now works five days a week at the cafe, sometimes on the weekends. She says it helps to keep busy. Sometimes I start awake at night thinking Dunc has come home for the school holidays. Could it be a premonition? I crawl to the edge of the bed, far away from Mum's hungry hands. I pick at my shin.

America has a handsome new president, a Roman Catholic. He has a beautiful wife with strange, wide-spaced eyes who wears little box hats on the back of her head. Miss Taylor wore a beaded box hat to hold down her veil when she married Joe Marciano. She wore a white lacy dress with satin buttons halfway down her back and Joe Marciano's sister from the city was the bridesmaid in blue; there was no flower girl.

Lizzie and I watched Miss Taylor arrive at the church with her father and walk out with Joe. They both looked so happy and smiling that tears prickled behind my eyes. Lizzie said weddings always make you cry; she's been to five, she should know.

I still can't think of Miss Taylor as Mrs Marciano. I can't think why women have to change their names when they marry. Or why they stop working and stay at home, like Mrs Marciano does, cleaning her new green and white house on the corner of Main and Macklin streets, and making a new garden. When I ride past on my bike, she looks up and waves. She has one of those new transistor radios with her in the garden, tuned to ABC voices talking, talking, sometimes someone singing. Mrs Joe Marciano looks like a prisoner behind her green picket fence. It is not how she should be.

*

It is 1962 and I have started high school. Dunc has been gone four years; in September it will be five. Pardie has not returned to Burley Point, not even for a visit. Pardie's mum has left Augie and moved in with Cele. Mum says don't let me catch you anywhere near those two or I'll have something to say. Elvis has a girlfriend called Priscilla who is only three years older than me. Colleen Mulligan has gone to boarding school in the city; I catch the bus to Muswell High, and now I get my monthlies, which I could do without. Faye Daley gets whatever she wants, squash heels, denim jeans, a Malvern Star bike, and, as soon as a transmitter tower is built in the Mount, she'll be getting a television too.

Mrs Marciano has had a baby girl. A baby girl without arms.

I avoid walking past her house: I cannot bear the thought of her baby. But one day after school, as I come out of the cafe, she is right there, pushing a blue pram. 'Hullo, Sylvie!' she calls, as if nothing's happened, as if everything's normal. 'How are you enjoying high school?'

There is no way of hiding, so I walk beside her, keeping my voice chirpy, telling her that I like Latin best, that Maths is good with Mr Kerford, that next week in Science we're dissecting frogs and I'll probably faint or throw up on the floor. I don't tell her how terrific it is not having Colleen Mulligan sneering at me. Or that every morning when the bus leaves Burley Point, I become a different sort of me. I don't tell her that I love my school uniform and the long socks that mostly hide my shin. I don't tell her any of this because the whole time I'm thinking: I will not look in that pram.

But as we cross the street near the post office, the pram wheels get stuck on the kerb, which means we have to stop while I help

Mrs Marciano lift it onto the path. And I get the quickest glimpse of a baby with a fuzz of black hair and a pink bunny blanket pulled up to her chin. I will not look again.

Next we're on the veranda of Reggie Patchett's grocery shop. 'Would you mind waiting with her? While I duck in here?'

I can see silver threads in Mrs Marciano's shiny brown hair. I can see Reggie's double swing doors are easily wide enough for a pram.

'Like this,' she says, jiggling the pram gently. 'I won't be a second.'

That baby must have ESP. The doors are still swinging when she wakes up with a yawn and a snuffle, tosses her head from side to side and kicks at the blanket. I jiggle the pram. She gurgles and looks up at me. I push the pram backwards and forwards, backwards and forwards, hoping she'll go back to sleep. But she smiles a big, gummy grin as if I'm the funniest thing she's ever seen. Then she does it again. And that little gurgling smile makes me smile too, which is why I stop pushing. I bend over the pram and see how pretty she is, with her mother's creamy skin and her father's black hair and happy black eyes.

'She's beautiful, isn't she?' says Mrs Marciano at my elbow.

'She woke up,' I say, springing back.

'She likes you,' says Mrs Marciano, smiling into the pram, her mouth exactly the same shape as that little mouth that was gurgling at me. 'She's such a good baby, such a happy little thing.'

Happy? How could she be happy?

'I've got to go,' I say, giving a quick wave, almost running away.

'Good luck with the frog,' she calls after me. 'Let me know how it goes. Tania would love to see you again.'

Tania? And then I remember Mum saying they called her Tania, probably after Tania Verstak, the first New Australian to win Miss Australia, and who might win Miss International. *Tania, Tania,* I say to myself all the way home. *How could she be happy?* Again and again I swallow the taste of tears but it's not until I rush through the gate and climb the kurrajong tree that I give in, and I cry and cry for that little girl with no arms, wrapped in her pink bunny blanket.

Friday after school, Mum is home early. 'Take this to the Old Girl,' she says, licking the envelope closed. 'I need to keep in with her.'

At least it's a birthday card, not another note asking for money. I will not be that kind of messenger again. Grannie's down-turned mouth. Muttering about Mum and maintenance payments and why can't she manage. Shoving a fat envelope into my hands. As if it was my fault. As if I was contaminated by Mum's asking.

Riding past the fish factory, I hear the survey plane droning overhead and then following me down Main Street like a silver buzzard spying on the carcass of the land. I like the word *carcass*. *'Let's carve him as a dish fit for the gods / Not hew him as a carcass fit for hounds.'* I've learned this by heart for my English test. Here there are sheep carcasses rotting in paddocks because last year's drought has lengthened into winter and there still haven't been good rains.

It's only a matter of time before oil is found under the carcass of our land, that's what everyone says. If it's been found in Bass Strait, why not here? Already geologists are snooping around Bog

Creek Road and Baldy's Flat, measuring whatever they measure to find where the oil might be hiding underground. Already there's a truck set up on Uncle Ticker's land, thumping away day and night, sending shock waves so far out that when Shorty pulls his pots near Ten Mile Rocks, he says the sea surface shivers like snakes under a rug.

After Uncle Ticker married Josie, Grannie moved into town. She said there could only be one hen in charge of the hen house and she'd better get out before feathers started flying. Her new house is on the foreshore with big picture windows to take in the view. Mum says she's welcome to it, and wait until the southerly busters hit, she'll have so much salt on her windows that she won't have a view. Or a garden. Because nothing grows that close to the sea.

Grannie has more birthday cards than last year. She arranges ours at the back of the sideboard, behind the open-mouthed fish vase with a bunch of red roses stuck down its throat. Hiding amongst her cards are photographs in silver frames.

'How's school?' she asks as she scuttles off to the kitchen to make me a cordial. 'Still top of your class?'

While she's gone, I look at her photos. Wedding portraits, others of my cousins in the city, the ones who go to posh schools, who I hardly ever see anymore. Since the divorce. Since I became contaminated. There's a photo of Uncle Ticker and Josie's wedding in the Mount with bridesmaids and flower girls in lemony green. Mum and I weren't invited. Because of Dad's bad blood. Or the divorce.

Where is my school photo? The one I gave her last year? There's a new photo at the front of Uncle Ticker's twins, Jamie and John, wearing blue bonnets and white buckle-up shoes. No photos of Dunc. None of me.

Can Grannie remember Dunc without a photograph? Or doesn't she want to remember?

As soon as I've finished my drink, she whisks my glass into the kitchen. Car doors slam. 'They're here!' Grannie rushes to the back door. 'Look at you,' she coos as the twins waddle towards her. 'My little sailor boys, don't you look handsome, aren't you the most handsome sailor boys I've ever seen?' She scoops up John and gives him a big kiss, puts him down and gives Jamie a sloppy one too.

Uncle Ticker says I've sure grown and how's high school? Auntie Josie tells Grannie she bought the sailor suits at John Martin's in the city. Grannie takes the twins' hands and leads everyone to the front porch. At the door, she turns to me. 'Hadn't you better run along now, Sylvie?'

Everyone waves, even the twins, because Grannie is crouched down, waving their hands for them. 'Bye-bye, Sylvie,' she says in a silly voice. 'Bye-bye, Sylvie. Byyyyyeee.'

I pedal fast to the corner. The wind off the sea slicks back my hair and makes my eyes water. When I look back they've all gone inside.

Cele takes an extra glass from the dresser and pops a champagne cork into the rafters.

'Careful, Lia,' says Jude, taking the bottle and catching the froth in a glass.

Lia is Jude's special name for Cele. Somehow it turns her into a stranger with locked doors and hidden keys and a *Keep Out* sign for me. They are celebrating something special, though they don't tell me what.

'Here's to us,' says Cele, showing me how to clink glasses. When I'm slow in taking a sip, she says: 'Go on, it won't kill you.'

The bubbles make me sneeze, and my sneezing makes them laugh. Cele sips and says, 'The Old Girl should mind her own business. It's my life I'm living, not hers.' Jude nods and the shadows beneath Cele's eyes soften into blue moons. 'So,' says Cele, turning to me, 'a little bird told me you've won a prize.'

'Nothing. Only Form One Latin.'

She says Latin's not *nothing* and asks what I'm going to do when I leave school. I say I might get a job at the paper mill in Muswell; isn't that what everyone does around here? Cele looks at me in disbelief. 'You can do better than that. You've got brains. Get out of here and get yourself a good job.' I forget and reach for my leg. 'And you've got to stop that too.'

My face turns purple. The sore on my leg is incurable, that's what I tell everyone. The doctors are searching for a cure because just as it heals it breaks out again; it's a medical mystery. But if I said that to Cele she'd say I was starkers. Trying to act casual, I drink too quickly and bubbles fizz up my nose, making me splutter and giggle.

'You look so much like Dunc when you laugh,' says Cele with sad eyes. 'Doesn't she, Jude?'

Jude nods. 'And like your father.'

I flush a stronger shade of purple. 'Who'd want to look like him? He's a born loser.' I want to rip rip rip at my leg.

'I don't think anyone's ever *born* a loser,' she says gently and Jude gives her hand a squeeze. 'He was never the same after

Darwin. That's what your mum says, so I'm not speaking out of school. People think war makes men out of boys but that's piffle.' Then she talks about Dad having a brother who drowned in a dam at Bindilla. I'm only half-hearing but I know this must be the boy in the photo at Grannie's. She tells me Dad was there when it happened. He was seven. She smiles with kind eyes. 'He's not a monster, Sylvie. He's just a man.'

I'm not listening. When I blink, I can make Cele disappear in a blur. Jude tilts her head back to drink and tiny blue veins shine through her pale lids; she looks like Pardie, a pale freckled angel without wings. On the wall behind, there's a photo of Pardie and Dunc, and one of me too. Blink. Now there are two Pardies, two Duncs, two faces of me looking back at me. There are two Celes filling four glasses, and no more for me.

'...hiding under Grandpa's bed...and then Brendan...'

Without looking at the photo on the wall, I try to remember Dunc's smile. It is a blur. He has been gone too long. Will he ever come home? I try to think of Dad's brother called Brendan, but the thought gets muddled with the photos on the wall and, although I blink and blink again, I can't think who is here and who has gone, and who is the lost child? I lower my head and look at the table where two Judes are stroking two Celes with too many fingers on too many hands. When I look up, Cele is smiling at Jude as if I'm not there.

Jude smiles too, soft and pretty. 'It's getting late,' she says, glancing at me. 'Time for Sylvie to go, or Nella will have us for dinner.'

How would Mum know? I won't be telling her.

'Wait,' says Cele, swivelling her chair to the dresser. Then a camera is on the table in front of me. *Brownie Hawkeye Flash*, I read as she leans forward and hangs the strap around my neck. 'For you.'

'Me?'

I look down at the camera against my chest and recognise it as hers. Why is she giving it to me? Sudden tears fizz into the space behind my eyes but I force them to leak down my throat. And all at once, I know she's wrong. He *is* a monster. He burned down our house. That's the whole point. That's why Dunc's disappeared. Can't she see?

Cele's voice drones on about shutter speeds and bubble lenses. 'There's a new roll of film in it. When you've used it all, I'll show you how to develop it.' She pats my hand and in a bleary kind of way I think: He should be punished; he should be made to pay.

Outside, they wave me off. I wobble about on my bike, suddenly happy and giggly in the cool air. 'Faack orf,' screams Fred.

I'm pedalling around the lagoon when Roy shoots past, does a wheelie and almost falls off. 'Hi,' he says as he rights himself. Then he thrusts something at me. When I look up, he's peddling away, his bike rocking from side to side as if it's a boat bobbing about in a storm.

A present? I tear off ribbon and paper. A bottle of 4711 perfume.

This means Roy's in love with me. I like Roy but I'm in love with Mr Kerford. Not that Mr Kerford even knows I exist. Not that I ever see him, except for Maths, and when he's on yard duty, and when he drives the school bus. But never on weekends when he's in Muswell, probably taking Miss Warner to the drive-in; I've seen her smiling in the corridor and flicking her widgie black hair

197

at him. And I don't see him in the holidays because he goes back to the city. And who knows what happens there?

I ride on home thinking of Mr Kerford's tight curly hair and pipe tobacco smell, his tweedy jacket with the leather elbow patches, the way his green eyes twinkle at me as if he knows I exist but only in a cute funny way and not as a girlfriend you'd take to the drive-in.

Next day, Roy and Chicken are waiting outside the Institute when Lizzie and I arrive for the Saturday matinee. I thank Roy for his present and he turns beetroot red. Then he punches Chicken and Chicken punches him and they dance around each other like a couple of dingbats. Inside, they sit up the back but as soon as the lights go out, Roy steps over two rows of seats to sit next to me. Chicken follows and when Roy Rogers gallops across the screen, we stamp our feet and chant: *Roy-Roy! Roy-Roy!* Then Roy stands on the arms of his seat, hooting and yelling, pretending to be riding Tigger like the real Roy.

Mr Stevens flashes his torch and yells that he'll stop the film if we don't shut up. When we quieten down, Roy's arm sneaks along the back of my seat like a night owl coming out of its hole. His fingers wriggle onto my shoulder, circle and swirl. My throat tightens, everything tightens. Next to me, Lizzie tries to read her Fantale wrapper in the light from the screen. I can hardly breathe. The Institute is stuffed full of sweaty matinee smells, Roy's Juicy Fruit breath, the breath of dead soldiers from the Roll of Honour on the wall behind our heads. Gradually Roy leans closer until our heads are almost touching. Lizzie gives me a poke. I kick at her feet and glance at Roy, who's staring at the screen as if his fingers have a mind of their own and he doesn't know they're slithering lower.

Should I stop him? If he goes any lower, he'll know I don't wear a bra. His fingers spread out like a fan and my whole body tingles. But right then, the film breaks, Roy's arm slides back into its hole and he boos and stamps and screams along with everyone else and doesn't even look at me.

When the film is fixed and the lights dim, I wait for Roy's hand to return. I wriggle around to let him know I'm still there. I know I'm not in love with him. But I like how it feels when he wants me.

In Min's Store, Mum heads for the discount table. Min sidles up, tall and thin with two pointy cones like Jayne Mansfield, though not as big. 'Can I help?' she says.

'Just looking,' says Mum.

'Just ask if you need me,' says Min, drifting off to dressing-gowns where she waits, ready to pounce when Mum's finished fossicking. It doesn't take long. She surfaces with two bras and Min rushes over. 'Brassieres for your daughter, dear? Would you like me to fit her?'

'No,' says Mum, 'these'll be fine.'

Outside, she looks all pleased. 'That didn't take long, did it?'

'Show me, show me,' says Lizzie next day on the school bus. She has been wearing C cups for almost a year. 'Where did you get them? What cup? What colour? You didn't get falsies, did you?'

We've just heard that Marilyn Monroe has died; everyone's talking about it, some of the farm girls are crying, so I make Lizzie wait until we're changing for Phys Ed, then I give her a flash. She frowns: 'What's that at the front?'

'Hooks. Where it does up.'

Lizzie is bug-eyed. 'That's a maternity bra. My sister wears one like that to feed her baby. Girls' bras do up at the back, not the front. That's why it's wrinkly and doesn't fit properly. Didn't your mother have you fitted?'

She is so keen to tell the whole world that she doesn't wait for an answer. Not that I have one.

Nor does Mum. When I get home from school, she's at the well, pumping. 'I thought they'd be easier to do up.' *Pump.* 'You shouldn't worry what Lizzie Campbell thinks.' *Pump.* 'It's comfort that counts.' *Pump.* 'You'll appreciate that one day.' *Pump.*

'They're too big!' I yell as she runs off with her bucket. Bert From The Bush—a stray from the lagoon who's decided to live in our yard—purrs around my ankles as if he knows all about bras. 'They're wrinkly too,' I tell her when she returns. 'They should be smooth.'

'You'll grow into them.'

'I'm not wearing them. I'm thirteen! I'm not having a baby! Can't you see? Can't you see anything?'

She stops pumping and looks at me. I am hot everywhere, face, hands, under my hair. But she is cut-up cold with tight lips. 'I can't get anything right with you, can I?'

On Fridays after school, I babysit Tania, mostly pushing her around the streets in her pram, sometimes taking her onto the jetty and walking her all the way to the end. I began babysitting her a few months after I met up with Mrs Marciano in the street. It was after I found out about thalidomide, after everyone knew.

I made myself go to see her. It was Easter Saturday and Mum was being ratty again, hardly speaking to me one day, snapping like a shark the next.

Tania was lying on the sunroom floor. Her arms were not as bad as I feared. One was a short little stump mostly hidden under the sleeve of her dress, the other more like a small arm ending at the elbow with a two-finger hand on the end.

Mrs Marciano didn't tell me she took the drug for morning sickness. She didn't have to: if you told one person in Burley Point, you told the whole town. 'We're lucky,' she said, looking down at Tania, kicking and gurgling on her rug. 'There's a little boy in the Mount with no arms or legs. Imagine how that would be? What would you do?'

I would die, I thought, I would want to die.

She reached across to straighten a curtain. Her sunroom is light and flowery, yellow curtains and cushions on a cane lounge with two bucket chairs where we were sitting. 'So many around the world…' She seemed to forget I was there so I shifted my feet and crossed my legs. 'Except in America. They had enough sense not to approve it.'

Her voice wobbled on the last bit. I couldn't look at her because while she was talking I was feeling wobbly too. Then she bent over and swooped Tania off the floor. 'Five months,' she said, bouncing her on her knee. 'Hasn't she grown?'

Tania gave me one of her gummy grins and kicked her chubby legs as if she wanted to run in the air. Her little arm waved furiously too and I tried not to stare. 'Would you like to hold her? While I make some tea?' And before I could say—*No! I don't know how, I might drop her*—she was in my lap and Mrs Marciano was showing me how to support her in the crook of my arm. 'You're a natural,' she laughed.

'Don't be long,' I said.

Tania felt small and warm, like Bert From The Bush when I patted him on my lap, but she squirmed and gurgled more than Bert ever did. Mrs Marciano had no sooner gone than Joe's ute pulled into the drive. She called out something from the kitchen, a car door slammed, the back door opened and Joe's voice roared through the house.

'Where are my two gorgeous girls?'

Tania almost leapt off my lap.

'*Three gorgeous girls!*' he said from the door. 'How are you, Sylvie? Marg told me you were cutting up frogs. Have to get you on to my bait.'

He kicked off his boots, dumped his jacket on a chair, then knelt in front of Tania and me. He smelled fishy and salty like my father used to smell. 'So, Sylvie Meehan, whaddya think of my little princess?'

'She's lovely,' I said shyly.

'She's more than bloody lovely!' He tickled Tania's toes with his big fingers and she wriggled ecstatically. Then he lifted her from my lap, held her high in the air and swung her about in circles like an aeroplane. 'She's bloody *bellissima* beautiful. Aren't you, Tarnie? You're bloody beautiful, and I just love you.'

'Don't swear in front of Sylvie,' said Mrs Marciano, returning with a tray of tea things.

'Heard worse than that, haven't you, Sylvie?'

With his laughing teeth and suntanned cheeks, Joe seemed to fill the room like a warm summer storm. He leaned over and kissed Mrs Marciano smack on her lips. I looked at my feet, my fingers; I didn't know where to look.

'Joe, you stink,' said Mrs Marciano as he tried to kiss her again. 'Go and have your shower.' But her eyes were laughing and proud, as if being with Joe was the same as being with a class of Grade Ones and Twos, just as wacky and fun.

'I'd better go,' I said, shifting forward on my chair.

'No, you don't,' said Joe. He plumped Tania on my lap and within minutes we could hear him singing in the shower, the 'Que Sera' song, over and over, the words splashing under water.

Mrs Marciano poured tea and asked if I might like to take Tania for a walk in her pram sometime; she said it would give her a chance to catch up on a few things. She asked if I'd thought of babysitting and getting paid for it, that she knew Bev Carter was looking for someone to mind Robert and Jimmie after school. She said I'd be good at it. What did I think?

I thought how nice it must be to marry someone like Joe.

18

After almost a year of searching and surveying, Esso decide to sink a wild-cat well on Uncle Ticker's land, the low-lying bit on Lake Grey's eastern edge. The school bus is held up for almost an hour because of the derrick being hauled down the road, with a truck either end, as slow as two soldier beetles shifting a twig. At Charlie Parsons's fence, half the town is hanging out, watching the trucks corkscrew down the lane, lumping their load over the low hills. I slide into the window seat next to Mr Kerford, but he's more interested in trucks than in me.

At the cafe, we push and shove to get off the bus and then grab our bikes and race each other out to the lake. Already I think I can feel oil underground, sloshing around, waiting to be found. Mr Kerford has stopped on his way back to Muswell and is watching the derrick being hauled onto the site. Why does Chicken have to ride so close to me? He bangs on the door of the bus like a ninny. 'Give us a ride, sir, or I'll report you for loitering.'

Loitering? I'm surprised Chicken knows what it means. He rides off down the lane, no hands like a circus clown.

Roy yells after him. 'You can't go in there. It's private land!'

'It's public!' Chicken yells back. 'Anyone can!'

Roy tells him it belongs to Bindilla and my uncle will give him a flea in the ear if he's seen. Sure enough, Chicken's hardly gone any distance when he comes back wheeling his bike. 'Mud's too soft.'

Roy kicks at his front wheel. 'Chicken's chicken.'

'Ask your dad,' says Chicken to me. 'It's open to anyone.'

My father's at the fence with Augie but I'm watching Mr Kerford reverse onto the Muswell road, hoping he'll wave.

'Loiterer!' yells Chicken. I give Chicken a look to burn through his brains. 'What?' he says, pinking up.

'You know nothing.'

But Chicken knows about oil. One of his brothers works on the Moonie rig in Queensland, so Chicken knows about generator sheds and storage tanks, rotary rigs and spudding in. And when the workers move into Hannigan's, he knows the name of every job: mechanics and tool-pushers, drillers, muckrakers and rough-necks, enough men to work the rig twenty-four hours a day.

At first we hang out at Stickynet every chance we get, watching the lacy derrick spike into the sky on the other side of the lake. But once the drilling starts, we get so used to the thumping that soon we hardly notice it pumping new life around town.

When Mr Kerford stops outside the cafe, he sometimes buys a meat pie or a strawberry milkshake that he drinks on the seat near the bin before driving back to Muswell. This day he's not hungry, or stopping, and Mum tells me Bev Carter's picking fish and needs me to babysit Jimmie. And do I want a milkshake?

'Paddle Pop,' I say over the heads of the kids at the lolly counter.

Her face sets. But it's not my manners that have turned her eyes into brown marbles: it's my father, sauntering through the swing doors like John Wayne doing his *Rio Bravo* thing. 'Camels,' he says to the shelf above Mum's head.

'I'm serving.'

'Young Spoggie Green doesn't mind if I'm served before him, do you, Spog?'

'No, Mr Meehan.'

'See,' says my father.

Mum ignores his palm, puts his Camels on the counter, then his change, hands me my Paddle Pop and turns back to Spoggie Green.

Outside, my father ignores me. Lanky Evans has Mr Scott bailed up on the footpath. 'Found it up at Moonie and Gidgealpa,' he's saying, 'why not here? Great blobs of it been oozing out the ground long as anyone knows. Ask Nobby Carter. He's had a bee in his bonnet about it half his life.'

'That's not oil,' says my father, 'that's bloody coorongite. It's vegetable matter, any nong knows that. There's no oil here.' Lanky shifts his weight on his stick. 'Now, Mick, they'd hardly bring in all that equipment and put up twenty folk at Hannigan's, with all of it costing a mint, if they weren't onto something, would they?'

'Why not? The world's full of mongrels looking for an easy quid.'

Listening, I think: Everything about you is a pain. I can feel the ache of you right through to my bones. And everyone should know what you did to our house. What's more, I'm not scared of you, not anymore.

Mr Scott from next door spots me standing there. 'How're you, Sylvie? Bit nippy, isn't it?

I agree and pretend I can't see my father climbing into his jeep. I cross the street and run through the playground to the fish factory where Jimmie is waiting with Bev. As always he wants to walk out to Stickynet. As always, we follow the sea wall, running from waves that threaten to drench us.

At the bridge, Jimmie drops rocks into the sea below. Gulls skim low on the lake, searching for fish. Further out, swans are black dots, the derrick framed against a pale sky. When a car thumps onto the bridge, I check that Jimmie is safe against the rail and half-turn, hoping it's not Kenny Sweet, who, since I've been taking Tania for walks, likes to yell at me as he hoons past: *Got a bun in the oven, have you, Sylvie?* What is it with him?

And as always, I'm half-believing, half-dreaming that it might be Dunc because I still see him everywhere. Driving a truck past Muswell High. A flash of his face at a window of a bus in the main street of the Mount. Once in the Reedy Creek footy team playing at Burley Point—until he ran right past me and turned into someone else.

But it's not Dunc. It never is. It's the FJ Holden ute that's been cruising around town for the past week, all turquoise duco and polished chrome. Faye Daley says it belongs to Will Pickles, a muck-raker on the rig who comes from a farm up near Coomandook. She says he's the spitting image of Elvis and, as the car slows in front of me, I see that she's right: Will Pickles has an Elvis curl that flops onto his forehead like a wobbly black tongue. He has thick black lashes, a dimpled chin, and a lazy Elvis grin. And that grin is grinning at me.

My heart thumps louder than the drill on the rig, louder than when I'm in the pictures with Roy, or when the new boy at school smiles at me. They're boys. Elvis is eighteen, maybe nineteen; he's a man.

I itch to pull up my socks. To be Priscilla with a hive of black hair. Sandra with a cute Gidget smile. Anyone except Sylvie Meehan minding a five-year-old kid on Stickynet Bridge.

With another lazy grin, Elvis winds up his window and flattens his foot. 'What's he want?' says Jimmie.

Me, I think, licking his dust off my lips. *Please let him want me.*

At seven months, Tania could use her stumpy arm to lift herself off the floor and crawl like a crab. At ten months she was walking. At twelve months she could toddle after a ball, bend over and clasp it to her chest. At fifteen months, she could kick it to me. Joe said Pele would have to watch out, whoever Pele is.

At eighteen months, Tania has a bush of black curls and pink cheeks that turn red when she gets angry: she gets angry often, lying on the floor or lawn or footpath, kicking and screaming. Then she picks herself up and lets me dust her off. With lungs like that, Joe says she'll be an opera singer. Move over Maria Callas. If Joe picks her up when she's angry, she thumps her stunted arm at him. He says she's so strong that soon she'll be taking on Cassius Clay and Sonny Liston, both of them together. And if she doesn't end up in the ring, she'll be Miss Universe, that's how gorgeous she is. Whaddya reckon, Sylvie?

I reckon Joe is sometimes plain crazy. Crazy stupid, not crazy mad. Once I took Tania to the playground and a kid called her a spastic. I don't think Joe understands that his daughter is a cripple. That she will be teased at school.

Mostly, when I'm babysitting, I push her down Main Street to the foreshore rotunda where we watch the sea and boats and gulls.

One day I show her a spider building a web between two rotunda posts. I tell her about the frosty morning at Bindilla. How overnight hundreds of spiders had spun webs on the low grass and, as the sun came up, the paddock glittered like a silver sea, just like the sea in front of us. Another time, I tell her about the black men who used to live in Burley Point before the whalers and farmers came. Slit up your eyes, I tell her, and you can still see them spearing fish off the rocks. She scrunches up her face and says she can. I tell her about their shellfish middens on the back beach, how in the warm hollows of the dunes you can feel tribes of them sitting around camp fires, having a good feed of shellfish or wallaby. I say I'll take her there when she's older and she can see for herself. 'Lub you, Silby,' she says, kicking her shoes excitedly against the footrest.

Tania has just started saying this—to her mum and dad, to Joe's old black dog—but it is the first time she's said it to me. 'Love you too, Tarnie,' I manage, despite a tug in my throat.

Next time we're in the rotunda, Grannie comes trudging along Beach Road. She has a good look at Tania in her pusher and says: 'Pretty enough. But what sort of life's ahead of her?' She drops down beside me and takes off her shoe to rub at her bunion. 'The Marcianos might have been here for a while but they're still Italians. In Rome one of them pinched me on the backside. *Bellissima* this and *bellissima* that. I stood on his foot with my heel. That put a stop to his *bellissim*ing.'

As I push Tania home, I wonder how anyone can think an old lady like Grannie is beautiful. And how Joe can think Tania could grow up to be an opera singer, or win a beauty contest. I wonder if you believe something hard enough, does it happen, despite everything.

In August, Mum loses her job at the cafe because Mrs Trotter's sister is returning to Burley Point and needs the work. 'Said she was sorry. Said she hoped I'd find something else. There isn't anything else!' Mum chews on her bottom lip as if she's trying to taste it. I hate the way she does this, it makes me feel sick. 'The Co-op's a closed shop…wives and widows and married women every one of them. Not that I'd be caught dead picking fish.'

My homework poem leaps off the page. *Tyger! Tyger! burning bright / In the forests of the night…*

'And I wouldn't be caught dead working at Hannigan's either. You might have to leave school and get a job.'

'I'm not leaving school. I'm going to be a teacher.'

Mum stares at me with fiery tiger eyes, forcing me back to my poem. *When the stars threw down the spears / And watered heaven with their tears…*But the words blur and Mum snaps down the blind and starts the washing up.

When the school bus gets in, Elvis is sometimes parked near the cafe. Or crawling down Main Street. Or accelerating towards the beach, sometimes doing a wheelie that dirties his duco. Soon I know his shifts, two weeks on days, two weeks on nights. Nights are best because he's usually hanging around when I get home from school. With Cele's old Brownie, I have an excuse for hanging around too.

Mostly I take photos of things close up—seed pods on a bidgee widgee bush, the crisscross pattern of the jetty legs from underneath. Cele says I have an interesting sense of perspective. She shows me how to compose a shot using the rule of thirds. Mr Kerford lets me photograph him hanging out of the school bus and one of my shots from sports day is used in the school magazine.

Right now, I'm interested in shells. I photograph a cowrie on the beach where the mine washed ashore in the war and the men from the city were killed when they tried to blow it up. This was just before the war ended, before I was born. While I'm on the beach, Elvis drives past so I tear back to Hannigan's and photograph the lacy iron on the balcony. He leaves for the rig without even glancing across the street.

I haven't picked my shin for three months and the scar is starting to heal. I am growing my hair. I change my part to the other side but it makes me look lopsided so I change it back again. I hate my gawky neck; it doesn't seem to match my face. I squeeze lemon juice onto my freckles every night for two weeks. It makes my nose peel. In the bedroom mirror, I practise different ways of smiling—full teeth, half teeth, Mona Lisa smile. Every way makes me look kind of crazy. Why would he want me?

Under my desk, I hold the paper plane ready. Mr Kerford leans into the blackboard and draws a triangle with an exterior angle in white chalk. He circles the angle in red then begins the calculation, talking, explaining. 'If the exterior angle is *ACD* and the adjacent angle is *ACB,* I want you to find the value of the pronumerals in—'

It lands on his neck like a wasp. It's so quick, I almost don't know I've done it. Perhaps I didn't. Perhaps it was Chicken or that boy from the farm out near Furner—please let it be one of them, not me.

Mr Kerford turns. 'Who threw it?'

Silence. Stealthy looks. Slowly I raise my hand.

'Sylvie?' Surprise. Then a quick frown of disappointment. He can't believe it—neither can Lizzie sitting next to me with her mouth hanging open—nor can Roy who gawps at me from the front row.

My face is a furnace. Why did I do it? I'll have to say it was an accident. That I'm learning origami and it just slipped out of my hands. He won't believe me. He'll think I'm crazy. Maybe I am?

'Stay behind,' he says.

Already my throat's closing up and my heart's beating so hard that I can't even hear Lizzie's whispering. Somehow I ignore her nudges and concentrate on indices and angles. You can hide in numbers forever if you want to. Words too.

'Sylvie?'

He's standing next to my desk, Old Spice aftershave, brown corduroy, so close to my nose that I could turn my head and sniff his leg. Why would I even think that? Outside, the playground shrieks. He sits on the desk opposite but I don't look up. I'm feeling too stupid, too sick.

'It's not like you,' he says softly. 'Is everything okay?'

I've got dirt under my nails like a five-year-old. *What can I say?*

'Did someone dare you?'

Glancing up, I see Van Gogh's sunflowers waving at me from above the blackboard, next to the portrait of the Queen. 'Fibonacci numbers,' I say desperately. 'I was wondering why rabbits breed in that number sequence. Sunflowers and shell spirals too.'

He stands. *Please don't go.* I stare at his corduroy leg, willing him to stay, remembering how he leans over my desk, the way his red pen marks my page. The way—just once—his hand brushed mine.

'How about I revise it next week?'

There's a smile in his voice. He's not angry! Quickly, bravely, I look up. I manage a choked kind of *thank you*. As I walk past, he reaches out and tousles my hair. He touched me!

Mum finds a few hours' work cleaning for the Bolands. For someone who likes cleaning our house, she doesn't much like cleaning theirs. She says beggars can't be choosers. I'd rather be a chooser.

After school, I meet up with her leaving the Bolands'. Her corns are playing up and I dawdle behind, pretending she's not my mother with her limping feet. Out of nowhere, Grannie Meehan comes barrelling along the lagoon path, out of breath. She nods at me and plunks her basket on the ground.

'Nella,' she says, looking over her shoulder as if she's afraid someone might hear. 'Can't you find something better to do than house cleaning? How do you think it looks for me, living around the corner from the Bolands? You'd be better off back in the city, wouldn't you?'

Mum stares at something behind Grannie's head. 'Sylvie's doing well at school,' she says eventually. 'And Dunc's here.'

'Dunc's gone. And Sylvie's a girl. She'll end up married.'

Mum and I give Grannie's lace-ups a good going over. *Bossy boots.* I wait for Mum to say something but she's taking her time.

Grannie glowers at Mum; Mum holds her ground. 'I've got work to do,' she says at last. 'I can't stand here talking all day.'

Grannie's mouth clamps shut like a trap. Mum limps off and I follow. When I look back, Grannie is powering along the lagoon path.

Mum says she won't move back to the city in a pink fit. She says Grannie's as hard as nails and everyone knows it. For the next week, she goes crazy scraping polish off the lino and starting again. She scrubs the bath and skirting boards, she picks dirt out of the cracks in the cement steps with the sharp end of a knife. She says I'm a dreamer, that I need to grow up and face a few things, that life's not for sissies. I say: A sissie's a girl, so what am I, a boy? She says I'm getting too big for my boots and I need taking down a peg or two. I hate the way she nibbles on her toast. I hate her blood on the sheets; we still sleep together and always seem to bleed together. I hate myself for not fighting to sleep in the other room. I hate myself for hating her.

Then she hears Hannigan is looking for a housemaid-waitress; she swallows her pride and heads up the hill. When she returns, her face is flushed, alive. 'It's the riggers. He needs me to do the beds, be there for lunch, have a few hours off then go back for tea. You'll have to eat straight after school, and do the washing-up. It won't hurt you.'

Elvis has a room at Hannigan's.

One night I set out my homework books on the table: it's soon after she starts working there and I'm not really planning it, not even thinking it, but the minute I can't find my pen, I'm out the door and heading up the hill to the pub. Bev Carter's mother waves me through the fatty stink kitchen into the cool dark dining room.

Mum is a white-apron dot in the far corner. 'What are you doing here?' she hisses across the tables. When I tell her, she says, 'We've got plenty of pens. Did you look?' She seems lost and little in the big room. 'Wait out there. I'll find one when I'm finished.'

In the foyer, noise from the bar is an animal roar. I'm tracing the gold swirls on the red carpet with the toe of my shoe when Layle sails out of the Ladies Lounge, lines up the front door and steers herself through. Before she can see me, I push open a door next to the stairs and find myself in some kind of storeroom with crates and glasses, a broken bar stool. It takes me a second to realise there's a half-open hatch and I can see into the bar.

My father is sitting right there, barely an arm's length away! I flatten against the wall. Augie's there too. And the rigger they call Wombat after Steppy Jones's father, who has the same bushy beard in the Council Chairman photo on the Institute wall.

'My old man used to reckon we were sitting on swamps of it,' says Augie, wiping off a froth moustache with his hand. 'Ticker'll be worth a bloody fortune.' He turns to my father. 'You thought of that?'

Dad frowns into his beer. 'Problem is finding it,' says Wombat. 'It's a bloody lottery. Twenty feet too far one way, a bad break in the strat, and you can drill forever and never see a drop.'

Without warning, Dad lifts his head and brays at the ceiling. 'I've said it before and I'll say it again. You've come here half-cocked. There's no oil here. Anyone who thinks otherwise is a bloody idiot.'

'Same as the parrots, Mick?' yells Bullfrog, further down the bar. 'Same as they're all gunna disappear?'

Everyone laughs and jeers and cheers and I can feel myself heating up in the cupboard, heating up for him being so stupid.

'You're the one who's half-cocked,' yells Bullfrog. 'Why'd they be spending this sort of dough if they hadn't checked everything out?'

'Because they're bloody greedy mongrels, Taylor, same as you. And mongrels'll do anything for money.'

Bullfrog looks like he's going to push down the bar to get to my father but someone stands in front of him. It's Dessie Martin's father. He owns the soldier-settler farm that borders Bindilla and he hates all Meehans since Uncle Ticker drained the swamp and destroyed his best lucerne block. 'Ya wouldn't know if your arse was on fire, Meehan.'

Everyone cheers. My father elbows Wombat out of the way and I'm afraid he'll punch Dessie's dad but instead he sweeps glasses and ashtrays to one side and leaps onto the bar.

'Get down,' orders Hannigan in his ex-cop's voice. 'Don't put your boots on my bar, Mick. I'm warning you.'

Hands on hips, Dad points a toe, threatening, teasing, enjoying himself, anyone can see. Then he yanks off his boots, drops them to the floor and laughs down at Hannigan. 'They're not on your bar.' And lifting and pointing, jumping and twirling, he spins round and round in a mad Irish jig.

My cupboard is suddenly hot with no air, the stink of beer. Why won't he stop? And then he does, abruptly, as if he was just doing it to get their attention. He yells down the bar: 'You know they've been finding oily blobs around here for years and thinking it's oil. My old man used to find it in the swamps at Bindilla, his old man before him. They still find it on the Coorong. It's why it's called coorongite. They've done tests, it's nothing but algae, not bloody oil. You know that, Augie. When we were kids we used to scrape it off our boots. It's a bloody weed.'

Someone roars: 'Doesn't mean the real stuff isn't here.'

'Doesn't mean it is, either. That's why you'd be fools to get your hopes up. You'll end up lookin' stupid.'

'You'll be the one lookin' stupid,' yells Bullfrog, ''cause Ticker'll be raking in the moolah, not you.'

Dad's off the bar in one leap. At the same time, Mrs Hannigan's voice shrieks over the noise: 'Kennedy's been shot!' Her words sink like a rock into a deep ravine. 'In Texas. In a car.'

President Kennedy? A mumble grows into a shriek of disbelief. I want to shriek too. *He's too young! He can't be shot!* Then above the shock and muttering, Hannigan yells: 'Time, gentlemen! Six o'clock! Time, please!'

Suddenly everyone's pushing and shoving, and Dad's back at the bar with two, three, then four pots lined up before him. Hannigan's wife is pouring and passing, froth running off glasses. 'Awlright! I'm not deaf! Wait ya turn.'

I can see Dad's throat pumping and guzzling, he's that close. Watching, I think: Doesn't he care? Then: He should pay for what he's done. There's a sudden noise in the foyer that might be Mum so I slide quickly out of the cupboard.

Elvis! On the bottom step. Pulling off his boots. That same lazy smile. Teeth divine. My legs turn to jelly and I can't think what to do, I can't move. Then I see Mum at the dining-room door. 'President Kennedy's been shot,' I blurt. She ignores me and glares at Elvis as if he's the devil, instead of someone whose bed she makes every morning.

'Here's a pen,' she says. 'Now get yourself home.'

Elvis gives her a goody-boy smile. 'See ya, Sylvie,' he whispers as he heads up the stairs.

He knows my name!

19

I wish I looked like Nancy Peters. She has perfect skin and honey-blonde hair and walks with a Marilyn wiggle. On the other side of the catwalk, Faye Daley whispers something to Colleen Mulligan and stares into my camera lens. I get suddenly interested in photographing Nancy because I can't bear Faye's cat's-got-the-cream face that she's been wearing ever since I saw her talking to Elvis near the bathing sheds. Snap. Snap. As Nancy turns at the end of the catwalk and walks back to the rotunda, Lizzie says, 'You look a bit like her.'

Sometimes I can't believe Lizzie. 'I've got brown hair.'

'Around the mouth.'

'I hate my mouth.'

'You'd think you'd be pleased.'

I'm pleased that Faye and Colleen have disappeared. The judges have their heads together at a table at the back of the rotunda; Mrs Denver is one of them. She knows about beauty queens because years ago she was one herself. When she walks to the microphone with an envelope in her hand, she keeps us guessing by telling us part of the Miss Regatta prize will be a wardrobe to the value of ten pounds from Min's Store in Muswell and a week's holiday in Sydney.

'I'm going to Sydney,' I tell Lizzie, 'if it's the last thing I do.'

'It probably will be,' says Colleen Mulligan right in my ear. When I turn around, she's sashaying away with Faye, smirking into her fairy floss. Back on the catwalk, Nancy is parading with her Miss Regatta sash draped over her swimmers, a gold cardboard crown on her head. I look at Nancy's mouth and think maybe Lizzie's right; if I wore lipstick—if Mum would let me—maybe I could look a bit like her.

After the blessing of the fleet, we buy ice-creams at the cafe and race back to the jetty to get a good spot on the rail for the Greasy Pole. Near the first landing, Lanky Evans lets us squash in next to him.

'Hottest Boxing Day on record,' he says. 'Too many bloody blow-ins for me. Might be good for business but I like me privacy.' He pokes about with his walking stick and flaps his bony elbows to make more room for us. 'Bloody blow-ins everywhere,' he says and just in case the blow-ins haven't heard, he says it again, louder. 'Bloody blow-ins.'

The blow-ins amble along the jetty in a sunny daze. Lizzie and I hold our cones over the rail and lick them as they melt. Strawberry drops fall into the sea and grow into greasy rings. There is a huge blue sky with cotton-wool clouds that hardly move; for more than a week the wind has been from the north with no summer storms to relieve the heat. And Elvis has gone home for his Christmas holidays: I know this from Faye Daley who knows everything about Elvis.

I'm leaning over the rail when someone jolts my elbow and almost sends my ice-cream into the sea. 'Sorry,' I hear.

Dunc's voice? Spinning around, I see a man shouldering his way into the crowd. A young man. Dunc's height, the same shaped head. The same walk! 'Hold this,' I say, shoving my ice-cream at Lizzie. Then I duck around Lanky and push through the crowd, around old ladies and under arms, barging through with a strawberry sick taste in my mouth. Mustn't lose him. Can't, not this time. Not with him heading towards the end of the jetty. Not unless he jumps off the end.

He stops suddenly and looks back. It's not him! Too old, ugly. Not Dunc. I turn away hopelessly. Everything feels drained out of me, the sky too bright and glittery, the jetty timbers suddenly rickety beneath my feet. 'Sorry,' I tell Lizzie. 'Thought it was someone I knew.'

'Who?' She hands me my ice-cream. 'Had to lick it to stop it dripping. Who?' she asks again.

'No one you know.'

'I know everyone you know.'

I distract her by dropping my ice-cream into the sea and pointing to Chicken and Roy, now fourteen and old enough to enter the Greasy Pole, both small and skinny compared with the fishermen, farmers and blow-ins who are waiting on the arm of the jetty with the lifeboat and crane. Bullfrog is there too, strutting around on his frog legs. Shorty has a little round belly, normally hidden under his clothes. My father, looking smaller than he should, brown arms and head, white body and legs. And Kenny Sweet, clowning around as usual. *Dunc.* The same hard lump. *He should be here.*

Denver Boland's voice echoes and fades through the megaphone, telling everyone that first prize is ten pounds and a grease and oil change at Grosser's Garage, and the winner is the one who gets furthest along the pole without falling off. This is decided by

Denver, who stands on a box next to the lifeboat. The blow-ins and two of the riggers are sent on first so they won't have a chance to copy the locals. They step gingerly onto the pole and before they're even aware of what's happened, they're in the water below.

When it's Roy's turn, I have my camera ready. Arms spread like a high-wire walker, he bends and wobbles, but manages to get ten feet along the pole before falling off. Chicken uses the pole like a slippery floor and slides as far as he can, ending up further along than Roy before falling into the sea with a crazy loud scream.

When it's Bullfrog's turn, he begins with a crab shuffle and is almost halfway along with no sound from the crowd, only the drone of a speedboat pulling a waterskier, the screams of kids on the beach—and shouts from Chicken and Roy, who should have come out of the water but instead are climbing the jetty ladder, bunching into balls and dropping with blood-curdling yells into the water below. As Bullfrog reaches halfway on the pole, Chicken drops with a deadly scream: Bullfrog wobbles and straightens, his arms swivel and spin, but there's no saving himself from a dipping.

He comes up spluttering. Chicken surfaces at the same time and swims with a lazy overarm towards the jetty. Bullfrog charges after him and Chicken's eyes widen with surprise as he is dunked by Bullfrog's big hand. But somehow Chicken escapes, a white tadpole with desperate arms and legs, disappearing under the jetty not far from where we stand. Lizzie and I scramble to the other side where the dinghies are moored by long landing lines. With a few angry strokes, Bullfrog is under the jetty too, catching Chicken as he surfaces. Holding Chicken by the shirt his grandma makes him wear even when he's swimming, Bullfrog dunks him again and again, letting him up for a spluttering breath, pushing him under again.

'Let him go, you bloody idiot,' yells Lanky in my ear.

'What's he doing?' says Lizzie.

Can't she see? Can't someone stop him? Denver bellows into his megaphone. 'Next entrant…a local lad…give Mick Meehan a big hand.'

I push back to the railing in time to see my father step onto the pole, but he drops straight into the sea, not even trying, and swims straight under the jetty. Back on the other side, Chicken is a limp biscuit, arms and legs hanging like worms beneath the water, hardly even a splutter when Bullfrog lets him up for air.

'What's Mick up to?' mutters Lanky, and I follow his eyes to a mooring line where my father is pulling himself along. Closer to Bullfrog, he lunges and grabs him from behind, pushing him under. Suddenly Chicken is free, he bobs to the surface, kicks to a mooring line and hangs off it by one arm, gulping air.

'On yer, Mick!' yells Lanky, rat-tat-tat banging his stick on the jetty. 'On yer!'

Denver is still bleating into the megaphone but now everyone is watching Bullfrog and Dad in the water, arms and legs and two black heads flying in a whirlpool of foam. Bullfrog is winning. He has Dad under his hand, and he dunks Dad as he dunked Chicken, again and again, holding him under, mushing him into the sea without mercy. Next to me, Lanky hops around, hands cupped to his mouth. 'Get him by the nuts, Mick!' People cheer and Lanky yells louder. 'Get him by the nuts, Mick. A nutcracker, Mick, give 'im a nutcracker.'

Bullfrog lurches back and his frog legs pump like pistons. Then he rolls onto his stomach and curls into a ball, legs barely kicking at all. Dad pulls himself along a mooring line until he reaches the jetty. Someone claps. And others join in. And the clapping gets louder and louder until soon everyone is clapping. There's a cheer in the clapping, a beat—beat—beat, as clear as the sea lapping the dinghies, as clear as Lanky's stick tapping the rhythm. Dad reaches the landing and Chicken and Roy lean over to help. I forget everything, and I'm clapping too, clapping and clapping until my hands hurt.

Parked near the lagoon on Sunday afternoon, engine running, he beckons me over. My stomach does its usual queasy thing. His lashes are the longest I've ever seen. I hope Faye sees him talking to me, wanting me. But what does wanting mean? Kissing? Going all the way? Would Faye? And what am I doing, standing here like a dummy?

'How old are ya now, Sylvie?'

'Sixteen,' I say, adding a year and a bit. 'Almost.'

He grins, guns the ute into gear and drives off, taking me with him in the silver trim.

I make my own darkroom in the lean-to behind the dunny shed. Tea chests for a bench, two blankets hung over poles to enclose the space from roof to floor. Cele gives me an extension cord, developing trays and an infra-red lamp. With money from babysitting, I pay for my own film and chemicals, which I have to keep in a sealed tin. Rats will eat anything.

For Tania's second birthday in December, I give Mrs Marciano and Joe a photo I took of Tania on the foreshore with the sea glittering behind. I crop it close to her shoulders so you can't see her stunted arm: that's when I discover that photographs can lie. But Mrs Marciano likes it so much that she displays it in a frame on the mantelpiece. Joe says I should enter it into a competition, and maybe I could become a portrait photographer like that Beaton guy, have I thought of that?

Sometimes Joe is just plain silly. But I borrow a book from Cele and look at the way Cecil Beaton does his backgrounds and lighting.

At first I think Mum's going to the dance by herself and I almost ask if I can go too. Faye's allowed to go when her father plays saxophone with the band. But in the mirror propped on the table, I can see Mum looking all dreamy and, before I can even ask, she says: 'Milan's taking me. He's a foreman on the rig.'

I choke on a mouth full of curlers. The New Australian? The Yugoslav who was here last week fixing the pump? They sat by the well smoking ciggies long after he'd finished. And last night he walked her home from Hannigan's: I was in bed and heard them talking. I thought he'd come to get his money for fixing the pump. How dumb am I?

I'm carving her scalp into squares and winding on paper and hair. I carve faster, harder. I don't know any mothers with boyfriends. What will people think? And doesn't she know about the Croats and Serbs, how they brought their problems here? Doesn't she read the papers? I slap perm papers and hair together and twang the elastic close to her ear. I get braver and push her head forward, jerk it back, roll a curler tight, tighter. I hate her white scalp, the scar from falling off the horse that hides on her crown like a white worm.

She hasn't been to a dance for as long as I can remember. She probably thinks the Twist is something you do with your wrist. I could teach her. But I don't. And when Milan arrives on Saturday night, she's in a total tizz because her perm hasn't dropped and she looks like a frizzed bear when she probably wants to look like Vivien Leigh, which Mrs Winkie once said she did.

When Milan gives her a bunch of flowers, so tiny you can hardly see them, Mum runs around calling it a corsage, as if she gets one every day. 'It's gorgeous,' she says, pinning it to her dress.

Gorgeous? She's never said *gorgeous* before.

'They're orchids,' he says with his dippy accent, making them sound like diamonds instead of bush orchids you can find anywhere. 'I find them near the lake. Who would kill an orchid, I think. It is awkward killing an orchid, I think, but for you I do.'

He brings flowers for me too. Mum looks pleased as if I'm meant to like him on the spot, which I won't, even though he's good-looking, with sad broody eyes, like a taller kind of James Dean. Besides, they're only old fairy flowers, as common as cows, I tell myself as they head down the drive, arm in arm, as if he's leading her down the aisle.

What if she marries him?

I let Bert From The Bush come inside. We've just found out he's having kittens so he's now Bertha, Bertie for short. She sniffs around on her belly before jumping onto the bed as if she's found Heaven. Mum says I have to find homes for her kittens or they'll

226

end up in a bag with a brick. She says Bertie's probably the reason Georgie Porgie turned up his toes: who wouldn't die of fright if that huge marmalade head looked into your cage?

I open her wardrobe. She's worn the ballerina with the diamante bow on the hip. I pick through the others, mostly pink: the lace one with tiny buttons and hooks down the back like a bride dress, the pale frothy silk with a net underskirt, and the halter-neck with the full skirt like Marilyn wore, but pink, not white. Five new dresses bought from the catalogue, all since she's been working at Hannigan's. How did she know she'd be going dancing?

I pull off my nightie, find one of Mum's push-up bras, and slip into the Marilyn dress. It almost fits. I crimp it in at the back and put on a pair of strappy heels, then pose in front of the mirror, big smile, legs apart, Marilyn on the vent. Bertie stares at me from the bed with unimpressed eyes. I agree and put Marilyn back in the wardrobe.

Then I remember I have *God's Little Acre*, which is being passed around school and is mine for the weekend, so I climb into bed and read the good bits. Reading them makes me wonder if Elvis might have gone to the dance. Would Faye be there? Dancing with Elvis while I'm in bed with Bertie? The thought is too embarrassing. I hide in the pillow and think how I'd like Elvis to be in bed with me like Will and Darling Jill in *God's Little Acre*. Next thing, Mum's at the door, waltzing in as if she's still at the dance. 'You awake?' she half-whispers.

'I am now.'

She's brought me a huge bunch of balloons that she ties to the dressing-table mirror where they float up like an A-bomb cloud. I can just see her after the last dance, jumping up and grabbing them, him laughing and helping. How old does she think I am? While she's undressing, I pretend to use the pot in the bathroom and sneak Bertie outside. Back in bed, I slide far over my side. She climbs in and I edge nearer to the wall. But tonight she doesn't cuddle me close: she lies on her back smelling of powder and perfume. And I lie on my side thinking: What if she kissed him?

Elvis is parked outside the cafe when the bus gets in. I bounce down the steps, forgetting to say goodbye to Mr Kerford, my eyes on the car in the puddle of shade beneath the pines. Faye's seen him too. She's talking loudly, laughing and calling out to Lizzie. Then she pulls her ponytail free and lets her hair flounce around her shoulders like a horse's mane. And somehow, without even thinking or planning, I walk straight up to Elvis. I'm shaking inside and can feel Lizzie and Roy gaping at me from somewhere behind. I can see Mr Kerford reversing onto the road and I imagine him watching in the rear-view mirror as he drives out of town. I don't have to imagine Faye; her fury is burning holes in my back.

'Like a ride home?' says Elvis, smiling, surprised.

Before I've even replied, he leans across to open the passenger door and somehow I walk to the other side and climb in. When he reaches over to pull the door shut, his head is so close that I have to pull back to stop it rubbing my nose. Black hair on his arms. The door shuts with a thud. As we pull out from the kerb, I press my knees together to stop them shaking. I can see Lizzie through the side window, mouth wide open. Roy is examining the wheel of his bike, not looking at me. What am I doing? And somewhere, a tiny voice in my head: Mum's got Milan, why shouldn't I have someone too?

'Took ya time,' says Elvis, reversing.

What does he mean? I stare at his hands on the wheel. Clean fingernails, cleaner than mine. He's wearing clean jeans and a red check shirt, brown desert boots. The car is clean. The dash and steering wheel gleam, the rubber mats beneath my feet are free of dirt and gravel. For a muckraker, every bit of Elvis is *incredibly* clean.

'What's a muckraker do?' I ask, my voice a squeak. Then I feel my face heating up: did I really ask such a stupid thing?

'Works ninety foot up the derrick—can see for miles, the bay, the lake, over your uncle's place—I watch the mud tanks, check what's coming up. It was me who spotted the bones last week. Next thing you know there's a bloody skeleton right there under the bit. Can't believe it. We get Bill Morgan to come and take a look. Then they get the cops down from the Mount. Still don't know who it is.'

But everyone's guessing: Chicken thinks they're roo bones. Roy says they wouldn't get the cops for a roo. Mum says Old Pat had a brother who disappeared from Bindilla years ago. He could easily have walked into the quaggy mud on the side of the lake and been sucked down. She says this with bright staring eyes and I know she's thinking of Dunc in Bunny's soak, the same awful way to go.

I wonder if Elvis knows about Dunc. If anyone in town has whispered to him about Dad torching our house. Then I hear him saying he'd rather be a muckraker for Esso than work for his old man on the farm where he's paid next to nothing. He says he won't be a muckraker all his life and if they don't find oil in Burley Point, he'll be moving on with the rig to the next well.

Leaving? 'But they'll find it, won't they?'

'Hard to tell.'

He stops at our gate and turns off the engine. With his back against the door, he grins at me. 'Well, Sylvie Meehan, maybe we'll go for a ride sometime. Whaddya reckon?'

When? I think. *Where?* Just trying to hold his gaze makes my hands sweaty. I shove them under my legs. What should I say?

He reaches forward and pulls the key from the ignition, shows me his key ring, a Maori tiki with an ugly twisted grin. But as I hand it back, it slips from my fingers and falls to the floor. I shift on the seat and lift up my knees, and he leans over and scoops up the ring. 'Hey,' he says, head low over my lap, 'what's this?'

'Nothing,' I say, trying to pull my skirt lower. 'I—I broke my leg. Once. Last year. It's nothing.'

'I broke my arm once but it sure didn't end up looking like that.' Gently he touches the scar on my shin, fingers soft and circling. A hole opens up inside me like a howl. 'I have to go,' I say, grabbing my bag and struggling out the door.

'I'm on day shift next week,' he calls after me. 'Finish at six.'

What's he telling me? I stare after him as he drives off. I want to tear at my leg but I don't.

20

Mum rushes in while I'm doing my homework at the kitchen table. She slides into the bedroom on her polishing cloths and slides out a few minutes later in her tatty house dress.

'Where've you been?'

She grabs saucepans, a knife from the dresser drawer, beans from the sink that she must have picked before she went out. She says I can top and tail them, but before I can even reach for the knife, she's doing it herself, cut, flick, cut, flick. Then I see her face. It looks flattened, like someone has punched in her cheeks. And there's something gone from her eyes that makes me frightened.

'What's wrong?' I say uneasily.

She sits at the table with a thump. 'They've found Dunc.'

My whole body seems to empty of air, as if it's been punched out of me like Mum's cheeks, as if Dunc is someone I can't quite remember. Then it seeps back in, filling me up with believing, with disbelieving, with not daring to believe, all of it mixed up in the dream of him returning. And a voice in my ears. *I knew it! I knew he'd be found! I knew he'd come back!*

'When?' I say but it's barely a whisper. 'Where?' I say, louder. 'Where is he?'

She jumps up and lights a ciggie, stands with her back to the stove, watching the door as if Dunc's waiting outside. I turn uncertainly. There's no one on the porch. *Talk to me! Tell me!* But then she puts her ciggie on the hob and starts scrubbing spuds, rough handling them, rubbing off dirt, fingers picking out eyes. With the sharp black-handled knife, she peels off skin in thick slices, dumps the peeled spuds into a saucepan and starts scrubbing more. *How many is she doing? Who will eat them all?*

Abruptly she stops. 'The oil site,' she says.

Her voice reaches me from a long way off. *He's got a job there? Working with Elvis? Milan?* A squeeze in my chest. *When did he arrive? Why didn't he come to see us?* Her fingers peeling spuds. Then I lift my head and see the horror in her eyes.

The bones Elvis found? Is that what she means?

Everything squeezed out of me. I can't breathe for the squeezing. *Please don't let it be him.* Under the mud. *He has to come home. I've been waiting so long.* A noise in my head that might be a sob, from Mum, me, I can't tell. Everything squeezed out of my bones, I can't breathe, the taste of mud, Mum's punched-in cheeks and hopeless crushed shoulders, the way she's back at the hob, cupping the long ash of her ciggie in her hand like a moth. *Please don't let it be him. Not him, not the mud.* A saucepan lid rattles far off on the stove. She tosses the ciggie into the fire and lifts the lid. Steam clouds her face. Now she's at the fridge, looking inside for a long time. *Shut it, you're letting the cold air out, that's what you're always telling me.* A lamb rack in her hand. Using the knife like a saw, slicing through bone. *Please. Not Dunc.*

'I used to think...' her voice, tiny and frail, '...not knowing was...' Her fingers curling chops into the frypan. 'Compared with...but maybe it's better...'

It can't be him. I thought he'd come home.

'I don't understand,' says Mum. 'He must have gone to the soak…his sock was there. All this time I had to believe…to survive. But why…why would he ride four miles to Bindilla without his sock?' She waits as if I should know the answer. 'Or his boots? They haven't found his boots. Or his bike. I told Bill Morgan, it doesn't make sense…unless…'

Unless? Her eyes are muddy brown soaks, the sizzling chops, the kitchen full of fatty smoke. Tears leak out of her eyes and drip off her chin. 'Maybe it's better,' she says. 'In the long run. Better to know.' She looks at me and I see how tired she is, as if she's run a long race and reached the finishing line and she's folding into herself with relief. 'Now we can bury him. Now that we know.'

But we don't know anything! She serves up our chops and I peck at my plate, squeezed tight with no tears. What about me? It's not better for me. Before it was all blocked out with not knowing. Now there's no hiding. From remembering. Imagining. From the mud. I don't want to know. It can't be true, can it?

He says he doesn't care what the dental records say, every nong knows there's mud on that side of the lake that sucks you down in seconds, and Dunc knew too. He would never have gone there. And how long did it take the oil team to build a platform so they wouldn't be sucked down? He says he's not going through a fancy-pants funeral with bones that could belong to anyone, even a bloody Abo, even a roo.

He doesn't say any of this to Mum. As far as I can tell, she hasn't spoken to him about Dunc, not at the inquest, not since.

The lagoon is a moat between them with battering rams and boiling pitch pouring down from invisible battlements and no hope of peace, no hope of anything. 'You'd better organise it yourself, Nella,' Bill Morgan tells Mum after the autopsy in Muswell. 'Doesn't matter what I tell him, he doesn't want to know. I reckon he can't take any more.'

'More likely he doesn't want to pay for the coffin,' says Mum that night. 'And how will I? That's what I want to know.'

My eyes stare at a page of *Twelfth Night*. I want to hide in the words but they keep smudging. I can't believe Sebastian could come back from the dead and be confused with Viola, even if they were twins. *I can't believe Dunc is dead.* I am stiff with the cold of stone castles. I should be in bed but the lino will be cold under my feet, the sheets will be cold, they will become as tangled as the plot of *Twelfth Night*, as tangled as my wide-awake thoughts in the night. Thoughts about what I said, and Dunc said, and what I should never have said.

'I'll have to ask the Old Girl,' says Mum. 'There's no other way.'

Grannie pays for a pine coffin with silver handles. She sits in the front pew on the other side of the aisle from Mum and me, the coffin on a stand between us. It is covered in carnations, roses, gladdies and lilies. I try not to look, not to think. I will not believe it. *I will not look again.* I pretend I have my camera and focus on the altar, the wood panelling, the coloured-glass window. I frame Jesus on the cross, red paint dripping from his hands and feet. I look down at my shoes; I need new ones, pointy toes with squash heels like Faye Daley's new ones. I examine the scar on my shin. It is lumpy and uneven. I will have it forever.

Again and again, I sneak looks behind. More people have come to Dunc's funeral than can fit in the church. Mrs Winkie and Lizzie, and Mary, who's taken the day off work. Roy's father and mother, Wanda the Witch. Mrs Marciano with Tania and Joe. Tania sees me glancing back and calls, 'Silby! Silby!' before Joe bounces her on his lap and distracts her. Cele and Jude arrive and take the spare seats in the front pew next to us. Cele looks at Grannie; Grannie looks at Dunc's coffin. *I will not look again.* Cele sits next to Mum and squeezes her hand. Mum's face crumples. Milan's hand reaches from the pew behind and gives her shoulder a squeeze. She straightens her face but doesn't turn back to him.

Milan is a mystery. Mum has known him for almost four months and been to four dances with him. He has never been to our house except to collect her for the dance, or to chop wood before taking her for a drive in his old Austin. Where did they go? Here and there, she said when I asked. Is he a boyfriend or isn't he? If he is, why isn't he sitting next to us in the front row? I feel sorry for him and turn to give him a little smile. He looks as if he's won the lottery. Straightaway my face heats up with guilt for not being friendlier to him, so I turn quickly back to the altar.

Mrs Boland has filled the altar vases with roses she's probably scrounged from farms all around. I focus on a pink rose with my camera eye, long-shot, close-up. Mrs Parsons starts up the organ, playing something dark and drawn-out as if she can't pedal fast enough to get it going. What sort of music would Dunc have liked? The Beatles, or the Stones? Maybe something different like the Dreamers? *Why am I even thinking this?* My mind flits about like a blue wren on a branch. Dunc prancing behind Mrs Winkie, wobbling his bum in time with hers. Mum telling Mrs Scott over the side fence: *It kills me every single day but I've just got to cope, I've got Sylvie to think about.*

The priest from Muswell enters and Mum nudges me to stand. Again I glance around. What sort of father doesn't come to his son's funeral? He should be making the speech called the eulogy, saying the words that Denver Boland is saying. What did Denver know about Dunc? Then I catch Grannie glancing behind and I look too.

He's there! A face at the side door, as white as the limestone walls, except for a whiskery shadow on his cheeks and chin. Abruptly he disappears. Is he coming in? No, he reappears closer to the door, still half-hidden. What is wrong with him? He should be sitting in the front row like us. Why isn't he coming in? The organ bellows and groans and the cold in me heats up with the shame of him.

The coffin is being carried down the aisle, Mum pushing me to follow. Why is Kenny Sweet a pallbearer? I'd rather be a pallbearer myself than have him. I stumble outside. People are spilling from both doors. Spoggies swoop from the pine trees, bare earth beneath the dark branches.

There is no sign of him anywhere.

He's not at the cemetery either. But as the priest begins to speak, Lizzie whispers to me and I see a man half-hidden behind Jude, head down like a dog. Pardie? Is it really him? He's wearing a bodgie black jacket and blue jeans, longish hair like Ringo's, a richer kind of red. It must be five years since he left. Jude has talked of him bumming around Queensland, working on prawn trawlers and cane-cutting. Did she know he was coming home? She must have told him about Dunc.

Then I see Kenny Sweet nudging up to Pardie. Straightaway Pardie slides through to the front row, leaving Jude saying something to Kenny. Whatever she says, Cele turns to glare at Kenny and he slinks off a short distance, his eyes never leaving the back of Pardie's head.

Dunc is lowered into the ground on long ropes by two men from Muswell in black suits. Amen, I say with everyone else but there's a muddy black taste in my mouth and I can't think why we're burying Dunc in dirt when he's just been dug out of it. I would rather believe he was drowned in the bottomless waters of Bunny Brennan's soak than know he choked to death in Lake Grey's stinking mud. And if they hadn't started drilling for oil and found him, we'd still believe he was in the soak, wouldn't we? Would it matter if we didn't know exactly where he was? What's so good about the truth if it's more awful than a lie?

Mum bends to toss dirt on the coffin and I look up at a sky full of clouds with long tails blowing in from the sea. In my coat pocket, I find the skull ring. Burying it with Dunc seemed like the right thing to do but now I want to keep it. I step back to let other people toss dirt and I see Grannie heading down the path to visit other graves, other Meehans, walking carefully down the slope in her good shoes, past headstones bulging and bent as if bodies are trying to break out of the ground, past rose bushes grown wild and scratchy, past graves with urns and angels on top that stare at Grannie with sad, stone eyes.

As people head back to their cars, I stand on the rise under the old black she-oak, waiting for Mum to finish shaking hands. Pardie leaves in a dusty white Ford with a badly dented bumper and a Queensland numberplate, and Kenny leaves soon after. I think: I want to run away like Pardie, to Queensland where it's always sunny. I think: It's my father's fault, and he didn't even come to see his son buried.

Then Lizzie is standing next to me, saying something about Chicken, who's walking towards us. Her voice is full of squeaky scorn because she thinks he's become a foreign species since he's grown sideburns and begun using his brother's aftershave. Roy sidles up behind Chicken as if not sure of his welcome, and why would he be when he's hardly spoken to me since Elvis gave me a lift home?

'Sorry about your brother,' says Roy, scuffing at the ground with his boot, still not looking at me. His cheeks have grown sharp bones and the freckles on his nose seem paler than before, hardly there at all.

'Do they know what happened?' asks Chicken, pushing in. 'You know? How he got there?' At first I don't understand what he means and then I realise he's referring to the inquest. But before I can speak, he tells me what he thinks. 'Maybe there's an underground river that runs from the soak. Maybe he got sucked down and it's taken all this time for him to flow out to the lake. Whaddya reckon?' His eyes are greedy, his face red and blotchy. Roy pings a scrap of gravel at him.

'What?' says Chicken, looking from Roy to me. 'What?'

'Misadventure,' I say.

'What's that mean?'

Now Roy gets stuck into Chicken, pinging gravel, making him

bend and duck. Chicken slides behind a headstone, ducking out to ping gravel at Roy. From the telephone pole near the gate, a pair of plovers swoops at a starling, *kekekekking* until they drive it onto the road. Mrs Winkie beckons from the car.

'It's like the resurrection, isn't it?' says Lizzie as we walk away. 'I mean with Dunc sort of coming back from the dead.'

I finger the skull ring in my pocket. It feels as if everything is coming to an end, or beginning, I don't know which. Chicken and Roy are still pinging gravel at graves, making the headstones talk. I think: How could he *not* come?

Next day, I follow the sea wall to Stickynet because the tide is too high to walk on the beach. There's a cold wind and a heavy grey sky, more like winter than autumn. When I push through the scrub to Cele's, I find Jude packing Pardie's car. Then Pardie comes out, carrying a brown duffle bag. He sees me and smiles a pleased, chipped-tooth smile, dimpling cheeks.

'Sylvie?'

I'm suddenly shy and can't look at him. I think: Why's he leaving already? Right then Cele comes out too and she's carrying a bundle of blankets that she loads into the car. Pardie dumps his bag on the back seat, Jude slams the boot closed and looks to the main road, listening, waiting. Cele and Pardie too.

Then the throb of a hotted-up exhaust, gurgling to a stop at the end of the track. Kenny Sweet's old Ford? It revs and snarls. Pardie takes car keys from his pocket, quietly, as if he's afraid of them jangling. Even Fred is silent. Then another noisy gear change and Kenny roars off.

'I'll be okay,' says Pardie, reaching for Jude. She buries her face in his shoulder and tells him not to come again, that she'll come to him. Cele tries to hug Jude and Pardie too and there's a whole mess of hugging and crying going on. And when Pardie pulls away, he looks at me, confused, as if he's not sure what I'm doing there and whether I should be hugged too.

'Sorry,' he says, opening the driver's door. 'I'll give you a lift home, if you like. We can have a bit of a yak on the way.'

With a quick reverse and turn, we drive down the track, Cele and Jude waving behind, Fred now screeching after us with every *faa-a-a-ck* he knows. At the main road, Pardie noses forward, frowning into the rear mirror as we head towards town. Is he watching for Kenny? At Stickynet, he swings the wheel sharp right, slamming me hard against the door. 'Sorry.'

'What's happening with you and Kenny? What's Kenny done?'

He doesn't reply. Soon we're on the track that runs beside the lake and connects with the road near the pub, the tea-tree a jungle of black trunks, writhing arms, cloud-leaf heads. Approaching Nobby's corner, Pardie checks nervily both ways before moving forward. At our gate, he turns off the engine and sighs over the wheel like an old man. 'What *hasn't* butcher boy done? That's what you should be asking.'

It's a second before I realise he's answering my question about Kenny. And that's when I see, really see, how much he's changed. The skin on his face is stretched tight. Thin lips. Tired eyes to match the sigh. Again he checks the mirrors. 'Sorry, Sylvie, I can't hang around here. I've really gotta get going.'

Everyone leaves. I look at the white tips of Pardie's ears poking out from under his Ringo hair and I remember him dinking me out to Five Mile Drain, my cheek pressed against his warm shirt. And Dunc dinking me home, the wind in my hair. The three of us, as it was before. And even though we've buried Dunc in the cemetery, I realise I'm still waiting for him to come home. 'Do you miss him?' I say.

His eyes lift warily. 'Dunc?'

Who else, I think, looking straight at him. But he turns away quickly. And I think: He looks scared. How could he be scared of me? And then the word *blame* rises up in me like the wave on the reef that tried to suck us both into the deep. It's not my fault, I want to tell him. It's my father's fault. If he hadn't burned down our house, I wouldn't have told Dunc. Don't you see? There'd have been nothing to tell. That's why it can't be my fault, can it? And while I'm saying all this, I try to hold on to the reef but my neck and legs hurt, my head is under water, under mud; somehow I'm holding my head down with my own hand. Then I can't hold it down, not any more. I see Pardie's fingers tap-tap-tapping on the steering wheel, and words bleed out of me like the cowardy custard I am.

'It's my fault he died.'

'Don't be stupid.'

'Everyone knows.'

Pardie's eyes lock onto mine. 'I was there,' he says harshly. 'I know what happened.' Somewhere Kenny's car revs and rumbles. Pardie's words come out in a rush, too many, too fast. 'I told him it was better to cross further on. I said the mud was too soft. But he wouldn't listen. He called me a pansy. Other people...said...but he never...I...I just rode off...I left him...'

His words fill the car like a fog drifting in off the sea. I don't understand what he's saying. I can't bear the hurt blue of his eyes. 'I heard him yelling…but I didn't know…I didn't look back…'

He was there? Is that what he's telling me?

'I never stop hearing him, Sylvie. Never.'

The fog clears, a little. I wonder if it's the same voice I hear. The voice that has paled into a prayer that I can't quite remember? In a rush I think: What's so bad about being called a pansy? And couldn't he tell it was a different kind of yelling? Couldn't he have looked back one last time? Couldn't Dunc have yelled louder? Then: If I was angry with Dunc, maybe I'd have left him too. And finally: 'Why didn't you tell anyone?'

'Because I was a fucking coward.' He glances in the side mirror, still watching, listening. 'I thought they'd blame me. Then I couldn't think straight and I almost convinced myself that he went back to the soak where we'd been earlier, where he dropped his sock. I wanted to believe it the same as everyone else. I thought, is it a lie? If they think he's in one place, not the other? But when they found him, when Mum told me…I knew I should've gone back…' He listens for the sound of Kenny's car. 'But there were other reasons…' And somehow I know Kenny is one of the reasons Pardie left town. But how could that be? 'Look,' says Pardie, 'it doesn't matter. I'm a bloody coward and that's all there is to it.'

The inquest? Shouldn't he have come back for that? But then everyone would have known. Should everyone know, now that I know? There are so many questions spinning around my head that I can't think which to ask first. Pardie's head is bowed over the wheel. I stare at the back of his neck, his pale freckles, and I remember when Uncle Ticker tried to save the emu, the way he was almost sucked down himself. I remember the day when Dad was drunk in the road, telling Layle he looked away for a minute and when he looked back Dunc had disappeared.

'My father. Was he at the lake?'

Pardie's head jerks up. 'No. Just me. Why?'

'What about his bike.'

'I don't know. Probably…with him.'

Again I think: If Dunc could have shouted louder. If someone else was at the lake. If someone had come along. But suddenly Kenny's car is on the road behind the school; we both hear it.

'Sorry, Sylvie. I've gotta get out of here.' He starts the engine. 'Tell anybody you want. I don't care anymore. But don't blame yourself. Blame me.'

I watch as he turns at the Patchetts' corner, a puff of dust then gone. Soon Kenny cruises past and I step into the shadows near the fence. When he's gone, I sink down on the grass and hunch into a ball. I think: *Death by misadventure.* That's what the coroner said. That's what *misadventure* means. An adventure that went wrong. And I hear Pardie's words: *Blame me.* His fault, my fault, Dad's fault, everyone's fault, no one's fault. I think: How can Pardie live with knowing? How can I? How does anyone? It still doesn't make sense. It feels too easy. Or too hard. I can't decide which. Then I remember Dunc with his cheeks full of birds' eggs, the funny way he wrote with his thumb tucked behind his pencil. I remember a big brown eye looking at me through a magnifying glass. The way he could do a warbler whistle.

A flock of silvereyes fly out of the pines. They drop over the lagoon like a lacy cloth. It's sunny now with feathery clouds moving fast along the ridge behind the houses. On the lagoon path, Bev Carter's little boys are racing each other on their three-wheelers, squealing and laughing.

21

Two weeks after Dunc's funeral, Mum stops seeing Milan. Without him to chop our wood, she goes wood-chopping mad and in no time at all has half the pile cut and stacked next to Shorty's fence. I offer to help but she says: 'Don't let me see you near that axe. I don't need anything else.'

One night I arrive home to find her at it again. I sit on the gate and wonder about her and Milan. And I wonder whether all men are water, as she says. Dad, of course, but even Elvis?

Nobby Carter walks past and doffs his hat. 'You shouldn't be doing that, Nella, it's no work for a woman.'

Mum watches him dodder off then slams the axe into a log. 'I don't see you offering to do it.' The axe gets stuck in the log and she has to slam it down again and again, until it splits open like someone's head. Nobby's head. Maybe Milan's.

Then I remember that last week she came home from a drive with Milan and lay in bed beside me like a log. Although I couldn't see in the dark, I knew she was staring at the ceiling, maybe even crying. Good, I thought, they've had an argument. Then: 'Milan's asked me to marry him.'

I held my breath and let it out slowly. 'Are you going to?'

She lay for a long time without answering, then turned on her side and said, 'No...I'll never marry again.'

And that was the end of Milan.

Now, with dusk creeping over the lagoon and her swinging and chopping in the half-light, she looks so small and alone—so like someone who might need a husband—that I wish I'd been nicer to Milan. I remember how he brought me fairy flowers that first time, and once an American book about film stars, even a magazine with photos of Elizabeth Taylor's wedding. And the whole time, I only grunted a thank you and treated him like a New Australian with no feelings.

As soon as Mum puts down the axe, I climb down from the gate and help stack the wood.

On her day off, Mum meets me after school in Muswell for a dentist's appointment, then we catch the train home. Hannigan is waiting on the platform when we get in. He's waiting for Mrs Hannigan but as soon as he sees us, he comes running.

'I'm sorry, Nella,' he puffs, 'but I'm going to have to let you go.' Puff. 'I don't really need you.' Puff. 'Anymore.' And he repeats himself without so much puffing. 'There's no work, Nella. Not anymore.'

Shock makes Mum stupid, me too. 'The oil?' says Mum.

He glances behind and sees Mrs Hannigan walking towards us, and now his voice is pleading, wheedling. 'You'd be better off back in the city, wouldn't you, Nella?'

That's what Grannie said. Mum's shoulders slump and suddenly I know what it means to have the stuffing knocked out of you. But she straightens quickly and eyeballs Hannigan; she doesn't say anything, but she doesn't have to.

Hannigan starts to squirm. 'I'll give you a good reference,' he says as Mum stalks off.

At home, Bertie has had her kittens, four tiny blind bundles, mewing and crying and climbing all over her on a pile of bloodied newspapers under the wash troughs in the dunny shed. I replace the papers with an old towel and Bertie immediately cleans every kitten. They're mostly ginger like Bertie but some are black, and one is a lovely tabby brindle. I'm glad there are only four because I've already found homes for two, and promised Mrs Marciano one for Tania for her third birthday at the end of December, so now I'll only have to find one more.

I sit on the floor, watching Bertie with her babies, fussy and busy one minute, sprawled out proudly the next while they suckle greedily. I tickle her behind her ears and she purrs happily. 'Clever girl,' I tell her, 'very clever mother girl.'

'Was it Grannie?' I ask Mum later. 'Did she say something to Mr Hannigan?' And thinking out loud: 'But why would she?'

Mum listens to the six o'clock news right through as if I haven't spoken—someone murdered on a farm, Margaret Smith winning the tennis somewhere, trouble in a mine somewhere. After the weather, she pours hot water into the sink. 'Because,' she says, as if I've only just asked, 'the Old Girl doesn't want someone with the same name as her cleaning houses and hotels. Because people might remember that's how she met Black Pat. And because she's never forgiven me for divorcing your father. She thinks I should have stuck it out...'

She washes one plate over and over. I want to tell her to stop. I want to ask if there's enough money to buy my marching-girl boots for the team that's just started in Burley Point. But she keeps

247

on washing and washing that plate, and I don't know how to stop her.

That night I'm reading in bed when there's a bump on the window and a loud scratching on the sill, making me jerk up in fright. I pull back the curtain to find Bertie balancing there with a kitten in her mouth, the brindle one I've chosen for Tania. As soon as I ease open the louvres, she leaves her baby and leaps down from the ledge. In no time, she's back with another baby in her mouth, and another, until all four are mewing and complaining on the bed. It's only then that she squeezes through the bottom louvre herself, fussing and desperate to sort out the whole furry mess of them.

Of course, Mum hears them crying and comes rushing in from the kitchen. 'They're not staying here,' she says, and straightaway bundles them in her apron and carries them outside, with Bert running beside her, crying pitifully. 'Filthy thing,' says Mum when she returns. 'What's she think she's doing?'

She thinks her babies should be inside, that's what she thinks, because Mum's hardly back in the kitchen before Bertie's on the sill again. This time I try to get the kittens inside quietly, hiding them under the quilt to muffle their mewing. But when Bertie arrives with the last one, she's so frantic that, before I can show her where they're hidden, she yowls like a cat banshee and Mum rushes in again.

When she sees them under the quilt, she practically screeches. 'I've got to sleep in that bed!'

'She's licked them all clean. We could put them in the spare room. I can make up a bed. Just for tonight.'

But before I can stop her, Mum bundles them back to the shed. This time she locks them in. I think I hate her then. I turn off the light and lie close to the window edge of the bed. My eyes are dry with tears of fury. Why can't I fight her? Why do my bones feel so heavy? And the hard lump in my chest getting bigger.

Next morning, when I go to the dunny, Mum is up before me, blocking the door, pulling it closed. 'Don't go in there,' she says.

'I need to pee!'

She tells me to do it on the nasturtiums where she empties the dunny can. That's when I see her pasty face, the way her eyes shuffle and shift. There's a sick hammering in my chest and I push past, knocking her shoulder, not caring.

Bertie's not under the troughs. No kittens, no sound. As my eyes adjust to the gloom, I see blood on the floor, a tiny foot, a kitten tail. Her voice behind me. 'I'm sorry.'

The kittens are dead. Eaten by rats in the shed.

'Bertie...?'

'She ran out...the lagoon.'

From a long way off, I hear her saying Bertie was a stray and strays are better off in the wild. It couldn't be helped, she is saying. I can get another cat.

I have been here before. It is a dream, a flash of half-remembered things, blood on a floor, a wall? I walk past her on robot legs. I get dressed and eat my cardboard breakfast. I walk down the drive and into the tea-tree with a thought walking beside me like a friend: I will punish her forever with the silence of my hate.

It is late August and the trees are still speckled with honey-white snow, the boobiallas and wattles blooming gold. All day, I hear myself calling, *Bertie! Bertie!* Birds chirrup and squawk. A stray flashes out of a bush, black with a patch of white, not her. All day I follow around the lagoon in a dream, searching in the stunted bushes near the tennis court, in the dense trees on my father's side, near the dunes where the scrub is thick and tangled. *Bertie! Bertie!*

By late afternoon, the dream is a fog rolling in from the sea, clinging and cold. I sneak into our yard and climb the kurrajong tree. I wait until she's screaming herself hoarse at the back door, not even bothering to look up the tree. I wait until it's dark and the spoggies have squeaked and settled around me, as if I'm a big bird roosting amongst them. Then I slide down the tree.

She turns from the stove. 'I've been worried sick about you.'

My stomach is heaving with hunger but I refuse to speak, or eat. In bed, I remember the warm smell of kittens and I think about killing myself. I wonder how I can do it without it hurting too much, and how she'll feel when I do.

Next day after school, she wants me to take a note to Grannie. I refuse and she looks like she's going to slap me.

Go on, I say with my eyes. Do it. Do it.

Her shoulders fold onto her chest and she asks me how much money I've saved from my babysitting, and can she borrow it?

I count it out on the kitchen table. I count it out slowly, making her suffer.

When I arrive, Mrs Marciano asks what's wrong. Nothing, I tell her in the fake happy voice I've been using for the past three days. After our walk, I leave Tania with Joe on the swing he's made for her in the backyard and, although I try to make a quick getaway, Mrs Marciano follows me down the drive, calling out that she's made coconut ice, would I like some before I go, reminding me that I'm leaving without my money.

I don't intend to say it—not then, not until I know exactly how I'll tell her—but as I'm nearing the gate, it blurts out of me. 'There won't be a kitten for Tania's birthday. They died. All of them.' Then the lie. 'They were stillborn.'

'That's awful, Sylvie. I'm so sorry.'

'Bertie's gone too,' I say stiffly. 'Back to the bush.'

'Poor little Bertie. Her first litter, wasn't it?'

'It was my fault,' I say quickly, not looking. 'I should have'—*Kept her in the bed. Got her out of the shed* —'looked after her. Better.'

'That's probably not true,' she says, pressing coins into my hand. 'Not everything is our fault.'

Her words make me look up, but she is gazing back at Tania strapped onto her swing, at Joe pushing her higher and higher. 'We'll get Tarnie a kitten from somewhere,' she says. 'It's the least of our worries.'

I walk home, trying not to hear kittens crying. Trying not to think of rats and cats and mice and mousey me. Yes, mousey me. I should have made her leave Bertie inside with her kittens. Made her. Made her!

Fake tan and short skirts. Kenny and his mates parked near the goal posts having a good gawk. Thumbs on wrists. Left, right, left, right. I'm not sure I even want to be a marching girl; I can't think why I let Lizzie persuade me. And while everyone's stepping out in new white boots, I'm strutting around in my school shoes with Faye out front, whistle stuck in her mouth, blasting out turns and *atten-shuns* like a sergeant-major.

Afterwards, Denver asks if I'll have my boots in time for the Muswell Pageant. I tell him they're coming.

When I get home, the power has been cut off because Mum hasn't paid the bill. Again there's toast and tomato sauce for tea. We've only just begun eating when there's a loud knock at the door. 'Ssshhh.' Mum pinches out the candle flame and creeps to the blind. 'Denver Boland,' she whispers. 'What's he want?'

Another loud knock. And another. He knows we're inside. He can see the smoke from the chimney; he can hear our breathing. His knocking seems to shake the house on its hinges. 'Damn,' says Mum. She flounces to the door and Denver almost falls into the kitchen, fist raised for another good knock. 'I've had the power cut off,' she says. 'That's why Sylvie hasn't got her boots.'

Denver's neck pokes about like a tortoise. 'Why didn't you say things were this bad, Nella?' He looks at me and lowers his voice. 'What about Mick…?'

'Hasn't paid a thing in three years.'

'I'll take care of the boots,' says Denver.

'It's work I need,' says Mum, sounding ungrateful, 'not boots.' Denver opens his mouth but Mum gets in first. 'I've tried the butter factory at Rendelsham. The fish factory. There's no work anywhere.'

Denver says it's the credit squeeze, businesses going bust every-where. He says oil's the answer; they're pumping it from Moonie to Brisbane, why not here? If they hit the jackpot it'll bring back the glory days when the train came every day, wool lined the wharf and ships called twice a week.

I can see Mum doesn't want a history lesson. She eases the door closed.

Next day, the power is reconnected. Again we're having toast and tomato sauce for tea. Again there's a loud knock on the door. This time Denver is carrying a large cardboard box and he has Mousie Tibbet standing behind him with more boxes.

'Got a bit of a surprise, Nella,' says Denver, and before Mum can ask them to take off their shoes, they're at the table emptying out Lions Club Christmas cakes, IXL jam, tins of Camp Pie, Lipton's tea, Arnott's assorted biscuits. And a big red bottle of White Crow tomato sauce.

Denver looks pleased with himself, as if he's the hungry one who's just had a good feed. 'That'll keep you going for a while.'

Mum stares at the sauce for a long time, too long. Doesn't she know she's meant to say thank you? Eventually she does. 'Thank you,' she says. Once.

Denver and Mousie look as if they're expecting more. To make up for Mum, I smile at Mousie and try to look grateful. Denver says: 'Anything you want, Nella, anything at all, don't be too proud to ask.'

When they'd gone, Mum puts the food away quickly, hides it out of sight in the cupboards. Then she takes out her tin of Wunderwax and rubs polish into the lino where Denver and Mousie have stood. From the fury of her polishing, I know she's thinking the same as me: *I'd rather eat toast and tomato sauce. I'd rather starve.*

She's making toast on top of the stove.

'You said you'd go.'

'I can't.'

'I'm getting two prizes. No one else is.'

'I'm not feeling well.' She spreads the toast with scrapes of butter that melt in straightaway.

'You don't look sick. Where are you sick?' But even as I say it, her face turns an oily white. She slides my plate across the table. We've eaten all of Denver's food and it's toast and tomato sauce again. If she won't go, I won't eat. I slide the plate back. And I won't beg. In the bedroom, I tie a perfect Windsor knot and I leave for Lizzie's house without another word.

Rattling along the Rendelsham road, I catch Mrs Winkie watching me in the rear-view mirror, pretending she isn't. Soon darkness creeps inside the car and makes me numb: I'm the fish-factory freezer with the door closed tight. The pine plantations near Muswell are black walls against the night sky and soon we're driving through the outskirts of town, porch lights, street lights, car lights.

People are milling in the town hall foyer. Faye's mother. Roy's mother and father. Even Chicken's grandma has come to see him win the footy prize. We sit with our class in the front rows, parents behind. The choir sings 'Michael Row Your Boat Ashore'. The head-master's speech is boring and long. When the prizes are presented, I manage to get onto the stage without falling over my feet.

I've chosen *The Complete Works of Wordsworth* and *I, the Aboriginal*. An excellent choice, said Mrs Truman when I returned from Ivy's Books and told her what I'd selected. Seated again, I open the covers and read:

Sylvie Meehan, Dux of 3A.

Sylvie Meehan, Intermediate English Prize.

When I glance up, Mrs Truman is smiling proudly at me from the steps near the stage, but I can tell from the look in her eyes that she knows there's no one there to see me receive my prizes. I open *Wordsworth* and read a line over and over: *Her eyes are wild, her head is bare / The sun has burnt her coal-black hair...*

'Your mother would be very proud of you,' says Mrs Winkie on the way home. 'It's a shame she couldn't come.'

Her eyes are wild, her head is bare / The sun has burnt....

In Burley Point, the sky is black with no stars and only a smudge of moon behind cloud. Mrs Winkie drops me at our side gate. As she drives off, the clouds move, exposing a full yellow moon that shines on the lagoon like a lantern. But the clouds are fast moving and, as I walk down the path, the moon fades, leaving a strange glow on the surface as if the moon has disappeared under water.

I sit on the step in the darkness for a long time, holding my books to my chest, hoping she's lying in bed worrying about me. But of course I get too cold and have to go inside. And although I thump around in the dark, although I tread on her legs as I climb into bed, she doesn't really wake up. Yet still she reaches over. I wriggle away and try to throw off her arms, but in the end—because I'm cold—because it's easier—I change my shape to fit hers and let her cuddle me to sleep.

*

A few days later, a strange thing happens as I'm walking past my old school. It's a steamy hot afternoon with cicadas shrilling all down the street. A sudden gust of wind slaps them into silence. As if he's right there beside me, I hear Dunc saying they've been stuck underground for anything up to twenty years and wouldn't you sing up a storm if you were finally free?

I lean on the school fence and my eyes travel from the big old red brick building to the shelter shed and tennis court, the basket-ball hoops. And suddenly there's a memory of running across the playground on another hot day, perhaps in my first year of school. I feel myself falling, sprawling, the softened asphalt oozing black beneath my hands. And as clearly as if it was happening before me, I see Dunc hurrying to help me up. 'You're all right,' he says before running off with Pardie.

The cicadas start up again in ear-splitting splendour. But something is different. And after a while, I realise what it is: I'm not waiting for Dunc to come home anymore. He is right here with me.

After Christmas, Roy's cousin comes from the city. Phil has long arms, horrible sunburn and terrible pimples. He looks like a Daddy-long-legs, spotty and scabby. He says he went to the Beatles concert and next day had the best possie outside their hotel, right behind a cop. When they ran for their car, he reached out and touched George. *With this finger*, he says, holding it up like a prize, *this very finger*.

Walking home from the beach with Roy and me, he sees my father's jeep parked outside the post office. 'Is it for real?' he asks and he's off, half-running, half-hopping, trying to stay in the shade of the pines so the soles of his feet won't burn. It's a scorcher. When we catch up, he's sliding his hand along the bonnet, practically drooling. 'It's in really good nick. You know whose it is?'

I'm about to tell him when I see my father standing just inside the post office door, his back to the street, Uncle Ticker facing him. Dad is half a head taller than Uncle Ticker and, although my father is older, Uncle Ticker has more grey hair. At first I think he's talking to Uncle Ticker and I'm so surprised I just goggle. Then I realise Dad is deliberately blocking Uncle Ticker's path, and Uncle Ticker is deliberately blocking his: it's a stand-off. Dad's not shifting, and Uncle Ticker's not shifting either.

Behind Uncle Ticker's head, the big black hands of the post office clock are pointing to one twenty-three. Mrs Patchett hesitates on the steps as she enters: everyone knows Dad and Uncle Ticker haven't spoken for years. I cringe behind the telephone booth, my face hot and hurting. And now my father leans in close and says something that makes Uncle Ticker's eyes flit around as if he's afraid someone might hear. Suddenly, unexpectedly, Uncle Ticker steps aside and Dad pushes into the post office as if he's just won the lottery.

Uncle Ticker crosses the street and climbs into the Bindilla truck. Dad returns to the door and yells after him, 'Done the dirty on anyone lately? Ya gotta be family for that?'

When I look back, Dad's face is puffed up and purple. It's the first time I've seen him since the day at the church and I can't believe his splotchy cheeks and pocky nose. 'Keep your pimply fingers off that!' he bellows at Phil before disappearing inside.

When he comes out a few minutes later, Roy is trying to drag

Phil away from the jeep. 'Is it for real?' asks Phil again, staring at Dad.

Dad drops a parcel onto the front seat. 'It's not bloody plastic, if that's what you mean.'

Back at the mailboxes, he stabs his key into a box and bends to peer inside. 'Ya finished sorting?' he yells into the opening. After a moment, he slams the box closed and wrestles with the key, pulling and jiggling. Suddenly he stops and curls against the wall, his head on his chest. Roy looks at me as if I should know what to do. I shrug like I'm not embarrassed out of my mind.

'You okay, Mr Meehan?' says Roy, stepping closer.

'Course I'm bloody okay.' He eases up, his voice thin and reedy.

'You don't look okay,' says Roy.

'Mind ya own business.' Turning back to the box, he reaches for the key and begins jiggling again. 'De-e-e-ell! How many times have I told you this lock needs oiling? How many bloody times?'

He's still hanging off the key when Dippy Dell appears at the door. She's called Dippy because even before you've asked a question, she nods; even if the answer is no, she nods. When she sees Dad at the mailbox, her head threatens to nod right off her neck.

'Some of them are a bit temperamental, Mick, it's best not to…'

'Tempra—bloody—mental! It's needed fixing for months.' He steps back unsteadily. 'Go on. You get it out.'

Dell steps around him as if he might bite. Reaching up, she gives the key a delicate wiggle and it comes free, easy as that. Without a word, Dad takes it. His face is grey and sweaty and he leans against the wall, breathing heavily. Dell's head dips furiously. 'You…you don't look well, Mick. Would you like me to…to telephone Layle?'

'What for?' He pushes off from the wall. 'Get the lock oiled before tomorrow or I'll do it myself.'

Phil is still at the jeep, stroking the metal rail behind the passenger seat. 'Did you get it in the war?'

I'm afraid Dad will blast him right off the street. 'Afterwards,' he says, climbing in. 'They were selling 'em off cheap.'

'It's in good nick.'

'Doesn't get much use, driving around here.' He turns on the motor and raises his voice above the roar. 'Maybe take ya for a spin. If I get time. If I don't cark it.'

22

'Why do I have to go? Why didn't you tell me before?'

'Because I didn't,' says Mum.

What sort of answer is that? We're on the way to the Mount *to sue the pants off* my father. As the train crosses Stickynet, we see the *Henrietta* bobbing about on her mooring and we watch it slide out of sight.

In the court house in Muswell, I'm the star exhibit, which I only discover when Barry Hodge, who left school a year ago and now works in the court, announces in a voice that's loud enough to be heard on the street: *Meehan versus Meehan.*

After Mr Drewe, Mum's solicitor, tells the whole world about our case, he nods at me to stand. 'The young lady in question is in court today. She is fifteen years of age and excels at the local high school where she is in Form Three. If she is able to stay at school, she has potentially a very bright future. Mrs Meehan submits that her daughter should not be denied such opportunities as can be provided by a father's support.'

A blur of faces peer at my potential. My neck prickles and I want to fall through a hole in the floor and never be seen again. At least my father is not looking at me: he's sitting at a table on the other side of the aisle, examining his hands. Outside the court, I did my best not to look at him. I tried not to see that the pants we were suing him for were baggy at the knees. That he looked thin and worn. As if I cared.

The magistrate tells me to sit. 'And who's representing Mr Meehan?'

'I am,' says my father.

'I am, Your Worship.'

My father grins. 'You are?'

A murmur runs around the room. 'No, Mr Meehan,' says the magistrate, 'I'm not. But I am *Your Worship*, so if you're presenting your own case, you'll address me accordingly. Stand, please.'

My father stands and leans on the table. Referring to a paper, the magistrate tells him that nine years ago when the court set maintenance payments, he had an inheritance of thirteen thousand pounds and an income, from operating a fishing trawler, of two thousand pounds per annum. Has anything changed?

'Plenty,' says my father. He had money put aside, he tells the magistrate, but things have gone bad and he's had to sell his boat and he has no way of paying anything to anyone right now.

'We've just seen it,' mutters Mum. 'How could he have sold it?'

'The best I can do is pay what I can if there's anything left over when the bloke from Port Lincoln coughs up.'

The magistrate says he's not interested in who coughs up what as long as my father pays a substantial amount of the arrears by— he looks at a page and chooses the third of February—and that regular payments are maintained thereafter. Case adjourned for a period of two months. Next matter, please.

Back in the street, Mr Drewe tells Mum he'll follow up with a letter. 'You're a bloody dill,' says Dad, barrelling out of the court house, 'if you think you can get blood out of a stone.'

Mr Drewe ignores him and shakes Mum's hand, mine too. When he leaves, Mum looks around helplessly. She has eaten off her lipstick and her lips are blue beneath. Winds off the farming flats whip along the street, snapping at our skirts, flapping the Christmas decorations already on shopfronts and telegraph poles. Suddenly she walks off and I'm forced to run after her, darting around people on the pavement, catching up outside the Farmer's Emporium where she's staring at wheelbarrows in the window.

'Why'd you just take off like that?'

She still doesn't answer. The window is full of flickering television sets all showing a man and four women at a big desk. One of the women says a man's entitled to put up his feet when he arrives home from work. The others laugh and squeal and the man tells them they're a bunch of drongos.

'Why did he sell his boat?' I ask.

When she turns, her face is bitter white: 'For the same reason he burned the house down. Because he'd do anything to get out of paying me a penny. Because he can't tell the difference between me and you. And because he doesn't care tuppence about you.'

Elvis cares tuppence, ten shillings, ten pounds. Two days later he slows on Lagoon Road and waits up ahead, motor humming. I walk towards him on jelly legs. 'Sorry about your brother,' he says and I notice the way he looks at me, hesitant, kindly. 'Didn't know it was him...you know...'

I blush and look away and think: *What is wrong with me?*

'I finish night shift Friday,' he says, and when I look back I can see the kindness is mixed up with something different, maybe the same kind of wanting as me. 'Got the weekend off,' he says. 'Saturday, we could go for a drive to West End. Whaddya reckon?'

I reckon the moon is mine.

Four o'clock at the jetty he said and already he's ten minutes late. I watch shapes rippling in the shallows below and try not to feel as if the whole world knows I'm waiting for him. A ute turns at the roundabout, slowly, taking its time, but it's only someone from out of town who drives by in low gear without even glancing at me. What if he doesn't come?

Kelp on the legs of the jetty drifts and clings with the tide, strong and free like I want to be. On the sea wall, a cormorant spreads out its wings to dry and studies me with a beady eye as if it knows I've been stood up. I'm thinking maybe it would be better to leave than be stood up, when Chicken skids onto the jetty in a spray of pebbles and dust.

'Whaddya doin'? Wanna go for a ride?'

Right then I hear Elvis throbbing down Main Street. By the time he rumbles to a stop at the jetty I'm standing by the side of the road, trying to act as if I've never met Chicken before in my life, pretending I can't see him gaping after the car as we drive off, tyre rubber screaming. Of course he'll tell Roy.

Thumping over Stickynet, Elvis nods at the rig. 'Close to findin' it. Down to three thousand feet. Soon know if it's there or not.' He grins. 'Didn't say that. Had to sign a clause sayin' I wouldn't. Between you and me.'

Between Elvis and me, there's a wide empty seat. 'Whaddya

doing way over there?' He pats the seat and I slide over timidly. He pulls me closer, tucks me right under his arm as if I'm a cushion.

He's changed his hair: he's lost the hair oil and curl; now he's all soft and shaggy. Elvis suited him better: he's too big to be a Beatle; he looks sort of silly. Chewing on a wad of Juicy Fruit, the wrapper there on the dash, he looks like Will Pickles from Coomandook. Suddenly I get a scared little lump in my throat and when he slows on a corner, I have a flash of opening the door and jumping out, but it's only a tiny lump that I force myself to swallow like medicine. Reaching across me, he turns up the wireless and taps a few beats on my arm with his fingers. The Beach Boys. *I get around, round, round, round…* Then he lifts my hand onto his knee and I tap a few beats on his leg too, like I know what I'm doing, which I don't. So I make myself sink back in the seat, trying to get calm. And I close my eyes for a second but maybe it's longer because when I open them, we've passed the turn-off and settled to a steady speed.

'You hear Pardie Pansy's been back?'

Pansy? 'Pardie Moon?'

His hand drops from my arm to my knee. 'They reckon he took off with that relief teacher. Someone Allen?' His fingers climb up my leg, tickling, prickling, a million ants on a mission. 'Heard Kenny and his mates really did him over for being a pansy before he left.' Pardie's face before mine, his panic to leave. The Four Seasons… *bi-i-ig girls don't cry-y-y…* Now his fingers at the leg of my shorts, poking, prying, my heart suddenly thumping too hard. 'Wouldn't be him if his marble comes up. Wouldn't be me, neither. Who wants to fight slanty eyes?' Suddenly his hand's back on the wheel, changing gears. 'I know a good place up here.'

264

I take a huge silent breath and let it out slowly. I see Pardie's face all battered and bleeding and have to force him out of the window. We're on a narrow track, overgrown with banksias and bracken that scratch at the car as we ram through. On a sharp corner, I'm lifted half-off the seat, thrown high and down again. Will laughs a silly-boy chortle, the sort I'd expect from Chicken or Roy. Further in we stop in a clearing full of casuarinas and she-oaks, dapples of sun trapped in the shade underneath.

The engine ticks into silence. He opens his window and lets the world in. I slide across the seat and do the same. The scent of she-oaks, dry and sweet, and far off the sound of surf running. 'Ya know who owns this land?' He reaches under and slides the seat back. And when I shake my head: 'Your Uncle Ticker.'

So? He sits there looking all pleased with himself. For the first time I notice his leg jiggling on the edge of the seat, and I wonder if he's as nervous as me, but why should he be?

The seat is warm and sticky under my legs and Will is looking at me with his blue Elvis eyes, but all at once I can't tell if he's Elvis or Will Pickles, or some kind of big Beatle. And I get this odd feeling that he's not really seeing me either, that somehow he's muddled me up with Uncle Ticker, and having a Meehan in his ute is some kind of prize, like finding a fiver. But how could I be any kind of prize for anyone?

He takes out his gum and sticks it on the dash. A shaft of light catches his cheek and he looks suddenly young, like a boy, like Roy, and I wonder if he's got a sister, if she's older than him, or younger? Could she be the same age as me? But maybe all this thinking is a way to stop wondering about what happens next, what if I don't want it, not really, and how will I know what to do?

Suddenly he's leaning over and I'm leaning back and I'm lost in his lips, sugary sweet, and now I can't think of anything except how different his kisses are from Roy's little kisses, how hungry and dizzy and drowning. I'm slipping down on the seat and again there's that scared little lump in my throat that might be a scream, but that is crazy because the rest of me is tingling all over, every bit of me burning up with the taste of him. And somehow he's unzipping my shorts and, although I try to wriggle out from under his weight, I don't try very hard, that's the thing; part of me wants to tell him to stop, but I don't want to do that either, not really. And all through the pushing and pain, I know he wants me; he wants me that much. And when he lets out a shuddering groan, almost a cry, a whimper, I'm so surprised and happy that a whimper rises up in me too and I want to hold on to him forever and never let go.

But straightaway he's clambering out the car door, and when I pull myself up, he's standing under a she-oak, wiping himself with a handkerchief. My fingers find blood on the seat, a smell like squashed tadpoles. A great empty hole seems to have opened up in my belly, then a rush of anger that has nowhere to go except out the window with Pardie, with everything lost and gone.

The sea behind the dunes is running, running, shadows swelling beneath the she-oaks, finches bickering. I watch him turn and zip up. Back at the car, he angles his head at the side mirror and combs his new hair. 'Bloody hell,' he says, checking his watch, 'ya know what time it is?'

After we drive off, I wait for him to reach out and tuck me under his arm like he did before, but we're back on the main road, he's humming under his breath and he still hasn't looked at me, not once. In the corner against the door, I clasp my arms across my chest to keep warm. I think of Pardie being with Dunc at the lake and wonder why I haven't told anyone. I think: Everything hurts too much. And suddenly I hate the way Will Pickles sings under his breath, the shape of his ears. When he leans over to twiddle the radio, the Seekers singing...*a new world somewhere*...I think: I didn't know it would be like this. I thought he wanted me. *Me.* Then a rush of other thoughts: Does anyone get what they want? But what do I want? Not Will Pickles, that's for sure. If he doesn't want me, I don't want him. I hope his marble comes up and he has to do National Service, and if they send conscripts to Vietnam and he's one of them, I won't even care.

It's dark when we thump over Stickynet. Lights from the oil site bleed into the lake, red, yellow, green. 'Wonder what's up?' The first words he's spoken. 'Might drop you off and take a geezer.'

As we turn at the roundabout, I see lights in the Institute, Mr Stevens setting up for the Saturday night dance. I slide down in my seat and stay there until we stop.

At first I don't see Bill Morgan's car at our gate. 'Shit,' says Will. 'What's he doing here?' His mouth works overtime on a new wad of gum. 'Better not tell anyone,' he says, leaning over to open my door.

'What's there to tell?' I slam the door hard on his scaredy white face and watch as he drives off, tail-lights winking around the lagoon like a red-eyed fox before disappearing at the corner.

Why is Bill Morgan here? I smooth down my shorts and try to tidy my hair. What could have happened? And then I think: I'm only a couple of hours late: she wouldn't, would she? I wipe at my lips and rub at the whiskery roughness on my cheeks. Do I smell of him?

267

Bill Morgan is at our table drinking tea. Mrs Winkie. Lizzie too. All squashed into our kitchen with Mum standing by the stove. When I walk in, her eyes shoot about as if they're loose on their stalks and I'm hardly in the door before she pushes forward. 'Where have you been?'

'For a drive.'

'Who with?'

'No one you know.'

Her face is flat and furious. She looks as if she's going to hit me but Bill Morgan moves between us. He's not wearing his uniform and I realise I'm almost as tall as him. 'Now, Sylvie,' he says in his sensitive cop voice, 'things are tough enough for your mother without you doing a disappearing act. Got enough on her plate, wouldn't you say?'

They all stare at me and I stare right back. Mrs Winkie is the only one with anything near kindness in her eyes. It makes me think she knows exactly what I've been doing and, for the first time, I wonder what things she did as a girl. 'You sure you're all right, Sylvie?'

But Mum jumps right in. 'Where've you been? Answer me! You think you can just come and go as you please. You think—'

Whatever I'm meant to think, it's interrupted by the foghorn, winding up like a windy gale, howling all over town, louder and louder, wailing a warning to ships lost in fog. Except there is no fog.

'What's set that off?' Bill Morgan pushes around Mrs Winkie to get to the door. 'Sorry, Nella. I'll have to leave you to it.'

Mum looks short-changed. Bill Morgan's footsteps disappear down the drive to the sound of the foghorn wailing and wailing.

But Mum's eyes are stuck on me as if there is no one else is in the room.

'Come on, Lizzie.' Mrs Winkie pushes back her chair and whispers to me as she passes at the door. 'Keep yourself for someone special, Sylvie. That's what I tell Lizzie.'

Mum waits until the side gate clicks closed then she comes at me. 'You're fifteen!' she screams. 'Barely fifteen!' Then she's hitting at me with wild, spinning arms. 'After all I've done for you.' Hitting me about the head, ears, face, neck, shoulders, arms, anywhere, everywhere. 'Who do you think you are?' *Hit. Hit.* 'You ungrateful.' *Hit.* 'Selfish.' *Hit.* 'Brat.' *Hit. Hit.* 'After giving up my whole life.' *Hit. Hit.* 'For you.' *Hit.* 'Putting.' *Hit.* 'You.' *Hit. Hit.* 'Before.' *Hit.* 'Everything.' *Hit. Hit.*

At first I hold up my arms to ward off her blows but she has a crazy mad look in her eyes that makes me feel half-crazy too. 'Don't hit me!' I yell. 'Don't. Hit. Me.' Our arms spin like windmills and I hit so hard that I can hardly feel where she's hitting me. I hit and hit but she keeps slapping and whacking until our arms are all tangled up in an embrace of rage and hate so huge that all I want to do is hit her and hit her and hurt her. For the dirty word divorce. For not being my father. For not being Dunc. For blaming me. For Pardie leaving. For Will Pickles not being Elvis. For him not wanting me. For the kittens the kittens the kittens. *For all she's done for me.* For *putting me before everything.* For sleeping with me. Smothering me. Not seeing me. And I hit and hit and hit until she stops. Then I stop too.

She leans over the table, shoulders shaking. The foghorn has stopped too and there's only the sound of our breathing, loud and uneven. Her hair is all messed up and I can see the scar on her skull, tiny and white. I wait for her to turn, to say something—anything—but she doesn't.

In the spare room, I pull back the bedspread and make up the single bed.

23

Burley Point has been partying. All down Main Street, balloons are bunched on telephone poles; coloured streamers litter the path outside the Institute and hundreds more are draped on top of the Christmas decorations on the roundabout pine. There's a white cowboy hat on the rotunda roof, and someone's pants are tied to the top of the flagpole, fat legs filled with a stiff breeze.

I prop on my bike and look over the bay. Everything seems the same. The usual Sunday morning quiet. A whisper of pink on the horizon. All the boats out. A few kids in the playground. Lanky Evans on the steps of his van in the caravan park. Yet something is different.

Me. I'm different. And Mum? The way she couldn't look at me, the flash of disgust in her eyes as she grunted: *Take this. Get me the* Sunday Mail *and a bottle of milk.*

Please? Of course, I didn't say it.

Pedalling around the lagoon, I tried not to feel the shame between my legs. Now I wonder: *What if I'm pregnant?* It can happen the first time, everyone says. I'd have to leave school. I'd have to get married. Would I want to marry him? Would I have a choice? But would he marry me? I keep getting lost in the questions. Then Roy is skidding to a stop next to me, wheels gouging grass.

'What happened to you?'

His eyes are innocent, interested, as if he doesn't know about me and Will Pickles. But he must. Surely Chicken would have told the whole town.

'Whaddya mean?'

'Last night.' Surely Will wouldn't have? Or would he? Roy smiles at me like he did in First Form when he knew a Latin verb that I didn't, the same dimply grin. 'You don't know?'

Perhaps he doesn't know?

'Didn't you hear the foghorn last night? They found oil, drongo. You missed the best party.' He lumps the front wheel of his bike around until he's facing the fish factory. 'I'm heading out to Big Tree, want to take a look?'

The siren? Not a fog warning. Not a false alarm. Red lights on the drill site: it all fits in. And, of course that's the difference: no thump of drill hitting rock.

Roy is already riding off when I tell him I'll take the milk home and meet him at the bridge if he'll wait. And then I fly along streets like a winged beast instead of a common hussy who has gone all the way with Will Pickles and might become pregnant. I pedal faster than I've ever pedalled before; the breeze slurps down my throat; my thigh muscles stretch like lacker bands ready to snap.

Mum is having a smoke on the back step.

'They've found oil. Last night. That's what the foghorn was all about.'

She looks at me for a second, surprised, as if she's forgotten we're not speaking.

'I'm going out to the turn-off.' She looks away quickly, stubs

272

out her butt, and doesn't even reply. As she disappears into the washhouse, my face burns hot. I want to race after her. I want to hit her—hit, hit, hit—like I did last night, like she hit me. But straightaway the crazy mad feeling leaves me and my stomach aches with a kind of empty shame. And the whole way to Stickynet, I try to pedal faster, faster, faster, to find the rage again.

Lizzie is waiting with Chicken and Roy. It's as if she's afraid to look at me, and I'm careful about looking at her.

If I'd expected oil to be gushing into the air and showering everything around, I'm disappointed. The lake is silvery bright in the morning sun and it's hard to see the rig on the other side: there's no burning flame, just greenish black smoke rising off to one side like rubber tyres burning, the same sharp smell.

'It fountained out last night,' says Chicken. 'Now they've capped it. I'm gunna leave school and get a job here.'

I watch Chicken carefully, wary of how he might treat me, but he's leaning on the bridge, drooling over the rig, not even bothering about me. 'So what happens now?'

'Your uncle gets rich,' says Roy as they climb on their bikes. 'Bet your old man wished he still owned it.'

Lizzie and I follow down the road. 'So where did you go?' she asks as the silence between us grows. 'What were you doing?' But before I can even open my mouth, she tells me how much I missed: that everyone—except us—went to see why the foghorn was wailing. That everyone—except us—joined the people at the dance and had a party in the street. That cars drove around town sounding their horns, and didn't I hear? And Chicken was drinking beer and threw up behind the cafe hedge. Then: 'So where were you?'

'With Will Pickles.'

Her front wheel veers off the road. 'Where?'

'West End.'

'And…?' She wobbles back.

Should I tell her? For a while I watch Chicken and Roy, now far ahead. Soon the silence speaks for me and she squeals: 'You didn't?'

Let her guess. And she does. A guess so momentous that she stares at me as if I've grown devil horns. 'How far did you go?'

Behind her head, a yellow vehicle crosses Stickynet and shapes into the council grader, coming closer, growing louder. We push to the side of the road. 'Five? Six?'

It's my father on the grader. *A Meehan working on the roads,* said Mum when she first heard he had a job with the council. *How the mighty have fallen. And what does the Queen Bee think about that?*

'Eight?' says Lizzie, her voice rising in disbelief.

I can't remember whether eight is letting them see your breasts or touching you down below, but the grader is barrelling down the road, smoke pouring from its stack and, before I can reply, Lizzie squeaks: 'Not ten? You didn't, did you? Not ten?'

For a moment, our eyes meet. I feel suddenly old. And Lizzie seems shocked and suddenly young, like the girl I was before I went to West End with Will Pickles. I wish I could be just like her again. But the grader is almost on top of us and the roar so loud that we both turn to watch as it hurtles past. From his throne above the road, my father waves. My head wrenches around in surprise. It was just a little wave—nothing special—a finger lifted off the wheel the way people do when they're driving. Straightaway

I tell myself I must have been mistaken. But as the grader passes, I hear a shout almost drowned out by the engine. *What did he say?* I glance at Lizzie but she's still looking at me as if I'm an alien with two heads and she doesn't seem to have heard. Anyway, what could he have to say to me? Except, *Get out of the way.* I stare after the grader until it disappears around the next corner and only the sound of its full-throttled whine lingers behind.

Lizzie doesn't linger. 'Well,' she says as she pushes her bike onto the road, 'you missed everything.' And without looking back, she pedals towards town, leaving me there like a leper.

I open my mouth to call her back, but then I close it again and watch her backside swivelling from side to side as she stands on the pedals and rides away fast. I'm glad I didn't really tell her about Will, glad I made her guess and, as I ride on, I have a big long argument with her in my head where she tells the whole world about me going to ten with Will and I accuse her of lying, of being jealous, of wanting him for herself. I say terrible things about her and, with every push on the pedals, I grind her into the ground.

The road shimmers into water far ahead with Big Tree pointing bare arms into the sky like a giant signpost. Riding towards it, I feel like a dot caught on a road between sea and land. Between Lizzie riding home and me riding away. Between Mum and me in separate beds. Between wanting Elvis and not wanting Will. Between growing up or not. That almost makes me stop. Do I have a choice?

By the time I arrive at the turn-off, Chicken and Roy have disappeared. I can't be bothered following them; no one is going to let them near the oil site, and I don't want to run into Will either. Then, hearing the sound of the grader further down the lane, I decide to ride on. Topping the rise, I find it nosed into a wire-netting barricade pulled across the lane as a temporary gate where the fence separates Uncle Ticker's land from the lake.

Who would have blocked a public road? Esso? Or Uncle Ticker? Why is Dad working on Sunday? And why is he just sitting there with the engine bellowing like an angry bull? The thoughts rush around with no answers and I'm almost ready to leave when I see the Blitz bumping through Bindilla's bottom paddocks, twisting and turning to skirt potholes and rocks, heading towards the grader.

Uncle Ticker arrives before me, jumps down from the Blitz and walks towards the battered fence, cautiously at first. Closer, he scrambles over the netting and runs at the grader, swings up to the cabin and reaches inside. The engine dies. In the sudden silence, lorikeets squeal and shriek past my head, circling back on themselves and then away again.

Uncle Ticker calls down to me, 'Bit of a problem here, Sylvie.' And that's when I see Dad slumped over the steering wheel. I find mud-caked steps on the side of the grader and climb up. What's he done now?

From the other side of the cabin, Uncle Ticker is reaching inside, trying to lever Dad off the wheel. I crawl onto the seat and try to push too, his shirt warm and clammy under my hands. He is too heavy. Then he groans and moves his head a little.

'Together,' says Uncle Ticker. 'Careful.'

Dad sags back in the seat, blinks at Uncle Ticker and me as if he's had a bad dream, then his head flops forward onto his chest. He looks awful, his face the colour of wet cement. Uncle Ticker scratches at his beard in a worried sort of way and gives me a little smile that's meant to be reassuring but isn't.

'Heart, I reckon. I'll get up to the house and phone for help. Be as quick as I can. You be okay here?'

The lorikeets are back, squealing and swooping at the grader as if they've found a new kind of tree. Uncle Ticker drives off and I want to shriek after him: Don't leave me. And sure enough, the Blitz is barely halfway to the house when Dad tips upright, looks around with huge glazed eyes and slumps onto the wheel again, right back where he was before.

What'll I do? I stare at the back of his neck. His hair is thick and wavy with hardly any grey. He has a soft brown mole near his ear. The Blitz is a speck disappearing behind the pines, the lake unmoving except for a huddle of black swans far out. Should I push him back? What if moving him isn't the right thing to do? Dropping my head below the steering wheel, I look straight up at his face. He seems to have gone to sleep. Perhaps that's a good thing?

But he hasn't. 'Shit,' he winces, lifting his head inches from me.

'You'd...better sit back,' I tell him, sitting back myself. I try to breathe deeply. Maybe that's what he should be doing? Breathe deeply: that's what the ambulance man told us at school after Eddie Jones collapsed in the change-rooms and no one knew what to do. 'Breathe,' I tell him as I kneel on the seat and again try to push on his shoulders, timidly at first and then firmer. He doesn't move; he's a great heavy lump of wood. He smells of tree stumps and wattle leaves and the strange earthy scent of summer heath. 'Sit back,' I say. 'Help me.'

He laughs. At first I think it's a snuffly sort of moan, but as he rolls back in the seat, I see there's a speck of dry spit at the corner of his mouth and a twist on his lips that is definitely a grin. And in a flash the oily smell of his hair makes me remember an emu egg, someone singing—him?—I can't remember the tune, the words. And then I remember him outside the post office with Phil.

His heart. What if he 'carks' it? What if he dies right here beside me? I turn to the side window, willing Uncle Ticker to hurry, seeing the red iron roof of the shearing shed, cattle nosing around the bottom dam, Herefords with early calves, red against the straw-coloured grass. Why is he taking so long?

'Sylvie.'

I can't ever remember him saying my name before. Is that possible? I turn quickly to find him arched back against the seat, the skin under his chin speckled with tiny black hairs. His colour is bad: it makes him look faded, smaller, as if he's shrunk into the skin of a stranger.

'That drop-kick rigger from Coomandook I've seen sniffin' around you. Reckon you can do better than him.'

His eyes are still closed. I'm not really sure he said it. Then an awful thought: was he in the clearing yesterday, hidden, watching me? But I realise that's just plain crazy: some busybody must have seen me in the car with Will and told him. So why do I feel so bad? At the same time, I think: Who does he think he is, telling me what to do? Why should he care? I should laugh in his face. I can do what I like.

A rush of wind shivers the grass and ripples a path across the lake, then dies. Further along the shore, smoke from the rig drifts towards town. It's where Dunc was found, just there. I don't want to be here. The sound of his breathing is suddenly shallow, and scarily uneven. I shake his shoulder hard, urgently. 'Breathe,' I tell him. And he does, drawing in air like a drink.

Then I hear the sound of a car, not Uncle Ticker returning but Bill Morgan bumping to a stop beside my bike. I'm so glad to see him that relief makes me stupid and I clutch at Dad's hand. It feels warm and dry, and strangely light, and I hold it; I hold his hand in mine. But he doesn't look up or open his eyes—he's probably forgotten I'm here—and then Bill Morgan is helping me down, finding a white hankie in his pocket, freshly ironed, and I don't even know I'm crying.

Out on the lake, a flock of black duck float like a feathered raft. The sky is a huge dizzy blue streaked with smoke from the rig. Everything seems too big, too confused. I think: I won't tell Mum I was here. She doesn't need to know.

24

He died three days later. He was still in Muswell Hospital but they couldn't save him. He was forty-six.

'You don't want to go to his funeral, do you?' Mum drops a fork and bends to retrieve it. 'What's he ever done for you?'

I don't think I'm meant to answer that. I can't anyway; it's the sort of question that grows octopus arms and squeezes me so tight that I can hardly breathe.

She splashes plates around in the sink. 'A heart attack. Drink more likely. Why else would it get him so young? Rushing in to sort out the world instead of sorting out his own life. Who cares if Ticker fenced a lane?'

My father, obviously. And why shouldn't he? The words stick in my throat. Her hands are hidden in the tea-towel, wiping the plates back and front, back and forth. I wonder what else my father rushed in to sort out that I don't know about. 'I've sold up,' she says.

'Sold what?'

'The house. We're moving to the city.'

I stare at her. 'But there's oil, now. There'll be work.' Her hands in the tea-towel. 'Won't there?'

'We'll starve if we have to wait for that to filter through.'

'But I'll be a prefect next year.'

'You can be a prefect in the city.'

'No one'll know me there. I don't *want* to go to another school. I like it here.'

She turns on me, eyes fired up. 'You want to be a teacher, don't you? Well, I can promise you it won't happen here. You'll end up picking fish and pregnant at sixteen. Is that what you want?' And when I don't answer, she leans over the table. A pulse in her neck ticks like a time bomb. 'Is it?'

Within days, she's on the bedroom floor packing tea-chests with newspaper parcels—three piles—things to be kept—to be given away—another for the incinerator that's been smouldering in the backyard all day.

'What about this?' She holds up one of my *Famous Fives*.

I snatch it from her. 'I want all my books kept.'

'You can't want this.' She tosses *Four Bad Hens* onto the bed.

I grab that back too. 'I won that in Grade Two. I want them all.' I hover behind, watching, not helping. I want her to stop, to look up and say she's changed her mind, to say we should go to his funeral. I want her to tell me what to do.

'And this?'

It's my jewellery box, which once held Easter eggs. I tip everything onto the bed. My old gold bangle that no longer fits. A string of green plastic Poppit beads. The Edelweiss brooch Grannie brought back from Switzerland. Dunc's heart locket with the coronation crown. Dunc's skull ring. The green beads go into the give-away pile. So does the gold bangle.

'If you have a daughter, you might want that one day.'

'Me?' I try to make my voice scornful and rude but my period came a few days ago and I'm so relieved that I reclaim the bangle and return it to the box. I also keep the locket and brooch. But the skull ring is really an ugly thing and I'm tempted to toss it; instead I turn from her and press it onto my finger. Now the metal bits barely meet at the back.

'Well, we're not taking these.' She dumps my comics onto the bed. There must be thirty of them. My mouth opens to argue, and then I change my mind. I'll give them to Lizzie. But even as I carry them outside and sit on the back step to sort them, I know I won't. There are Dunc's old *Phantoms*, Pardie's too—the ones left on our doorstep the night before he left—and more recent *Archie*s and *Mad*s. On the cover of the latest *Archie*, the gang is singing folk songs in a big city high school, a school that looks as frighteningly foreign as I imagine my new school will be.

For some time, I nurse the comics on my lap, thinking of a blur of things. Mrs Winkie saying she hopes I'll come back to stay with Lizzie. *There'll always be a bed for you. You too, Nella.* My old autograph book saved from the fire. Dunc's curly writing: *If all the boys lived over the sea, What a good swimmer Sylvie would be.* Tadpoles in jars, watching them grow legs and turn into frogs on a window ledge at school. My father's hair at the lake, thick and wavy. I think: Is this who I am? All of these things? Do they add up to me?

My eyes find a wisp of smoke drifting skywards from our incinerator, a forty-four-gallon drum on bricks close to Shorty's fence. I walk past the old shed, step under the clothesline, around the climber beans, between the cabbages. At the incinerator, I peel the comics from my chest and drop them into the drum, one by one. At first pages tremble and flutter as if they're alive and crying out to be saved. I don't save them. As flames leap and roar, I return to the kitchen, take my camera from the table and cross the road into the tea-tree.

The lagoon has begun its summer retreat and the path near the water's edge is covered with a carpet of dry white weed. Further around, it's still damp and spongy and I'm forced to leap onto tree trunks that lie about like drunks. Alert for Bertie, always hoping, I hurry. Although there is no hurry. It's cool and dark beneath the trees and I'm glad they're still clouded in their winter green. I don't want to be seen. The path leaves the scrub on the other side of the lagoon, not far from my father's house. Cars are nosed into the fence, along the drive. *What's he ever done for you?*

I have stopped being careful of snakes. I climb the track through the dunes, stepping on pig face and muntries, pushing through snotty gobbles and old man's beard. High on a dune, I look down. Black specks are moving about the rig on the other side of the lake. For a second, the horizon tilts and blurs, then steadies. There's no smoke. No oil. The well ran dry after only two days. The specks are trucks and men dismantling the rig, getting ready for the move north to Lake Claire.

See. Mum's voice. Pleased. Redeemed. *All that effort. What a waste.*

I take a wide shot—too wide—I know it won't work. Then I turn to the back beach, the long sweep of it. The tide is low with reef and rocks exposed the whole way to Seal Island, sea and sky the same colour, almost merging. A gull wheels and screams above me as if I'm bothering its nest. Beyond the lighthouse, three boats are coming through the reef, returning early for my father's funeral.

I will never cry for him.

At the base of the dune there's a dip of sand, a beckoning beach. I stretch out my arms like angel wings and then I leap and slip and slide down the slope to the bottom. A wave licks up the sand then falls back, leaving a froth of foam in its wake. All around is blue sea and breaking surf. Clear light and birds shrieking. The wind holding me. I think: I could walk to the edge of the reef and wait for a wave; that's how I could do it. And for no reason, I think of Tania holding her teddy bear with half an arm.

Further up the beach, I sink down on soft sand. Way to the north, sea and rocky outcrops vanish in a salty mist. I want to disappear into that mist. Or burrow into the sand like a sand crab. Instead, I photograph the sun lowering in the west, frame after frame, until I run out of film. Until the service is over. Until he's buried and gone. And when the waves soften on the reef and the wind dies, I know Mum is right.

What's he ever done for me?

Nothing.

Returning over the hill, I see Cele leaving his house. There's no avoiding her; she sees me coming and waits at the side gate. She's wearing a black dress. Closer, I see she's pinned a glittery brooch to the collar, a sunburst of glass that might be real diamonds, the sort of brooch you save for special occasions. Like funerals. All of a sudden tears try to sneak up my nose but I keep them away by staying focused on the brooch. I think: I won't look at her. I won't let her see.

'Hey,' she says in her warm, funny voice. And somehow, her

arms are around me and I'm squashed against the glittery brooch, her voice soft in my hair. 'It's okay,' she says. 'You didn't need to be there. It's okay.'

I can smell her green perfume, her sweet sweaty skin. She is soft and hard, fragile and strong, all at the same time. 'Did,' I say into her neck.

'Didn't. Funerals are for the living, not the dead. From what I hear, you did your bit on the grader.'

That's when I feel something shifting inside, a sob. And somehow I know Mum is wrong, I just know. 'Didn't,' I say, pushing hard to get out of her arms.

'Hey,' she says, surprised. We're hardly any distance apart and she's smiling, but her eyes look tired, as if she's been crying, her lids swollen and smoky. And I just stand there with the sob like a rock inside me. I think: She knew him when he was a boy. When he sang at the Institute dance. When he was someone else. Is that why she cries for him?

Reaching for my hand, she examines the skull ring, angling it against the sun. Then she says it. 'He was very proud of you.'

It's so ridiculous that I don't even reply.

She lifts her eyes. 'It's true. When I saw him at the hospital, he said you bossed him around at the lake, made him sit up and breathe, really looked after him. He was tickled pink.'

I know she's lying. Tickled pink is not his thing. But I so want to believe her that I almost do. At the same time, I think: How dare he be proud of me. He has no right to be proud of me for anything, ever. Then I look at her puffy eyes and remember he's gone. That's all there is.

*

As the train pulls slowly out, Cele shoots onto the platform. 'Nella-a-a-a!' Dropping her bike, she runs to our window and pushes an envelope into Mum's hands. 'Photos. You gave them to me years ago. You should have them.'

I watch and wave until Roy and Chicken, Tania and Mrs Marciano, Cele and Lizzie and Mrs Winkie disappear in the curve of the line. As we rattle past the fish factory, and as the bay comes into view, I try to suck it all in behind my eyes—the jetty, a flash of Seal Island before it slides behind the point, the spires of the foreshore pines pointing into a high white sky.

When I turn from the window, Mum is staring ahead, the envelope on the seat between us. As I reach for it, she does the same. Her hand hovers and falters then flinches away; she sinks back into her seat and crosses her legs. Yet I know she's watching as I remove three photographs.

They are faded sepia, all three of my parents and Dunc, taken at the bottom gate with the lagoon behind. In the first, Mum looks like a girl, hardly older than me. She has a ribbon in her hair and holds Dunc on her hip. Dad is standing a little apart, hands behind his back. On the ground, their shadows touch.

In the next, Dad has Dunc half-hoisted on his shoulder and all three are frowning at the camera as if they'd been caught before they're ready. Dunc has a cowlick curl on top of his head, those huge brown eyes; Mum's arms hang uncertainly without her son to hold.

I pass the photos to her. 'How old is he?'

She barely looks before handing them back. 'About twelve months. Just before your father went to war.'

He looks too young to go to war, a skinny boy with striped

braces holding up his pants, pleats at the waist, cuffed bottoms sitting on black polished shoes. In the final photo, he has Dunc settled safely on his shoulders. Dad's elbows are angled awkwardly behind his head. Without Mum in the frame, Dunc and Dad are grinning fit to burst, Dunc's cheeks fat with dimples, a crease in my father's cheek, the same dimpled chins.

This is not the father I knew. He is not the one who died. I shuffle the photos together and turn to the window. I have missed Stickynet and the last glimpse of the bay. Somewhere beyond the lake are Bindilla's bottom paddocks. Somewhere between the dunes and the train lies the cemetery, but I can find no landmarks to anchor me. Somewhere behind the green wall of boobialla, Dunc and my father are buried close to the sea. As the train gathers speed, I think of the flowers on my father's grave that were still there yesterday and the lump in my throat dissolves into slow trickling tears.

I'll come back, I tell the blurred trees. I will come back.

ACKNOWLEDGMENTS

Sincere thanks to Barbara Turner-Vesselago and Shelley Kenigsberg, whose support from the beginning showed me the way.

Special thanks to Writers Victoria for a mentorship with Andrea Goldsmith, who gave me invaluable help.

To Elisabeth Hanscombe, I owe an immense debt of gratitude: her kindness and belief never wavered, when mine often did.

Thank you to Michael Heyward and the dream team at Text Publishing, and most of all to Penny Hueston, my brilliant editor, whose guidance and great care informs this book.

Love and appreciation to my brother, Malcolm, whose remarkable knowledge of country and creatures inspires my own.

Above all, heartfelt thanks to Stan, whose love made it all possible.